DESTINED
BRYN

THE BLACKSTONE BROTHERS

Z.L. ARKADIE

ISBN: 978-1-952101-53-3 (2nd Edition)

✾ Created with Vellum

Author's Note

This second edition of *Destined* combines *Crave* (book 1) and *Destined* (book 2, first edition) into one book.

Also, as of August 15, 2022, the surname/last name of the main family has been changed from Christmas to Blackstone.

Enjoy!

One

BRYN BLACKSTONE

I sat on a stool at the airport bar, eyes glued to my cell phone screen as I swiped through images of the interior of the next house I'd been paid to design. It was still hard to believe beautifying people's homes was my profession. I, who had never truly believed I would amount to much beyond being good at spending the family fortune, had found myself a real career. My flight from Newport, Rhode Island, to Denver, Colorado, had been scheduled to take off three hours earlier. The last announcement said I would be boarding soon, though. It was the third of January, and travelers were flying home from wherever they'd spent the holidays, but overnight, torrential weather—the sort that disrupted life on the ground—had sailed in from the north.

All three of my brothers had tried to convince me to fly on an aircraft from the family fleet, but I preferred traveling commercial. Growing up a member of the Blackstone family had been such a lonely existence that I took every opportunity I could to be around people I didn't know. Plus, I wasn't as well known as Jasper, Spencer, and Asher. Only on rare occasions was I recognized as "the Blackstone heiress." So far, even in my hometown, no one had requested to take a picture with me or asked if I was indeed Bronwyn Henrietta Blackstone. I'd been able to sit at the bar in peace while sipping a martini and getting a lot of work done.

"I thought that was you," a man said.

Keeping my eyes on my phone, I stiffened. I recognized the voice, even though I hadn't heard it in a long time. Slowly, I turned until Jamison Cox and I were gazing into each other's eyes.

"Wow, you." I was having an out-of-body experience, and the words came out of my mouth by accident.

Jamison absentmindedly wiped at his mouth. "Well, hi."

It was the moment for us to either shake hands

or hug. We did neither because I was unable to move. "Hi," I replied in a flat tone.

My head felt light as we continued to stare at each other. Soon, I would have to say something. *But what?* I was looking at someone I thought I'd never see again.

"What are you doing here?" I unthinkingly asked.

"How are you?" he asked at the same time.

We both looked away from each other to chuckle bashfully. I didn't want to behave like a schoolgirl with a crush on the wrong boy. But that was exactly how I felt. Frankly, I'd never understood my attraction to Jamison Cox. His face was always clean-shaven, and all the hairs on his head were perfectly combed into place. His shirt was still crisp and white, and his slacks were dark and had a crease. As with the last time we'd been together, he carried the scent of fresh laundry and cologne that gave me the same feeling as biting into the sweetest fruit and pausing to let the flavors swell in my mouth. He looked conservative. Randolph, my father, hid behind a conservative appearance. Therefore, I was prone to distrust him and would have never pursued a relationship with him. Until one night, I did.

My memory flashed me back to the first time I laid eyes on Jamison Cox and how he'd had no effect on me at all. It was roughly eight years earlier at Becca Smith's wedding. The ceremony took place at a castle nestled against Lake Como in Italy. I was certain that Becca's parents were in charge of the guest list and I'd been invited because of my last name. Having a Blackstone seated on the bride's side at their daughter's wedding made for good optics. At first, I declined their invitation by simply tossing it into the trash bin. However, Randolph insisted I go and gave Jasper the job of making sure I followed his orders.

I shook my head adamantly. "No way."

"Bryn, a destination wedding at Lake Como? This is not a battle you want to fight," Jasper said.

As usual, his point got through my thick skull, and I flew to Italy to attend Harper Rebecca Callahan Smith's impending nuptials. On the day of her beautiful and high-priced sunset wedding, she was a no-show. Jamison Cox, the groom, was literally left standing at the altar. I observed him as he waited, and I wondered what was going through his mind. He seemed so relaxed, as if he hadn't a care in the world. Then Dorothy—Becca's mother —and one of her sisters approached him and his best man and whispered something to him. Jamison barely nodded and then shrugged before the four of them escaped the scene. I never forgot how indifferent he looked. A groom whose bride was a no-show should have looked angry or upset. I concluded that he was no different than most of us who attended the wedding—empty on the inside and going through the motions. The next time I saw him was at a restaurant in Santa Barbara, California. Jamison was a campaign manager, and my sister-in-law had met with him to ask if he would spearhead my brother's congressional run for office.

But there we were again, running into each other randomly at an airport in Rhode Island. "So, it's true?" he asked.

I braced myself to look at him again. And when his handsome face filled the frame of my eyesight, my heart raced like a brisk wind. "What's true?"

He smirked, flashing straight white teeth—the trademark of a genuine California boy. "You're the only Blackstone who flies commercial."

I looked away from his sultry eyes to break the spell his gaze was putting on me. *No, Bryn. Remember what he did. He's not to be trusted.*

"You look good, though—beautiful, as usual," he said.

Damn it. I was forced to gaze into his eyes again. I cleared my throat. "Thank you." Working hard to remain the picture of calm, I dropped my cell phone on top of the bar. "But I just don't understand what happened."

His eyebrows shot up in surprise. "You mean between us?"

I could feel my pulse speeding. "Yes, and are we supposed to be talking? After all, your father not only tried to tarnish my family's reputation but also inferred that I committed a crime. Also, you tried to torpedo my brother's political campaign, which leaves me wondering, was I part of your plan?" I felt relieved. I'd been wanting to say all of that since the night Spencer informed me of Jamison's double-dealing.

Jamison rubbed the back of his neck as he sighed. I didn't think he realized he did that, because from what I remembered, Jamison intentionally remained the picture of calm whenever he came under fire. That was one of his strengths. However, I'd given him a lot to chew on. I didn't enjoy being in his face as much as I would have in the past, but it had to be said. My continued recovery depended on me always addressing the pink-polka-dot elephant in the room so that it wouldn't eventually end up squatting on my chest.

"No, Bryn, I was never using you. I could never do that," he finally said. "I apologize for the role I played in the debacle with your brother's campaign. That sort of divisiveness is not what I'm known for. As for my father, I can't apologize for him."

I unfolded my arms, allowing my cooler head to prevail, and thought of my own controlling and despicable father, who was fortunately dead and buried. "I understand, and I accept your apology."

Jamison's Adam's apple bobbed. "Thank you."

We stared into each other's eyes again. I didn't want Jamison Cox to set off fluttering sensations in my chest or make my soul quiver, but he did just that. Suddenly, I felt irritated, and a tiny part of me wanted him to go away already and forget I'd ever existed. But that was a very, very, very small part.

"So, what are you doing in these parts, anyway?" I asked.

He looked down at his feet while wearing a sheepish grin. My pinched face gave me a slight headache. He was being cagey, and that was annoying. "You don't want to tell me?"

Our gazes met again. "What? Huh?" he asked.

"You don't have to tell me. And you don't have to stall. As a matter of fact—"

Jamison shoved his hands into his pockets. "So, what have you been up to these days?"

I paused to study him. *Did he hear what I just said?* Jamison's face was red, and his gorgeous eyes seemed a little wild. If I had a mirror, I would probably see that I appeared just as flustered as he had. I felt jittery, and the parts of me that hadn't tingled in a long time had been activated. It was apparent that we still had strong sexual chemistry, but that could be resolved by putting distance between us. I wouldn't be making a healthy choice if I got involved for the second time with a man who had loved me and left me. The wisest decision would have been to get as far away from him as possible, but still, I wasn't ready to leave him just yet, and that worried me.

"My brother Asher got married this weekend at the family estate," I said.

He nodded. "I heard. It was a big deal, wasn't it?"

"I don't know about that, but the day was magical for us. Being that it was a new home and the old memories had been…" I smashed my lips. That was enough talk about me. "What about you?

I mean, do you have connections in Rhode Island?"

Jamison shook his head and pursed his lips.

His evasiveness annoyed me. "You can't tell me because you're doing your father's bidding, I presume." That was prickly, and I immediately wanted to take back those words.

A cynical sniff accompanied Jamison's smirk. "No." He licked his kissable lips, and gosh, it was so sexy. *Get a grip, Bronwyn Henrietta Blackstone. Get ahold of yourself.*

"Visiting a girlfriend?" I asked. *Damn it, I am on a roll.*

He shook his head and, after a two-beat pause, said, "No."

Bingo. I'd hit the nail on the head. "So, you do have a girlfriend, then?"

His eyebrows furrowed. "Did I say I had a girl-friend? I don't think I do."

"Well, you're not referring to her as a 'girl-friend.' But you've flown all this way to be with her, so she may believe you're her boyfriend."

Jamison tossed his head back and laughed. "I see you're still creative."

"Am I wrong?"

"You're wrong."

"About which part?"

Our gazes locked. It was as if the chatter, glasses clinking, and voices calling flight numbers over the loudspeaker had faded to silence. I felt my chest rise and fall with each breath. His nearness was slaying my heart, and I couldn't stop it from happening if I stayed in his presence for too long.

"Bryn." His whisper echoed so loudly in my ears. "Again, I'm sorry."

I opened my mouth then closed it. I couldn't speak, because if I did, my heart would betray my head. But I did appreciate his sincerity. I was sorry, too, but I was too choked up to say it.

Then I heard, "Flight 3345 to Denver, Colorado, is now boarding."

"That's me." My tight throat made my words come out strained.

"You live in Denver?"

I eased off the stool, and then we were standing close enough that the strong connection between us completely overwhelmed me. "No," I barely said. "I have a client."

His eyebrows flew up and stayed there. "A client?"

I nodded gently. "Yes."

"What are you doing these days?"

My lips wanted his, and I could sense that his wanted mine. But I wished I'd never run into Jamison Cox, because there could be no future for us as a couple. It was apparent that he was still working for his father, Boomer, who was a bad man and a foe of my family. I couldn't be stupid. Jamison's father would have been happy if my brother and I had gone to prison for something we hadn't done. To Boomer, that would have been a win. But was that the real reason I was afraid to let my heart get attached to him again? I didn't know.

"Good seeing you. Take care of yourself, Jamison." I quickly turned my back on him and walked away as fast as I could, trying not to run.

"Bryn?" he called.

I wanted my feet to keep shuffling, but they stopped and turned me around. We stared at each other. *Why do I want to cry? Why does my heart feel shattered by him for a second time?*

He rubbed the back of his neck. "See you around."

See me around? He would never see me again. I would make sure of that. So without another word, I turned my back on Jamison Cox and finished making my escape.

Two

BRYN BLACKSTONE

The airplane soared steadily through the sky after a bumpy start. I was seated next to a girl who was about eleven or twelve years old. The last time her cell phone had been out of her hands was right before takeoff. She had sat her device on top of the bin between our seats to scarf down two complimentary preflight hot chocolate chip cookies. Once we reached cruising altitude, her eyes were fixed on the screen. I loved sitting next to kids on airplanes, but she was obviously not in the mood for conversation, so I sparked up my laptop, hooked into the secure onboard network, and tried to do some work. Unfortunately, I couldn't shake thoughts of Jamison Cox. It was strange how being in his presence was like being swaddled in a warm, soft blanket. I let the possibility of us being soul mates sit in my mind just so that I could deconstruct it.

After Jamison had been exposed as a conspirator against my brother's political campaign, he never got in touch with me. Granted, I'd lost my cell phone while vacationing in Borneo, but I still had email, and the address was on the contact sheet. My ex-boyfriend, Dale Rumor, had torched my heart by being a selfish prick. But although I'd been with Dale longer, the break between me and Jamison hurt more.

Jamison was supposed to be the good guy, my first healthy pick. And that one night he and I spent together had been out-of-this-world amazing. I'd put a lot of effort into trying to forget the details of our lovemaking. My breasts tingled as I recalled how his wet, warm tongue rubbed the tips of my nipples. Jamison wasn't an overeager or coarse lover. His mouth, body, and movements had been soft and sensual. I recalled how he savored his way down from my mouth to my ribs then sank his tongue into my belly button. My back had curled, my body tense with novel sexual pleasure, and I nearly fainted when his wet, warm mouth devoured my flower, bringing me to the most potent orgasm

I'd ever experienced. Dale hadn't known how to eat vag. Jamison had.

Gosh, he was good in bed. Or maybe it was our chemistry that took our lovemaking to a level that was beyond our universe. Sexual attraction wasn't our only bond, though we weren't an obvious match. I was carefree, and he was conservative, at least in appearance. Our connection was emotional. On the one and only night we made love, when he wasn't inside me, we lay shoulder to shoulder and talked.

"What makes you tick?" he asked. "I've been trying to figure that out from the day we met."

I chuckled, feeling buoyant. "Are you referring to the day we formally met?"

"When did we informally meet?"

"On your wedding day." Then I twisted my mouth thoughtfully. "I guess I met you. You didn't meet me."

He chortled. "Then yes, I meant when we met at the restaurant, which might be the best day of my life."

We stared into each other's eyes again. I agreed. That had probably been one of the best days of my life too. Lighthearted, I pondered his question. *What makes me tick?*

"In regard to your initial question, I'm still trying to figure that out," I said.

After a long pause, he whispered, "Me too."

Our confessions were our first dive into the well of emotional trust. We talked about money and how having a lot of it had never brought either of us true happiness. I revealed how lonely I'd felt growing up with Amelia Blackstone as a mother. He shared that after all these years, he was trying to figure out what sort of person his mother truly was, but he never said more than that about her. I talked about all the schools I'd been kicked out of. He was a straight-A student and high school valedictorian. I shared that when my father would dispatch me to do my Blackstone-daughter duties by showing up to some silly event attended by ladies and daughters who lunched, I would pretend to have an accent that came from no particular country. Jamison found that very funny. As night turned to morning, we made love once more. When he left, we planned on seeing each other soon at the campaign office. Of course, that had never happened. But even after learning of Jamison's betrayal, I'd wondered if he was the soul mate who got away.

"Hi," the flight attendant said cheerily.

I opened my eyes and stopped smiling as if I

was high on good drugs. "Um, yes." I shifted in my seat. I must have looked ridiculous.

He served me the cappuccino I'd ordered before takeoff and gave the girl next to me, who hadn't taken her eyes off her phone, another Coke.

After a quiet sigh, I decided not to think about Jamison Cox ever again. Instead, I focused on the lovely wedding weekend that had just passed. My twin brother, Asher, was now the husband of intimidatingly sexy Dr. Penina Ross. I never could picture him having a wife. I couldn't picture myself as any man's blushing bride either. Despite trying so hard to have healthier relationships, I couldn't shake the belief that I was too damaged to enter a partnership that was built to last a lifetime.

But maybe I wasn't too damaged. Maybe I just didn't know how to go about the business of meeting and mating forever and ever. Regardless, the redesign of our childhood home was a hit with my family. A house that carried the energy of a castle torture chamber and imprisoned the meanest, dirtiest, angriest ghosts had been torn down. The historical society wanted off with my head for demolishing the structure without their permission. The old white stone Blackstone mansion had been built during the Gilded Age, and many sightseeing tour buses would pause outside the iron gates to get a look at it while listening to an account of our family's lineage that started out palatable but ended with the guide mentioning my sister-in-law Holly's book, *The Dark Blackstones*. Fortunately, Jasper got the history police off my back. I respected historical relics, but not in the case of our personal hell on earth that was the mansion we'd grown up in. I never asked what Jasper had done to make my problems go away, and frankly, I didn't care.

I hired Rina Ito, an architect who married East Asian and Scandinavian contemporary styles, to redesign our home. The new mansion had three levels, each separated by hip and gable roofs like Shinto shrines. The new home felt light and open, a stark difference from the bulky old colonial structure.

It took four months for the frame, walls, windows, and flooring to be erected. The builders worked long hours to get it done. The final seven months were spent on the interior. My goal was to make sure those who entered couldn't experience a stitch of what it used to feel like to walk inside the Blackstone manor. For inspiration, I took a trip with Rina and her friend Yana to Greyson Highland State Park in Virginia. Rina had suggested the excursion. As we strode along the pathways through meadows and emerald forests, we spoke very little. I remembered everything I could about each of my brothers—who they'd been when we were younger and the men they'd become after Randolph passed.

Truthfully, none of us had liked who we were when Randolph was alive. We were like lab rats, always racing in multiple directions with nowhere to go and always part of a furtive lab experiment. What happened when the rats were set free? They scattered, and that was exactly what we'd done. When we came back together again, we were all different. We had evolved.

When designing the interior, my goal was to convey our transformations. We used to be blood-red, black soot, and shadowy gray. With Randolph out of the picture, we'd become precious metal for strength, softened by fire and molded into fine human beings.

So I hired Mendes Lee, an LA-based artist famous for her metalwork. Mendes flew up to Newport and stayed with me in the guesthouse for two months. Together, we moved from the bottom to the top floors, crafting with our theme in mind. Thoughtful design went into the tiniest details— knobs, handles, lightbulbs, types of glass and wood.

We even considered the light flowing in from the sun, moon, and stars when selecting window frames, paint, wall art, and other design features. In the end, we had an ultramodern and stylish yet comfortable place to live. Gone were the depravities of the past, all replaced by hope for the future.

Mendes was so proud of the scope of what we'd been able to accomplish that she contacted two of the most popular art-and-design publications in the world. After Mendes had hosted house tours with several journalists, the story "The Monstrous Mansion Reformed" caught on like wildfire.

Mendes never failed to give me most of the credit for the majority of the interior design concepts. "Bryn Blackstone was very detail orient- ed," she would say. "Bryn was thoughtful about how art merged with use in every part of the house, from the windows down to the bathroom medicine cabinets."

I hadn't realized I'd been so immersed in the project until she mentioned it. What I liked most about the renovation was the idea of destroying the old and ushering in the new.

Then, one day, Mendes called and asked if she could hire me to help with the design of her London flat. The theme would be *Standing firm against the raging wind.* I already knew a lot about Mendes from the days we spent living in the guest-house. That job led to another and then another, each as enjoyable as the last. When I became certain I wanted to make interior design a career, I went to see Jasper at the BFE—Blackstone Family Enterprise—office in Lower Manhattan to seek his assistance for coming up with a solid business plan. Jasper listened to me attentively, asked questions about my goals, and wanted to know about the challenges I'd faced during some of my past projects. His expression remained stern as I gave my answers. After a final brisk nod, he typed feverishly on his keyboard. Seconds later, his secretary entered his office with a complete business plan. He went over it with me. It was amazing how he could come up with a solid blueprint in a matter of minutes.

"Then you want to implement it?" he asked.

"For sure," I said, and Mindful Interior Notable Design—MIND by Bryn Blackstone, for short—had been added to the BFE portfolio for the small-business sector.

That meant my employees were privy to a complete benefit package, which included all the bells and whistles. Their salaries were extremely competitive too. I had seven employees—one project assessor, three craftsmen, and three associate designers. Four of my employees lived in LA, and they were finishing up two projects in the county. I was on my way to start a third job. My associate designer Alana and the builder, Alex, who lived in New York City, were scheduled to fly into Vail, Colorado, the next afternoon. I liked to spend the first day on the job alone with my client to get a better feel for the house with the person inside it. After that, I would figure out how to bring our theme to life.

In the case of Eden Newell, she couldn't think of a theme. I'd promised to help her come up with one. Manuel, my assessor, had traveled to her vacation home in October of last year, two weeks after Eden and I met in person. He'd taken pictures of each interior and exterior space and uploaded them into a design app that BFE's technological team had made for me—another perk of being in the conglomerate. The app allowed me to shop catalogs and virtually insert products into the spaces. It made my job a whole lot easier.

I was working on preliminaries of the first-floor spaces when the stewardess returned to take my coffee cup and ask if I wanted another cappuccino. Remembering that once the airplane landed, I had a long drive ahead of me, I said yes. Then dinner was served. Absorbed by my work, I had no space in my head to think about my surprise encounter with Jamison Cox. He was out of sight and out of mind, forever forgotten, and that was exactly how I preferred it.

———

"YOU DON'T NEED THE RECEIPT, MISS BLACKSTONE. I have your reservation in the system," the guy behind the counter said.

I was standing at the car-rental counter, rifling through my purse. My cell phone had to be in there somewhere. I hated when I misplaced my things, especially my cell phone. I froze, trying to remember the last time I'd seen my device.

Then I sighed. *I left it on top of the bar at the airport in Providence.* "Thank you," I said wearily.

It had been a mentally taxing day, so I had no energy to kick myself for losing my phone. I had just enough left in me to make it to the finish line, which was the two-hour drive to Vail.

We finished our transaction at the counter, and once I was in the large SUV, I shuffled through pop music stations on satellite radio and took a quick listen to the songs that were being played. I knew how my mind worked. I would obsess over losing my phone and running into Jamison if I didn't keep my thoughts occupied by something like music I knew and could sing along with.

None of the songs were doing the trick, so I took my iPad out of my briefcase and used Bluetooth to hook it up to the car stereo. *Ding!* My iPad rang, letting me know I had messages. Gripped by relief, I remembered that I could lock my lost phone from my iPad. But first I saw that I had one message from J. Cox: *I have your phone. When can I return it?*

I flopped back in my seat, palm pressed over my overly beating heart. "What the hell?" I whispered.

At least my cell phone was in safe hands. However, it was being safeguarded by the last man in the world I wanted to see—or at least, I was trying to convince myself that I felt that way about him.

I gripped the steering wheel, wondering what to do next. I wasn't ready to reply to Jamison's email. "When can I return it? Is he serious?" *His face. Those lips. His seductive eyes.*

I shook my head like a rattle and started the engine. "No more Jamison Cox," I whispered and turned up the volume on a song by Sam Smith and sang along.

IT WASN'T THE FIRST INSTANCE IN WHICH I'D DRIVEN from Denver to Vail, although I hadn't planned to make the journey so late in the day. My flight had been scheduled to arrive seven hours earlier, which would have allowed me to make the drive in daylight. Snowflakes struck the windshield, but my handy-dandy wipers shoved the ice off the glass. Snow-covered fields were illuminated in the darkness, making navigating the large SUV with snow tires feel less intimidating. In fact, I felt as snug as a bug in a rug.

I wasn't a music buff, but over the years, I'd acquired a collection of songs by my favorite artists. Sam Smith and Adele topped my list. As their songs played and my heart connected, all I wanted to do was fall in love with Jamison. I needed a different effect, a reminder that I should always protect my heart when it came to him, so I called up Siri on my iPad and asked her to play "Uninvited" by Alanis Morissette. Once the dramatic beginning of the song had rolled, I let myself think of Jamison again, but in a different way.

It was evident that he was still working for his corrupt father, Richard "Boomer" Cox. Boomer had no ethical barometer when it came to business. He struck me as the sort of human being who not only knew he could get away with murder but would attempt the act just to prove it. Even after learning that his father had tried to smear Asher and me with a lie, Jamison had stayed with him. The fact that he hadn't chosen to separate himself from that kind of person, father or not, spoke volumes about his own character. I needed to believe that in order to keep myself from giving him a second chance to break my heart.

I still owed Jamison a response to his message, though. But first, I had to remember that he was uninvited and not allowed back into my heart. And so I sang the words, putting all my heart and soul into them. When the song ended, I told Siri to play it again. When I stopped in front of the resort's lobby, I could barely keep my eyes open, but I felt like a mighty warrior, dressed for battle and ready to resist Jamison's charm and good looks.

AFTER FINISHING THE FORMALITIES WITH THE valets, I stepped out of my car into the icy air. Exhaustion and the altitude made me slightly dizzy. I could have enjoyed all that the resort offered, and more, by staying at our family's Vail estate. Also, I wouldn't have had to go through the process of checking in at the front desk and ordering the early risers' breakfast to be brought to my room in the morning. However, ever since the mansion had been built, I'd learned how much it cost to maintain the utilities and caretaking for properties as large as the ones owned by my family. Upkeep cost tens of thousands of dollars a month. I'd also purchased my own homes: a luxury but not overwrought apartment on the Upper West Side of Manhattan and a cute mid-century modern home—less than a quarter of the size of the one I'd grown up in—on Mulholland Drive in LA. With a full-time chef who came with the property, along with groundskeepers and housekeeping, the Blackstone estate was not only more convenient than the resort but closer to the job site too. However, the resort was easy enough and far more cost-efficient. I couldn't believe I'd become so sensible when it came to money. Becoming cash conscious was easy for an heiress like me, who never felt as if her father's money came without strings attached. There were no strings attached to what I'd earned on my own.

When I walked into my suite, which was suited for long-term stays, I tipped the bellhop, lugged myself to the bedroom, and plopped down on the bed. The moment I'd been anticipating had finally come. I took my iPad out of my briefcase, called up Jamison's message, and replied: *Thanks for securing my cell phone. Could you send it to me by mail, please?*

I added the name and address of the resort. Then I sat still, waiting for his response. Minutes ticked by, and I became sleepier. Jamison was either away from his phone or asleep. As I remembered, he was the sort of person who went to bed early and rose early. Figuring I should have his response by morning, I followed his lead—I set my alarm and went directly to bed.

Three

BRYN BLACKSTONE

I rose before the alarm sounded. I'd gotten a solid seven hours of sleep, and other than the fact that I was starving, I felt ready to tackle my day. I was extra thrilled about the possibility of seeing Jamison's response to my message. It was stupid and reckless of me to be so excited to hear from him, but regardless, I was. Wrapped in a towel, I trotted out of the bathroom and into the bedroom to check my iPad. Disappointed, I sighed. He still hadn't replied. I checked again after my shower—nothing. I couldn't pout, though—time was breathing down my neck.

I dressed for comfort and warmth, putting on a loose-fitting pair of jeans and a soft light-blue cotton T-shirt under a thick cable-knit sweater that

I could easily take off, since walking through the home, along with the reaching and squatting my work demanded, tended to make me warm. I gave myself a final once-over in the bathroom mirror, and I approved of myself for being comfortable and quite stylish in the West Coast manner that I'd adopted when I'd moved to LA after my father died.

I trotted into the bedroom to check and see if Jamison had finally responded. Still nothing. I pursed my lips. I needed my phone because it was my lifeline to my family and work. I decided to give Jamison until the end of the day to respond before driving into town to shut off service on my cell phone and buy a new one.

As I was considering this plan, I was surprised to hear a doorbell ring. I hadn't realized the suite came equipped with one. The sound was akin to a meal bell. Knowing exactly who the caller was, I rushed to the foyer. I'd scheduled a seven thirty breakfast delivery. When I opened the door, the aroma of an egg white, spinach, feta, and roasted roma tomato omelet with home-style basil, citrus sweet potatoes, and a hot pot of Columbian coffee made my stomach growl.

It felt as if time was speeding up faster than I

could manage it. I ate while racing around the room, making sure I'd brought the correct flash drives—sorted according to design styles—which contained catalogs of vendors for lighting, furniture, and appliance vendors that worked with MIND's design app. Alana and Alex, my assistant and crafts-man, were flying in from New York and bringing the trunk loaded with textiles, fabrics, woods, metals, cements, porcelain, and other tangible samples. By the time I did another time check, I had only ten minutes to be at Eden Newell's house. I sent her a quick message to let her know that I'd misplaced my cell phone and that I was on my way.

Her response came immediately: *Take your time. Would you like breakfast?*

If only Jamison had replied that quickly. I answered: *I've already eaten. Thanks for offering. I promise we'll hit the ground running as soon as I get there.*

She texted back: *Can't wait.*

With the bag full of modules on one shoulder, my purse and computer case hanging from the other, a briefcase in one hand, and keys in the other, I paused to make sure I hadn't left anything else. Satisfied that I hadn't, I hurried out into the hallway and toward the elevator. When I reached the porte cochere, I was further delayed because I'd forgotten to call downstairs and let the valet know I was leaving.

When I was finally on the road, I was flustered and could have used another cup of coffee. Also, I rarely drove to work in the morning without answering a barrage of phone calls. I was anxious about not having my cell phone, being late for the first day on the job, and Jamison's silence. To calm my nerves, I focused on my surroundings. Tall, thin pines rose up out of the snow-layered ground and mountains. A light mist settled in the atmosphere. The place was freezing cold, and I was wondering if it was feasible to start an interior design project in a high-altitude mountain town.

My iPad chimed, and I tensed up. I had a hunch the message was from Jamison, but with the sloshy ice on the roads and the gray weather conditions, there was no way I was going to fiddle with my briefcase so that I could check and see if I was right. My device beeped two more times while I was driving up West Forrest Road. Finally, the voice on the navigator app instructed me to make a right turn. I stopped in front of a wooden gate and rolled down the window. A pillow of cold air ambushed my face, and I retreated a bit more into the heated cab of the SUV after hitting the call button at the gate.

There was loud dialing, and then Eden said, "Hi, Bryn, is it you?"

"It's me."

"You'll see an open garage. Park inside it just in case it snows. Then you'll see the entrance to the house on the right. A staircase will take you to the first floor. I'll meet you there."

"See you there," I said, making sure I sounded professional and friendly and not distracted by wanting desperately to see what Jamison had to say.

After a buzz, the gate slowly began to roll open. In the brief seconds before driving onto the property, I quickly retrieved my iPad from my briefcase and saw that I had received several messages that were indeed from Jamison: *Your brother Asher called. Also, your sister Kat. She's on her way to Houston for a conference. Wants to know if you're able to join her for a day or two. Told her you're working in Colorado.*

A laugh escaped me while I read the message again. *Is he for real?* There was no mention of him putting my cell phone in the mail. Instead, he was taking the role of a glorified message taker, even to the extent of indirectly informing Kat that I wouldn't be able to join her in Houston because I was starting a new job.

The gate was wide open and ready for my entrance. I huffed, knowing that at some point when I had a moment, I would have to respond to Jamison and insist that he mail my cell phone to me.

As I pressed my foot gently on the gas pedal, my iPad chimed again. Another message from Jamison appeared on the screen: *Your mother called. I told her you made it to Colorado safely. I assumed you had.*

I couldn't stop shaking my head as I drove up the driveway. *What sort of game is Jamison playing?* I wanted to blow my top, but I couldn't. My work had already started. The outside of the house and the grounds reflected how the inside should look. Built into a hill and bordered by tall fir trees, the structure reminded me of stacked blocks made mostly of glass and stone. Even though its shape was ultracontemporary, it appeared to be at one with nature. With one look, I knew that I would have to leave at least half of my design ideas by the wayside.

Overwhelmed by thoughts of Jamison and all the calls I had to return to the people I loved, I clenched the steering wheel and took a series of deep breaths. "You will get through this day," I whispered.

My iPad chimed again, and I glanced back and forth between the driveway and the screen to read Jamison's message: *Jasper called. I didn't answer. Letting you know.*

I rolled my eyes as I groaned. At the end of the day, when I was back in my room, Jamison would be the first person I contacted. It was just weird that he had my phone and was taking messages for me. However, I had to admit, it felt exciting to know that he was in possession of something I owned and we were in contact with each other again.

He's uninvited, remember? I reminded myself.

I drove into the garage. As soon as I turned off the engine, the garage door lowered. I collected all the things I needed for the job. As I slammed the vehicle door shut, I whispered, "I remember." I didn't sound at all convincing, though.

EDEN NEWELL MET ME IN A SPACIOUS FOYER THAT had a glass-top roof showcasing a view of the gray sky. Like most Hollywood actresses, Eden was classically beautiful, with light-blue eyes, which were striking in combination with her tousled chestnut hair. Beneath her round and high cheekbones was a wide mouth that made it impossible to miss her smile, even the pensive one she held as I walked into her house. I felt as if I'd interrupted her in the middle of trying to complete one last task before my arrival.

"Did you have any trouble finding the house?" she asked, scratching the back of her head.

I smiled. "Not at all. I used the navigational system just in case, but you don't live that far from my family's property."

"Oh, the Blackstones are my neighbors?"

I chuckled. "I guess so." There was no use explaining that we owned hundreds of multimillion-dollar properties all over the world, all purchased by Randolph, who'd used them as his sex lairs.

She squeezed her palms together as if nervous about something. "Wow, so it's finally happening. We're going to do this."

I frowned, concerned. "Did I catch you at a bad time or something?"

"Hey, hon," a guy said.

I jerked myself into a straight position. There was no way in the world I was hearing who I thought I heard. The guy was behind me, and Eden was watching him.

"I see that the interior designer's late but here," he said. "I guess that counts for something."

The voice. I knew it, and I knew it well. *Holy crap.*

"Hey, babe," Eden said in her lackluster tone.

I turned my head slowly, feeling as if it was time for the big reveal on a game show. Then I saw him. My stomach tightened in disbelief as I inhaled sharply. I was looking into the eyes of my ex-boyfriend from hell, Dale Rumor.

Four

BRYN BLACKSTONE

My eyes felt as if they were spewing enough fire to scorch Dale Rumor alive. I wanted to ask why he was there, but the words would not come out. Dale wrapped an arm around Eden's tiny waist and looked at me as if he'd never seen me before in his life.

"Can I get you anything—coffee, tea, water…?" he asked.

I could have choked with embarrassment, not for me but for Eden. I knew what came after "water." It had been a habit of his to say, "Coffee, tea, water, or me?" He only proved he was the same scoundrel of a boyfriend for Eden that he'd been for me.

"I'm fine," I said, glaring at him. I didn't like the emotions I was having.

I could have bet a million bucks he'd orchestrated the present situation without her knowledge. He was sneaky in that way. He'd put me in a severely awkward position. I didn't hate Dale, but no one could push my buttons like he could. The last time we'd seen each other, we fought because he'd decided to fire me from the film project we were both producing. I screamed—admittedly crazily—that he couldn't do that because we had a contract.

He told me I should have read the fine print. "Plus, working together isn't working, Bryn. It's ruining us, and you know that."

"You're ruining us," I shouted and then called him every derogatory name in the book.

He called me a nutjob who had extreme rapist-father daddy issues. Then I jumped and clung to him like a spider monkey and clawed at his face. He pulled me off him and held me down.

One of our neighbors had called the police, and when they arrived, I was still yelling and screaming that I was going to kill him. While I was trying to spit on Dale, my spittle landed on one of the officers, and they arrested me for disturbing the peace.

When they put me in the back of the squad car, I was lethargic and unable to stop crying. One of the officers thought I was high on drugs, but I wasn't. I was merely having another mental and emotional breakdown.

My memory of that night remained foggy, to a certain extent, but I recalled one of the officers saying that they weren't taking me to the rich people's station—I was going to Twin Towers in downtown LA. One of them mentioned my pretty little face that liked to spit.

One of them said something about saving my spit for a blow job. "Is that what you like to do?"

His tone was salacious, aggressive. He said that he would teach me a lesson. He had no idea how much I wanted to learn that lesson. I didn't want to be Bronwyn Henrietta Blackstone. I hated that girl. I felt I deserved hell on earth, and Dale was just a start. Out of all the children my father had produced by inflicting violence on innocent girls, he'd chosen to use me and the brothers I'd grown up with to make him appear normal. My name was evidence of that. Blue-blooded. Rich. Lofty.

Screw my father and Dale, I'd thought back then. *Screw her too. Screw Bronwyn Henrietta Blackstone.*

I never made it to Twin Towers. The officers

received a call while en route. A man with a gruff voice ordered them to take me to the Lighthouse Recovery Center. One of the officers shouted that it was too late—I was as good as booked.

"What… Take her!" the guy over the radio said. "And nothing better happen to her, or your asses are grass. And you don't want to start nothing with her brother."

"Who's her brother?"

"Jasper Blackstone," the voice blared.

It got deathly quiet in the car. My brother's name repeated in my mind. Then, as further evidence of my mental breakdown, I started crying for him.

There was no more taunting or talking after that. I was taken straight to the recovery center. That wasn't my final stint in rehab, but it was the last day I saw Dale Rumor. I later learned that Dale had called Jasper to let him know I'd been arrested. It wasn't that he was looking out for me, though. He was afraid that if Jasper found out he'd been the reason I was taken to jail, he would incur the wrath of my brother. I doubted that would have happened. Jasper would never have let me spend more than a day in jail, but he was all about me taking responsibility for my inappropriate behavior.

Even though his motives were selfish, calling my brother was the last good deed Dale had ever done for me.

I didn't want to lie to Eden, but it didn't feel like the appropriate time to tell her the truth about my past relationship with Dale. A pinch of anger raced through me. I didn't let it catch fire and burn down all the progress I'd made by getting happy. But I had to think it was strange to run into Jamison on Sunday and Dale on Monday. *Is that a good or bad sign?*

"That's right," Eden said jubilantly. "The two of you know each other."

I forced a smile. I was right on the money—he hadn't told her everything about us. If he had, her tone would have been the direct opposite of happy.

"Hi, Dale." I kept my voice deadpan.

"Good seeing you, Bryn." He sounded cordial and casual, as if there was no reason to let his girl-friend know that we used to be an item.

I pressed my lips together.

Eden patted him on the shoulder. "Now, go. Bryn and I have work to do."

I found it interesting that Eden hadn't picked up on the cold formality between Dale and me. I wondered if she was ignoring it on purpose. *What did he tell her, anyway?* At least I strongly believed the ambush had been Dale's doing—which, again, wasn't at all surprising. I would have to tell her about us at some point. Hopefully, she was more intuitive than I was giving her credit for, and at some point during our long day together, she would ask, "So, what's the deal with you and Dale?" If that happened, I felt like I would tell her everything —the bad, the worse, and the ugly.

EDEN AND I HAD HAD OUR FIRST IN-PERSON MEETING on October 27 the previous year. We ate lunch at a vegan restaurant in the Venice Beach area near Abbot Kinney—her choice. She pointed out six well-known actors, who were seated around us, all dressed as if they'd just finished a spin or yoga class at a nearby gym. I took note of how she brought her fellow thespians to my attention. I could tell that she liked being in the mix but didn't want anyone to perceive how much she enjoyed it. She herself looked pretty casual in a pair of tight navy blue stretch pants and a blousy T-shirt with the word Lollygag across the chest, with her hair pulled into a high ponytail. She capped off her outfit with the usual celebrity's touch—mirrored aviator shades. The purpose of our meeting was to find out if we had enough chemistry to design together. My philosophy was that I was merely the part of my clients that could step outside them and see their truth.

Eden told me her story. She'd been born and raised in Toledo, Ohio, the middle child of six siblings. After graduating from high school, she'd left home for Colorado State University.

She gazed off, unfocused. "One day, I packed my car, got behind the wheel, and just drove. I didn't let myself think about what I was doing. I just kept going. I ended up in LA. I had three thousand dollars in my savings account. It took me three days to find a job waitressing. I went back and forth between living in my car and staying in a hotel near LAX. They're cheaper there." She said that with a nostalgic yet proud smile. She was on a roll, retelling the story of her humble beginnings.

When Eden finally had enough money to pay the security deposit and first month's rent, she moved into an apartment in Sherman Oaks. "Thank God I wasn't fresh in town by then. Live in Hollywood for more than a month, and you'll know better than to live there while broke."

One of her coworkers, another waitress, invited her to improv one evening. She found making up her own words—shuffling through her thoughts to bring a random scenario to an onstage performance—exciting. She kept going and then took a class on how to be better at improvisational acting. Less than two weeks in, her instructor had challenged her to go on an audition for a national commercial.

"He said it was good practice," Eden recalled. She'd gotten the job. "I was good at acting. I never knew it until I left Colorado for LA."

"Oh, maybe you did," I suggested. She frowned at me questioningly. "Of all the places in the world, why did you choose Los Angeles, and more specifically, Hollywood?"

Eden became pensive. The waitress showed up and served us our bean-and-sprouted-greens burritos and refills of chicory coffee. Eden then changed the subject by asking me a barrage of questions about growing up a Blackstone and the bestselling book about my family. I was very much aware that she was done talking about herself, and I respected her boundaries.

"So, what's the verdict?" she asked as I took care of the bill.

I looked up from signing the receipt and smiled at her. "I will definitely take you on as a client."

I could see by the look on her face that she wanted to ask why, but she only said, "Thank you," and then asked if I'd ever taken a local spin class.

I learned that her house was in the neighborhood, and when I asked if I could see it to get an idea of what she liked, Eden had said perhaps another time. "It's a pigsty. Plus, I want my vacation home to be something I could never have imagined."

So there we were, finally designing her multimillion-dollar vacation home, which was the first over-the-top purchase she'd made since landing a leading role in a hit sitcom and thereby making it big. When Eden and I were left alone, we moved to our first space, the living room, which already had a large gray U-shaped sectional, a mahogany mid-century modern coffee table, and a pendant-style floor lamp with an aluminum hood. I guessed that she was into modern sophistication with a touch of hidden humility. I asked her to stand in the middle of the room and tell me what was the first thing that came to mind, no matter how gory.

Arms folded and looking up at the ceiling, she said, "Cockroaches."

I interpreted that one word to mean that to her, the room felt cold, murky, desolate, and uncomfortable. She'd tried to get rid of that feeling with the furniture that was already there. However, the heavy, clunky sofa and blocky coffee table only made it worse. So I showed her renderings of how the room could be if we added furniture and design pieces that complemented the trees and the view of the snow-covered mountains not far in the distance.

We moved from room to room, performing the same exercise. Time flew by. We only saw Dale twice. The first time, he found us in the kitchen and asked Eden if she would like him to go into town to get her something to eat. She told him she wasn't hungry. Then he came back an hour later and asked her the same question. Eden and I were too involved in what we were doing to want to stop to eat, so she said no again.

"Well, I'm going into town." He sounded irritable, as if Eden had forbidden him to do what he wanted. I was very familiar with Dale's disposition. It used to give me anxiety.

"That's fine. See you later," Eden said, keeping her attention on the lighting catalog.

He glared at me before turning his back on us and plodding off. Once again, I waited for Eden to ask me about my past relationship with Dale, but she didn't look away from her shopping. Since we were alone, I considered bringing it up, but I chickened out. Instead, we continued with our activity.

A few hours later, when Dale returned, we were in one of the bathrooms on the third floor. He informed us that he had hero sandwiches with Dijon mustard, extra tomatoes, and sweet pickles, with the bread lightly toasted.

"That's awfully specific," Eden said.

I could feel my skin flush as I tried to hide my shock. Years before, we'd driven to Providence for lunch and had come across a sandwich shop. I rarely ate outside the mansion in those days because we had the best chefs in the world cooking in our kitchen. But I ordered a hero sandwich because I was blinded by love and called Dale *my hero*. I ordered it with Dijon mustard, extra tomatoes, and sweet pickles on a lightly toasted kaiser roll. I found the sandwich so tasty that after that, I often had our driver take me to the same shop at least once a week. I stopped when Amelia came into my room to tell me that I was getting fat and Randolph had noticed and didn't like it.

"You know what he does when he doesn't like something," she said.

47

I knew. I'd never gone back to that shop again. Regardless, by ordering that sandwich, Dale was being sneaky and disrespectful to Eden, once again showing me that he hadn't changed a bit.

"And I don't eat sandwiches. I have a TV show, you know." Eden turned her attention to me. "The camera really does put ten pounds on me, and the producers are always checking my weight." She shook her head. "I hate that."

"Don't worry, babe. I bought you green goddess salad, no chicken. The sandwich is for me, and for the heiress if she likes." His eyebrows flew up twice. He was flirting with me, and poor Eden couldn't detect it.

I knew the tactic very well. The boundary he'd just crossed pushed me farther down the rabbit hole. I had to tell Eden about his and my past relationship. I wanted to say something then, but she was smiling and in a good mood. Plus, I had to figure out how to tell her the truth that her boyfriend had kept from her. I wished I'd said something that morning.

I focused solely on Eden, pretending Dale wasn't in the room. "How about we leave the modules where they are, and tomorrow morning,

I'll have my team members with me, and we'll finish up and then get into some really fun stuff."

Eden looked incredulous. "Oh, are you leaving?"

I intensified my fake smile. "I am."

"You sure you don't want to stay and eat something with us?"

I hung my purse over my shoulder and swiped my iPad off the counter. "No. It's late, and I have dinner plans for tonight."

Eden raised an eyebrow. "Oh? Preferably with a hot guy who's worthy of having you."

I was happy that my smile was genuine. Her compliment had not escaped my attention.

"She's a Blackstone, babe. They have private chefs and all the other bells and whistles, I'm sure," Dale said before I could respond to Eden.

"You have a private chef?" Eden asked.

Do not look at him.

"Not this time. But"—I clapped my hands, signaling I was bringing all communication to a halt —"I'll see you tomorrow." I thumbed over my shoulder. "And I'll find my way out."

"I'll escort our guest," Dale said.

"Nope," I insisted. "No escorting necessary. Good night." I turned my back on them and got the hell out of there. I was certain that Eden was baffled about why I'd turned down her lemon of a boyfriend's offer to walk me to the car. Apparently, she had no idea what he was capable of, or she would never have so genially offered his services.

When I made it to my car and turned on my engine, which caused the garage door to slide up, I was only thinking one thing. *God, I hate that he's seen me naked.*

Five

BRYN BLACKSTONE

Alone in my car, I narrowed an eye at the road. "Eden, Dale and I used to be a couple. Did you know that?"

"No, but why didn't you tell me this yesterday?" I said, imitating her high-pitched but sultry voice.

I sighed. That was a good question. "Sorry. I thought that should've been his responsibility. But I do have something else to ask you."

I pictured her looking at me even more incredulously than she had before I rushed out of her house. "Like what?"

I took a breath. "Were the two of you together back in October of last year? Was he the one who suggested you contact me? Because that's so in his manipulative little wheelhouse."

I massaged one of my temples, hating that I'd gotten so worked up over a hypothetical situation. I wanted to know the answer to my last question, though. *Or maybe not.*

For the remainder of the short ride back to the resort, I forced myself to ponder what to do about my cell phone. It was probably a good sign that I hadn't received a message from Jamison since that morning. My fingers were crossed that he'd put my device in the mail and I wouldn't have to go through the arduous process of turning off my old phone and buying a new one.

Instead of using the valet, I self-parked. That way, in the morning, I wouldn't have to wait around for someone to go fetch my car. As soon as I entered the lobby, the concierge informed me that I had messages at the front desk. I yawned and dragged myself over to pick them up. I was starving to the point where I could have actually eaten the messages, and I was dreaming about making it back to my room, stripping out of my clothes, and wrapping myself up in the fluffy white robe. Next, I would call room service and order something fattening and greasy that could compete with the hero sandwich I'd turned down. Then I'd shower.

The girl behind the front desk smiled when I

approached her. I read the name on her tag, and before I could ask Kara for my message, she absent-mindedly handed me a slip of paper.

"Thank you." I grimaced at the front of the note before turning to view the back. "This is blank. Are you sure you gave me the right note?"

Kara's smile grew very large, and her face turned red as I waited for her to address my concern. "Sure," she replied, staring googly-eyed at something that was happening behind me.

I twisted my body to see what had stolen her attention. My mouth fell open, and then I closed it to swallow. The tall drink of water who had captured Kara's attention wore a black wool duster over a white cable-knit sweater and black slacks. His figure and face were things of beauty. He stood at least ten feet away from me. I blinked, guessing that my mind was playing tricks on me.

Jamison Cox's sexy lips smirked, and then he waved. "Thanks, Kara. Job well done," he said without ripping his hypnotizing gaze off me.

I could hardly breathe. I didn't know what to say. I resisted the urge to pinch myself to make sure the moment was real. Finally, words found their way out of my mouth. "When I sent you my address, it was for mailing my phone, not hand delivering it."

Jamison's smirk turned yummier as he made his approach and then stopped in front of me. "I wanted to see you."

Oh, his presence. My God, his presence.

A lump formed at the back of my throat. I hadn't noticed Jamison's long fingers handing me my cell phone until then. My hand shivered as I took it. Embarrassed about that, I gazed up at his classically handsome face.

"You didn't have to." The words came out in a whisper even though that wasn't my intention.

His devilish smirk made my lips want to mug his. But I couldn't. He was there uninvited, just like the song. *Remember that, Bryn.*

"You should really password protect that," he said.

My eyes expanded and then narrowed. "Did you go through my messages?"

His dimples looked more delicious than ever. "I wanted to. But I didn't do it. Hey, let's grab a bite to eat," he said as if inviting me to dinner had suddenly popped into his mind.

I could feel Kara's attention and sighed when I

turned to glance at her. She was staring at us, her cheeks still red as a tomato.

I shook my head, knowing that before I arrived, Jamison had worked his magic on her. "Poor thing. She didn't know charm is your superpower."

He stuffed his hands deeper into his coat pockets as he leaned toward me. "Ha. I'm charming? That's news to me."

"Well…" I felt my eyebrows fly up. "At least, when you want something." My eyes were flirting with Jamison Cox, acting against my more cautious brain.

His chuckle sounded like a seductive song. "Are you hungry?"

It was just like Jamison to try another angle. My stomach growled, and hunger pains punched me, but I was certain he couldn't hear the ruckus in my belly. "A little."

"Then let's get a little food, talk, and catch up."

I sighed forcefully. Like a gnat, Jamison was a man who wouldn't stop until he got what he wanted. Before our first and only hot night of mad, passionate… *Sex?*

Now way.

That doesn't capture what went on between us.

Skin on skin, soul on soul, Jamison and I had made love.

Gazing into his eyes, I was experiencing shadow effects of his manhood stretching me. I knew one thing for sure—if I spent any more time with Jamison Cox than our brief encounter in the lobby, he would end up in my bed, or I'd end up in his.

"No, um, I'm fine. I mean, I'm tired. So… thanks for my phone." Walking away from him felt like the worst mistake of my life. But I had to do it. I tried to will my feet to move me away from him, but they stayed stuck to the floor.

Jamison took his hands out of his pockets and motioned as if he wanted to touch me, but in a split-second decision, he chose to rub his palms on his pants instead. "Come on, Bryn. I came this far, and this is it?"

I moaned contemplatively while gnawing on my bottom lip. He'd come a long way to return my cell phone, though I was pretty sure that wasn't his sole purpose in being there. But I'd never asked Jamison to fly all the way from San Francisco to Denver. *Am I obligated to spend time with him?* For certain, I wasn't. He'd gambled on me providing whatever he sought from me. *What is he looking for, anyway? Sex? Friendship? Forgiveness?*

But still, I liked Jamison a lot. I cocked my head, narrowing an eye, ready to bargain. I was starving and curious about what he'd been up to since we last parted.

"Dinner, and then I go to bed, in my room, alone?" I said, more to instruct and convince myself than to inform him.

Jamison's sexy brown eyes were aglow. "Deal."

I waited for him to take at least one hand out of his pocket so we could shake on it, but he didn't. I wished he had, though. A handshake would have given me a reason to touch him.

He turned to examine the sign behind him. "Peak 54 Grill?"

I shrugged. "Sure."

"Then after you."

As I passed Jamison, he pressed his hand against my back, and my insides fluttered. It was going to be difficult trying to downplay my attraction to him. Indeed, I was playing with fire.

Six

JAMISON COX

THE DAY BEFORE

I saw the abandoned object in my peripheral vision. My chest tightened as I hoped like hell Bryn Blackstone didn't suddenly remember she'd left her cell phone on top of the bar. As she walked away, I focused on her long legs and elegant body. The bartender was busy gawking at her too. I didn't blame him. She was a sight for sore eyes.

I didn't have long to decide. The bartender was too busy looking at her to pay attention to what she'd left behind. If he saw it first, by the looks of him, either I'd be out the five hundred bucks it would cost me to pay him off and let me keep the phone, or he'd pretend to be a decent and moral guy and refuse to take my money. But he wouldn't return her phone to her or take it to lost and found. The guy had to be aware that Bryn Blackstone was above his pay grade. Therefore, he wouldn't try to call her. He was afraid of being rejected by such a beautiful woman. He'd keep her device and look through her photos. But he'd be disappointed. She wasn't the kind of person who took personal photos with a cell phone. I knew this, because from the moment I met her, she'd ignited my curiosity, and I watched and studied her as though she were a new client.

When I first met her, it took me less than twenty-four hours to devise an initial report on her. Firstly, she wasn't interested in me. She saw me as a preppy, and she knew what that meant. My conservative and clean appearance—the physical manifestation of trust and sobriety—was a front for concealing deeply buried pain that was opposite of what I was presenting on the outside. She was right to prejudge me that way. I'd grown up in that world. I should have been that guy. But when nature and nurture fought to claim me, I'd tried hard to be nothing like my father had been, and I'd succeeded. To change Bryn's mind about me, I laid bare the parts of myself that I wouldn't usually show others whenever I was around her.

Secondly, I suspected by the way her eyes passed over me that she liked what she saw but wasn't interested in getting to know me better. I chose to wear her down and remain close to her as much as I could. During the weeks we worked together, knowing I would see her every day gave me butterflies in my stomach.

Then, one night, after dinner with her family, she rewarded me for my efforts. Her heat and wetness overwhelmed my senses with a pleasure I'd never known. I wanted to come in less than five seconds. The enjoyment of my cock thrusting in and out of her became the best kind of torture as I fought not to explode. I couldn't look her in the face, but I did. I couldn't kiss her, but my lips wouldn't leave hers alone. She was finally giving herself to me. I wanted to take it all. Her soft, warm skin… her engorged nipples, hard and tasty against my tongue…

I forced my eyes off her cute little ass walking down the corridor on her way to catch her flight. While the bartender kept ogling her, I secured Bryn's cell phone.

"Damn," the bartender said, finally looking away from her. "She's a goddess."

"Agreed," I said, sliding her phone into my pocket. Agreed.

I'D BEEN ON MY WAY TO CATCH MY CHARTERED flight when I caught a glimpse of her sitting alone at the bar. At first, I hadn't realized the leggy blonde was Bryn. The light from above caught the side of her face. She was engrossed in whatever she was doing. I wasn't one of those guys whose tongue hung out of their mouths every time they caught sight of an exceptionally beautiful woman, but after doing a double take, I stopped in my tracks, rubbed my chest over my heart, and muttered, "Well, damn." It was her.

Coming off the taxing weekend I'd had with the Lovells, and considering the fact that Bryn was the last person on earth I thought I would see at an airport bar, I'd taken her presence there as a sign.

Sitting in the airplane, I held her cell phone, rubbing the back of it. There was no signal thousands of miles up in the air at cruising speed. I pressed the home button. Just as I'd guessed, her device wasn't password protected. Having her phone made me feel as if she was sitting beside me. I was craving her beyond reason. After I ran into Bryn, I'd forgotten about how my weekend with the Lovells had worried the hell out of me. I didn't want her worrying, though, so without crossing the line by infringing on her privacy, I pulled her phone number off her device. I knew the old number didn't work anymore, because I'd tried calling it dozens of times to no avail.

Then I sent Bryn a text message letting her know that I had her cell phone. I would have flown out to Colorado to be with her that night, but I had a meeting in LA that I couldn't miss. I was going to be sitting down with Pedro Santiago, a political candidate and long shot for winning as mayor of Alhambra, California. My father didn't know about the meeting.

I read Pedro's profile, digging up as much information about him as I could. He was my kind of candidate, not Boomer's. When it came to candidates, the pickings had become slim for the sort of candidates my father liked to manage ever since he'd chosen to go to war with Jasper Blackstone. But Boomer wasn't worried about the business going up in smoke. He was flushed with cash, and he wanted me to be the son who kissed his ass and ate from his trough. I never had to bend the knee too much as long as I kept Cox and Cox Management afloat though. By all estimations, we couldn't survive another year without winning a political race. We needed people to see that we weren't out of the picture. If I made an unknown candidate a winner, that would send a strong message to those in the political world.

I squeezed Bryn's phone, choosing to keep my mind on her rather than on what would happen to me if Pedro decided to decline my services.

I WAS SERVED AN IN-FLIGHT MEAL OF CRACKED-ginger-and-honey-braised short ribs, citrus-butter risotto, and green beans. The meal was a favorite of mine. I declined dessert. The only sweet thing I wanted was Bryn Blackstone in my mouth. I couldn't wait to taste her again. I had no doubt that soon, I'd be indulging in her body.

"Excuse me, Mr. Cox, but you have a call from your father," the flight attendant said. I hadn't noticed her standing by my shoulder.

Do I want to talk to my father? Hell no.

"Tell him I'll call him back," I said, closing my eyes as I pressed my head against the seat.

"Yes, sir. Um…"

She hadn't moved, so I opened an eye. "Could I help you with something?" I asked.

Her gaze penetrated me. "Can I help *you* with something else?"

It took a moment for her question to seep in. The stewardess stepped closer, her thin hips inches away from my face. She was offering herself to me. That wasn't shocking. The airplane belonged to the company. Boomer preferred a different standard of service than I did. I knew what kind of man he was, and so did Stephanie, my mother.

The one and only time I'd told her that my father was a cheater, her answer was, "Well, that's relative, darling. And while you're at it, it's perfectly fine to mind your own business when it comes to that sort of thing, okay?"

I was rendered speechless, but I wasn't surprised that my parents had an arrangement. My mom had grown up in the sticks of Oklahoma. She was beautiful, regal, and mature, and my father liked his women young and thin as nymphs, the kind of chicks who'd ride him, make a lot of noise, and try to convince him that his cock was magical. As far as

Boomer was concerned, when it came to casual sex, my mom's kind of striking beauty wasn't required. The stewardess's average attractiveness was all he needed.

I looked down at my package. The stewardess must have noticed how dense my cock was. It had nothing to do with her, though. It had everything to do with having Bryn Blackstone on my mind.

"How about this?" I said.

She raised her eyebrows, and her eyes gleamed with hopeful curiosity. The prostitutes my father hired to play stewardess would have rather had me bang them than have him do it. But I never touched them. Pay to play will never be my style.

"Yes?" she sighed.

"You leave me alone, and don't come back in here unless I call for you. Nobody comes in here unless I say so. Got it?"

Her lustful gaze turned confused. "Um, sure. Is that all?"

"No."

"No?" she asked.

"With all due respect, don't ever try that again. I don't pay to play."

She tilted her head and brushed a hand through her hair. "What about for free?"

I jerked my head back, surprised that she was bold enough to ask me that. "Not interested."

Her gazed dropped to my cock. I'd lost my hard-on.

"I'll leave you in privacy, then." She walked out of the cabin.

Once I knew for certain that I was alone and would not be bothered, I lifted Bryn's phone off the seat beside me and smelled it, taking in a faint scent of her. Then I rubbed the damn thing against my cock. Instead of making me feel embarrassed, it made me horny as hell. I undid my pants and envisioned my cock charging into her silken haven. I'd never forgotten how that felt. With one deep inhalation along with a squeeze of my cock, I was experiencing Bryn Blackstone anew.

TWICE, I FINISHED TO MEMORIES OF MAKING LOVE to the one woman in the world I craved. The act wasn't satiating, though. I needed more from her— the total Bryn Blackstone. But at least I got a few hours of shut-eye. Before my flight landed, the stewardess's voice came over the intercom, asking whether I was ready for her to clear the cabin for landing.

With a woozy head, I said yes. I wasn't a slob, so other than a general walk-through, there wasn't much to clean. The stewardess avoided eye contact. I was fine with that. I'd probably never see her again. As I was disembarking, she stood by the door to say goodbye, in customary fashion. Before I made it out, she stepped in front of me and grabbed my cock.

"One day, after you marry your boring, pretentious, uptight wallflower, you're going to need this. I just slipped my card into your pocket. Call me. I want you." Then she walked past me. I didn't turn to get a look at her.

I wondered why the hell she'd said that to me. *What did she overhear while servicing Boomer? What does she know?*

I had to get independent faster than I'd planned. Landing Pedro as a client was more than a wish—it was a necessity. I had a feeling my father was cooking up some sort of scheme with the Lovells. I never wanted to see any of them again, especially Jimmy. And Bree left a bad taste in my mouth too.

Before I'd made it down the ramp, my phone

rang. I was certain it was Boomer. I couldn't put him off any longer. He wouldn't stop calling until he got ahold of me. I knew he wanted to know how Newport had gone.

"Hello," I said.

"Is this Jamison Cox?"

I stopped before my feet hit the concrete. I knew the voice because it was my job to recognize it. "This is he. Is this Mr. Santiago?"

"It's me." He sounded weary, and that worried me. "Sorry, but I'm going to have to cancel our meeting in the morning."

I stood straighter, but that didn't feel like the right position, so I tilted my head back to gaze up at the overlit LA sky. "Well, do you want to reschedule?"

"No. That won't be necessary."

My jaw was so tight it threatened to lock on me. "I don't understand."

"Thank you for thinking of me, but I can't use your services."

His words felt as if they punched me in the gut. "Can I ask you why?"

Pedro paused for a few beats.

"Is it because of Mr. Blackstone—Jasper Black-stone?" I asked.

68

"Who's that?"

I rubbed my eyes, experiencing some relief. Pedro was a young and idealistic candidate, with good ideas and the energy to fight for them. He wasn't familiar with those who were woven into the establishment. That was why I needed him. He would be my first step in a different direction. And because old candidates wanted to appeal to new generations, they would seek me out too. Boomer would get pissed. He would want to cut and run, and I would let him. *Peace out, old man.*

"What is it, then? Because, Pedro, we can win this. I can win this for you."

"It's your father," he said abruptly. I heard bitterness in his tone.

"My father? He's not in this. It's only me…"

"Just, I'm out. Let it be."

"Wait. What happened?" I asked.

"Good night. Good luck." Pedro hung up.

I wanted to wring Boomer's neck. The driver in the motorized cart sat behind the wheel, waiting to take me to my hired car. I needed a moment to figure out what to do next. I was back to square one. It would take months to find another viable candidate. Then it hit me. I knew what I needed to do.

I talked to the pilot. We couldn't fly out to Colorado that night, but we could head out at eleven o'clock in the morning. I took that deal and stayed in a hotel near the airport. Once I got settled in my room, I saw that Bryn had sent a huge gift— the address of where she was staying.

Seven

BRYN BLACKSTONE

T he echo of our footsteps in the hallway disturbed instrumental music that sounded like indie rock playing in the background. I was trying to think of something to say. We'd gotten all the formalities out of the way at the airport the other day. Even though Jamison was his usual drop-dead-gorgeous self, I could sense something had changed since we last saw each other. I was contemplating asking if everything was okay when we made a right and walked down a short set of steps, and the girl at the hostess station, dazzled eyes pasted on Jamison, welcomed us to the restaurant.

"Just the two of you?" she asked Jamison.

His tired eyes lapped me up, and I pressed my

lips together, still wondering what was going on with him.

"Somewhere quiet," he said. "We have, um, a lot of catching up to do."

I rubbed the side of my neck. My skin felt flushed as I looked away from him. I was too attracted to him to win the battle against keeping it casual. I glanced at the steps that led away from the dining room. There lay my last chance for escape.

"Okay, please follow me." The girl started walking.

Jamison wouldn't move until I stepped in front of him. *Why am I so afraid of my attraction to one man?* I needed to get a grip and grow up, so I smiled and followed the hostess.

She took us to a table near the window. Jamison pulled my chair back. I leaned away from him as I sat, but he leaned toward me, refusing to lose the opportunity to be close. The hostess told us the glass was warmed, so we wouldn't feel the chill from outside. It was dark out, but the haze from that morning had lifted enough to give us a majestic view of snow-covered mountains.

The hostess glanced at Jamison. He was staring at me, so she set her focus on me too. "Your waiter will be with you shortly." She'd just gotten her attention redirected by a pro. It reminded me of the biggest reason I'd fallen for him—because Jamison was smart and so damn good at influencing people. I often pondered how I'd gone from having a fleeting interest in him to admiring him to finding him so scorching hot that I could hardly look at him without wanting him to do me.

"Thanks for always being a gentleman," I said as I got comfortable in my seat.

"You smell good."

So do you. I smiled. "Thanks."

"How was your day?" he asked.

A picture of Dale and Eden standing beside each other came to mind. I wanted to groan and complain about how I'd felt ambushed by Dale and completely believed Eden had nothing to do with it. However, seeing him sitting there brought another question to mind. If we were going to sit down together, have a meal, and reconnect, then it would be ludicrous to ignore the past.

"Um… fine."

"You never told me who your client is."

"Jamison," I blurted.

He snapped back in his chair. "Yes, Bryn?"

"We didn't leave things on good terms a few years ago. I know you had your issues with my

73

brother, but if you cared for me, you could've called me, come looking for me, or something. We had such a great connection that night, I thought."

He frowned thoughtfully. "Well, I did call you, but you didn't answer my calls."

"But that was after I lost my cell phone four days later. You could've called me the day after we made love."

His body tensed up. "We were up all night, remember?"

"I do."

"I wanted you to get some sleep. However, I was going to call you later that night and invite you over, but then all hell broke loose."

I frowned as my memory came up with a rebuttal. "But you didn't learn about Spencer's endorsement of Mike Dunn until the following week."

Jamison sighed. "We had some intel about Spencer being in the desert. Boomer went straight through the goddamn roof about it."

The fatigued expression that had been on his face when I encountered him in the lobby returned at the mention of his father. "But you remember what you said before I left, don't you?"

My confusion intensified. "Enlighten me."

"You said, 'Let me call you.'"

My mouth fell open as I tried very hard to remember how Jamison and I had parted that morning. *I did say that.* I'd been afraid of what I felt for him. It was too much too fast.

"Good evening. I'm Brent, your waiter for this evening."

My head felt floaty as I turned my attention to the tall and lanky waiter named Brent. Jamison's explanation had left me breathless, and I was still recovering from that. I'd never tried to view what had happened from his outlook, only from the one that supported him being selfish and willfully letting whatever we'd been building collapse.

"Can I get you started with drinks?" Brent asked after spying our closed menus.

I already knew my order because I'd been dreaming of it all day. Only, I'd planned on scarfing down my burger and fries with a glass of wine while uploading new catalogs into the design app from vendors who sold furniture, lighting, and home-decor items that would better suit the choices we were making for Eden's home.

"I'll have iced tea, unsweetened, and truffle fries with a cheeseburger." I restrained myself from ordering alcohol. I didn't want anything to lower my inhibitions.

"An Angus cheeseburger?" the waiter asked.

My mouth watered. "Just a big, fat, juicy cheeseburger with grilled onions, ketchup, and nothing else."

Jamison smiled bemusedly at his menu. "I'll have the T-bone steak with the house salad."

"Anything to drink?"

"Just water."

The waiter thanked us and walked away. We were alone again, and Jamison's explanation hung in the air, ready for me to respond.

"By the way, I'm sorry," I said.

He narrowed an eye. "For…?"

"My part in our demise."

After a few beats, Jamison cleared his throat. "I have a proposition for you."

"Okay," I whispered.

"How about we forget the past? At least for tonight."

I inhaled sharply. He was asking me to forget that his father and my brothers had a lot of contention between them. *And what about his trip to Newport?* I still suspected a woman was involved. At least, that was what my instincts were telling me. I could've been wrong. *And what did he mean by "At least for tonight"?*

"Are you still working for your father?" I asked, since Boomer was the real reason another attempt at relationship between us would be strained.

He looked away from me to scowl at the dark. "Yes."

"What's going on between the two of you?"

Jamison faced me, the sides of his sexy mouth turned down. "We shouldn't talk about him either."

I felt my eyebrows flit upward, and I forced myself to bite my tongue. I'd hit a nerve. The curiosity about what was going on between Jamison and Boomer was killing me. But I was one for respecting boundaries.

"Okay." I was thinking of what else to say when the waiter interrupted us to serve my iced tea and Jamison's water and then let us know that our dinner would arrive soon.

Then Jamison said, "So... interior designer, huh? I thought you would go into politics. You were good at having your brother's back." He chuckled.

"No, I was just..." I pressed my lips together.

"You were just...?"

I shrugged. "I don't know, proving myself to my brother." I held my breath as his gaze explored my face. "What?"

He shook his head. "And did you?"

I couldn't look away from his sexy mouth. Small talk wasn't helping to quell my lust for him. "Did I what?" I whispered.

"Prove yourself to your brother?"

"Oh…" I adjusted in my seat. The answer was part of a long story regarding my relationship with Spencer. I'd been wrong to want to prove that I was worthy of his love and acceptance. "I didn't have to."

"Knowing Spencer, I don't think you had to prove yourself to him either. He put a lot of trust in you."

"Yeah… he did."

We were staring at each other again. My sex quivered, begging me to let down my defenses so that Jamison could enter me, screw me, make it feel alive.

I abruptly shifted my position in hopes of getting rid of the tingling. That didn't help. "What about you and the girlfriend you were visiting in Rhode Island? Whoever she is must have the Boomer stamp of approval."

Jamison snorted as he looked down at the table, once again proving to me that I was right about there being another woman.

"There's no girlfriend," he said, looking up again.

"Whatever you say."

"You don't believe me?"

I shook my head slowly. "I don't."

He smirked, making his dimples more pronounced.

Damn, he's sexy.

"That's because you don't want to believe me."

He was wrong—very wrong.

"Bryn, I still like you. A lot. I haven't been able to stop thinking about you. I think there was something… I don't know, pretty amazing happening between us. Don't you?"

I swallowed the lump in my throat. Jamison was reeling me in yet again. He was an expert at it. I couldn't think. I had to change the subject.

"What about you?" I cleared my throat. "What have you been working on recently?"

Not until he sat back did I notice he'd been leaning in toward me. Jamison shook his head. "A lot of craziness?"

I grunted thoughtfully. "Are you still working with Agent Tammy Preston?"

He looked confused. "Who's that?"

"Kristen. I mean Bree. That was her real name."

"Bree Lovell? Why are you referring to her as Agent Tammy Preston?"

"*Twin Peaks?*" I said as if the answer was obvious.

"What's *Twin Peaks?*"

I raised a finger, chuckling. "Give me a second."

Jamison wiggled his eyebrows. I could feel him studying me as I searched for a clip of Agent Tammy Preston on YouTube. Brent returned with our dinner.

"How about a bottle of your best red," Jamison said.

"Mes Fleurs première classe?"

"We'll take it," Jamison replied.

I looked up with a grin as Brent walked away. "Then you're going to drink a whole bottle of wine by yourself?"

Jamison focused on my mouth and then wet his bottom lip. I narrowed my eyes at him even more. *Goodness, he is a dangerous fire to be playing with. Who am I kidding with that question? Not him.*

I had the video ready to go and handed him my phone. "Here you go." I cleared the frog out of my throat. "Press Play."

His long, strong fingers brushed the back of my hand as he took my cell phone. "This is a good sign."

"What's a good sign?"

"I give your phone back to you, and you give it back to me."

"Why is that such a good sign?"

"We're building something here," he said.

I had no idea what he meant other than that we both had large grins pasted on our faces. After a few seconds, he looked away from me to view the video. I felt released from his spell as I watched him.

I shouldn't do this. I could do this. I want to do this.

He let out a laugh. "Wow, she does have Bree's mannerisms," he said, still watching.

I sniffed. "I know. It's crazy."

When he gave me back my phone, I made sure our skin didn't touch. "She was jealous of you," he said. "She tried to convince me to fire you from the campaign several times."

I scoffed. "Spencer would've never let that happen."

"That is true."

"Plus, not only did she want to bang my brother, but she wanted to bang you too. I actually thought the two of you were getting it on."

Jamison sneered at me. "Are you fishing, Miss Blackstone?"

The smoldering look in his eyes made my heart beat faster. I tilted my head, going with the flow, willingly playing the game of cat and mouse. "Maybe."

"Never."

"You've never had sex with her?"

He shook his head.

"Have you wanted to have sex with her?"

Again, he shook his head. "She's not my type."

I snorted. "Not into banging Agent Tammy Preston?"

"I prefer Helen of Troy."

"She's a myth."

"So is Tammy Preston."

"Not as far as Bree Lovell is concerned."

Jamison chuckled. "Touché."

Brent was back with the wine and poured a glass for Jamison and one for me too. I didn't refuse my glass and didn't want to. Jamison was saying something about Bree having several personalities. Suddenly, I saw him and me together. My breath hitched as I visualized his hands roaming my body and his mouth stimulating my erogenous zones, finding hot spots I never knew existed. My womanhood was experiencing a sense memory of his girthy erection plunging in and out of my ready depths. I shut my eyes tightly, pushing the image out of my head.

"Are you okay?" he asked, sounding concerned.

"Mm-hmm," I said, nodding erratically, and took a sip of wine.

"So, here's what I want to know," he said, smiling smugly. I was positive Jamison knew he was getting me all hot and bothered.

I took another drink of wine. "Hm?"

He smirked. "I'm a busy man, but my cell phone doesn't ring nearly as much as yours."

On cue, my attention snapped to my device as it rang while sitting on top of the table. We laughed at the strange coincidence. I looked to see who was calling and then picked up my cell phone.

I raised a finger. "I'm sorry, Jamison. Could you give me a moment?"

Grinning, he nodded. The way he wasn't a jerk about me taking a call in the middle of our dinner made me want him even more. I knew my skin was flushed, but I couldn't help that.

"Hey," I said, curling away from Jamison for privacy.

It was Alana, one of my assistants. In a frantic

rush, she told me that they couldn't fly out of New York that night because the storm had blown in faster than forecasted. "It's really bad, Bryn. Alex and I think we should just get home while we still can and wait this one out."

I nodded feverishly. "I agree. Eden and I have plenty to do tomorrow. If I need you for something, I'll call you, but for now, get home. We'll stay in touch."

"Thanks. Love you."

"Love you too," I replied.

I ended the call and then faced Jamison, who was frowning. "You love Alan?" I detected regret in his tone.

I chuckled and rolled my eyes. "You mean Alana, my assistant?" I explained the weather conditions to him and how I'd been expecting Alana and Alex that night.

"Then you'll be alone tonight?" he asked.

My mouth opened, but nothing came out, because my brain was experiencing a traffic jam. I wanted to say yes or maybe no. Fortunately, Brent arrived at our table with our entrées. My plate hit the table, and I wasted no time plopping a hot, crispy, delicious truffle fry into my mouth. After one went in, then went another and another. Brent poured more wine for me and Jamison. I bit into the sweet bun with tasty cheese, sautéed onions, and savory meat. My body became more satiated with each bite.

"Then you were hungry?" Jamison asked.

I paused and paid attention to myself. My posture was slumped, and I'd been tearing into my food like a lion with a fresh kill. Laughing, I sat up straight. "Yeah, I was." I took another bite of burger.

He watched me with an adoring smile. My heart, mind, and sex loved the way he looked at me. "Remember the dinner at your brother's house?"

I nodded, putting another fry into my mouth.

"The food was good," he said.

"Yep."

"You enjoyed it."

"I did."

"It was so damn sexy."

I stopped midchew. Our gazes penetrated each other. There was no doubt about it—we'd gotten to the point of no return.

Jamison tapped on the table and then abruptly leaned toward me. "I didn't get a room because you have a two-bedroom suite," he whispered, his gaze penetrating me.

I cleared my throat, smirking. "Poor Kara at the front desk. She didn't even know what hit her."

Jamison chuckled. "I'm just a man who knows how to get the information I need."

I narrowed my eyes seductively. "And what you want?"

His Adam's apple bobbed as he swallowed. "Bryn?" He sounded out of breath.

I leaned toward him. "Jamison?"

"How about we take all of this to go?"

The stillness and silence between us reigned. My sex throbbed, and my nipples stiffened, both responses making me squirm in my chair. If we let our guard down and got it on, I would be choosing to bed Jamison despite his father and my brothers.

My head felt as if it was floating to the ceiling when I made my final decision. "And you don't have a girlfriend or anything?"

His focus on me remained steady, deep. "No, beautiful. Not yet."

Eight

BRYN BLACKSTONE

rent arranged to have room service bring our dinner and another bottle of wine to my suite. Being the perfect gentleman that he was, Jamison carried my briefcase and slung my purse over his shoulder as we walked to the elevator. I'd never had a guy carry my purse. The very small, considerate gesture made me feel taken care of in a gentler way. My heart loved it. I liked him. I could no longer ignore that fact.

With Jamison standing so close to my backside, I could feel the heat coming off him. He reached around me to push the elevator button. The doors opened, and my head maintained the wooziness as, with his strong fingers cradling my waist, we stepped inside.

"The sixth floor?" he asked, his breath warming the back of my neck and his voice thickened by lust.

I swallowed. Unable to speak, I nodded. My body remained caught in suspense as I kept my eyes on the floor. I heard Jamison pressing the button and the briefcase hitting the linoleum. His hands seized my hips and guided me against all the firm parts of him. I stifled a gasp, tossing my head back against his broad chest. All my defenses and inhibitions were so distant it was as if they'd never existed.

"Yeah, dude, that was gnarly," a guy said followed by the sound of the doors reopening.

Regaining a little bit of my willpower, I turned to face Jamison. Our melded gazes didn't allow me to be cordial to our new arrivals. The longer I looked at Jamison, the more euphoric I felt. Then he trailed a finger down the side of my face. I closed my eyes and tilted my head back to drink in the sensations.

"Yeah, the powder is pristine." I could hear the nervousness in the second voice.

"Right… yeah." The first guy sounded just as anxious.

Unfortunately, they'd walked in on a heated

moment that couldn't be extinguished. I was certain our raw sexual desire for each other thickened the air. The elevator remained silent. My heart pounded, and fluttering sensations ignited in my belly. The elevator dinged. The doors slid open, and the people who were enclosed with us were out in a flash.

We only had one more floor to go. Jamison tugged me against his rock-hard body, and then his warm, delicious tongue was rounding mine. We breathed heavily against each other's mouths as our kissing turned more intense. I ran my fingers through his neat but windswept hair, and he did the same with mine.

"You're so…" Our greedy kissing wouldn't let him finish whatever he was going to say.

His stiff chest and cock against me and his strong arms wrapping around me made me want to burst into flames. It had been so long since I'd been that close to a man that I'd forgotten what unadulterated sexual desire felt like. Not even the loud *ding* could bring me back to my senses.

Jamison ended our kiss by dragging my lower lip between his teeth and then whispered, "Let's go."

I fell fully under his spell when he picked up my

briefcase and took my hand, our fingers interlaced. There was nothing left to say, no small talk to be had. I knew what came next. I let myself glance down at his package just to make sure I was right about my assumption. Jamison's crotch was so swollen. I was so wet. There was no turning back.

We made it to the door of my suite, and Jamison handed me my purse. "The key," he said without lessening his deep and prolonged eye contact.

Gosh, he is so sexy. I hated looking away, but I had to so that I could fumble my keycard out of my wallet with shaky fingers. I almost lost it when Jamison pressed himself against me, laying soft, wet kisses on the side of my neck. My knees felt weak as the door beeped. He reached around me to turn the knob.

Unable to control my desire, I rotated to face him. Our lips mashed against each other. Next, tongues. My fingers tousled his hair. He bunched up my hair, pressing my mouth harder against his. Panting, tasting, Jamison lifted my feet off the ground. The door slammed closed.

We're inside.

CLINK.

Clomp.

Heavy breathing.

Smacking.

His tongue swirling around mine.

Suction.

My back hitting the sofa.

His heaviness on top of me.

His cock rubbing against me, letting me know what it craves.

Knock. Knock. Knock.

"Room service."

"Damn it," Jamison said against my mouth. "I'll get it."

As soon as he got up, I got up too.

"In the bedroom," I said and trotted up the hallway before he could object.

My body was trembling when I made it to the bedroom. Shaking, I plopped down on the foot of the bed, running my fingers through my hair and then over my breasts. My nipples were hard as pebbles. My desire for Jamison was too overwhelming, and I needed to control it, especially since there was something I needed to remember.

What is it?

I sprang to my feet when I heard Jamison say, "Put that in the kitchen with my bag over there."

My panties!

Jamison continued whatever conversation he was having with room service. It sounded as if he was talking to more than one person. I had seconds to get my comfortable granny panties off.

I pushed my jeans down and stomped out of them. Next came the pale-pink cotton panties. The crotch was soaked.

I tugged my sweater off over my head and then my T-shirt. Then off came my full-coverage, bland white bra. Jamison said final goodbyes to the guys in the other room.

"Oh no," I whispered and kicked my unsexy underwear under the bed then climbed on the bed and stretched out on my side, head resting on my palm, torso twisted, hip high, and toes pointed—a total come-get-it pose.

Jamison's footsteps came to a halt when he stopped in the doorway. "Woe," he whispered, his eyes drinking me in. "Don't move." He darted over to the nightstand and set a box of extra-large condoms on top of it. My sex shuddered as I remembered that they were the right size for his magnificent cock.

"That's pretty presumptuous," I joked. I was more nervous than I'd been a second before.

Jamison chuckled as he snatched his sweater off over his head and then his T-shirt, revealing his bare chest, which only had a sparse amount of hair on it.

That's sexy.

"I arranged a box," he said.

I had no snappy comeback. Instead, my breathing quickened as he pushed down his trousers then undies, and his enormous erection sprang up, tilting toward his stomach.

Jamison appeared dazed as his eyes explored my body, starting at my shaved vag and then moving up to my face. He licked his lower lip and then grabbed his manhood. "I've been dreaming about this," he whispered.

I swallowed and was so excited that I mashed my thighs together, squirming. I released a sigh, feeling a surge of pleasure race through me. He hadn't even put his hands on me yet, and he was driving me wild.

He muttered a string of curse-words as he attacked the box of condoms, ripping the cardboard. Then he tore one off the attached roll of ten. I flipped onto my back, sucking air as he rolled the rubber over his erection. Jamison separated my knees. Our eyes remained locked.

Here he comes.

JAMISON COX

I'm standing on my knees between her legs. My breathing is all over the place as I stare at her fuzzy mound. I need a moment. If I go in now, I'll blow. But the heat rising from the insides of her thighs and her sweetness is driving me crazy.

I swallow the moisture pouring into my mouth. I want to taste what I'm looking at, but I want to be inside her more. But first, I'll touch it.

I slide a finger up and down her slit. Her sexy lips part, and her pretty face shows how much she likes what I'm doing. The suppleness around her firm clit drives me wild. I want it in my mouth. But later… I'll taste it later.

"Mmm…" she moans, squirming, as my thumb rounds her knob and fingers sink into her balmy, wetness. She's so goddamn receptive. So ready. "Ahh…" Her pelvis tenses as her hips rise to my fingers. Bryn's eyes close, the skin between her eyes pinched. Her mouth opens, soft, sexy lips ripe for kissing.

I rub. Around. Faster.

"Jam..." she cries and then sucks her lower lip.

Damn.

"Oh... ha!" she cries out, and her thighs quiver.

I'm beyond hard. I can't take it anymore. "Oh yeah..." I snatch her by her thighs, separating them and slamming my cock deep inside her.

"Oh..." Her wetness swallows my cock. "Damn."

I shiver as I pump in and out of her. I don't want to shiver, but I can't stop.

Her hands brush up and down my back. Her breaths waft against my ear. Every thrust sends billows of pleasure through me. I'm too overstimulated.

I'm going to come, though...

No.

I close my eyes and concentrate on stopping my release. "Just," I mutter and pin her to the bed, holding her hips still.

It makes it harder when she touches me that way. But that doesn't stop me from feeling her warm, soft body. Her sexy tenderness gets me excited, too, but I can't do anything to get a reprieve from that part of her. It's her soul, her spirit, her being. And then she moans into my ear and whispers, "You feel so good."

Damn...

I ram my cock deep inside her and then surge in and out. I see white light as orgasm seizes my cock. "O-O-Oh!" I call, my lower half convulsing because it feels too damn good. "Bryn," I whisper when it's over, and I don't want it to end.

BRYN BLACKSTONE

We remained motionless. Jamison was still on top of me, inside me. Our hearts beat hard against each of our chests. Our heavy breathing needed time to calm.

"That was amazing," I said.

It was actually better than amazing. Our sex was spiritual, life altering, the sort of lovemaking that marked the beginning of a couple's forever. But I couldn't say that out loud.

Jamison's lips sought and found mine and led me into deep, soul-rousing kissing. We rolled all over the sheets, messing them up. His scent of citrus, vanilla, soap, and raw masculinity made me hornier. Without our mouths breaking apart, Jamison rolled me on top of him.

I tossed my head back, releasing a long sigh when he gripped my torso to lift my right breast to his mouth. The erotic sensations of his soft, wet, warm tongue and the gentle nibbling of his teeth sent sizzling pleasure through my womanhood.

I had no idea if he was building a new erection, but I squeezed my walls around his manhood and raised my hips, searching for…

"Ah…" Orgasm streaked through me.

Jamison's manhood stretched me. He'd risen again, his cock gliding in and out of me.

Back arched, head back, eyes expanded, staring at the ceiling and caught in wonderful euphoria, I sighed.

Round two.

LATER, I LAY WITH MY HEAD RESTING ON JAMISON'S broad chest. I could hear his heartbeat, and whenever he spoke, it sounded as if his voice was magnified. I clung to him because I chose not to think about the consequences of what we'd just done. The first time Jamison and I made love, I noted that it was different than any other sex I'd ever had. Granted, I'd only had a handful of sex partners in my life, but I'd been pounded by guys who'd wanted me so much they orgasmed within a minute. I'd engaged in clawing, biting, ravishing-each-other, down-and-dirty sex. But after the second time with Jamison, I could honestly conclude that the soulful sensation that had occurred when we first made love hadn't been a one-time thing.

While rubbing my shoulder, Jamison kissed the top of my head and then planted a delicately deep kiss on my forehead, even using a small amount of tongue.

"Now what?" he asked.

"Meaning?"

"What are we going to do next?"

I sighed. "Well… I have a lot of work to do, and I'm on a tight deadline. My assistants are delayed, so that's going to set me back…"

"Hey, how about I be your assistant for tomorrow?" Jamison said.

I chuckled.

"I'm serious, Bryn. I'll do whatever you want. Coffee run, sex—you name it, I'll do it."

Parading Jamison in Dale's face would be the best revenge. Jamison was the kind of man Dale thought he should be but was too screwed up to ever become. Dale was the classic American tragedy. He had a critical father, Jim, who he could never please even after spending most of his life trying to do just that. Dale attended Harvard, graduated at the bottom of his class, and then clerked for Judge Herbert Nylander, all to make Jim happy. It didn't work. Jim put him down even more. Dale's mother, Loriann, had always been too busy making sure the insufferable perpetual-asshole Jim was happy and still paying attention to her.

Setting aside thoughts of Dale, I asked Jamison if Boomer was expecting him in the office in the morning, and he went silent. I waited for him to say something.

"Randolph Blackstone has been dead for how long? Six years?" he finally asked.

I raised my head to look into his eyes. "About seven years. Why do ask?"

Jamison wrapped his arms around me, our bodies readjusting until he was behind me, sliding his manhood between my thighs and against my opening. "Damn, you're so wet." He sighed.

Tickling sensations trailed through my nipples and activated the nerves through my sex. "Then what are you waiting for?" I whispered.

"Babe, I want to make love to you nonstop. But I need breaks or else."

I chuckled. "Or else?"

"Or else I'll run out of steam and…"

Jamison went silent. I could have urged him to finish whatever he was going to say, but I already knew what came next. He would run out of steam, and that would be it—we would be done.

"But why did you ask about Randolph?" I asked in an attempt to change the subject.

"I think…" He sighed, rubbing his burgeoning erection against my slit.

Somehow, my clit got stimulated, and I whimpered. "You think?"

He did it again and then sighed, pulling me against him. "I think your brothers are lucky that he's gone."

I agreed with him. "And so am I."

Suddenly, Jamison's body stiffened. "Did he ever touch you?"

I pondered Jamison's question, and something occurred to me. "Do you know, you're the first person, other than my brothers and my therapist, who's asked me that question."

He stopped stroking my hip. "Then he did touch you?"

"No. He tried, but Jasper stopped him, and from then on, he pretended I didn't exist."

Jamison grunted thoughtfully.

"What?" I asked.

"Nothing. Just, you make sense to me now, that's all."

I frowned. "I don't get it."

"You're so damn beautiful, Bryn. Women who look like you know their power and use it to get whatever the hell they want. But you don't do that."

I grunted thoughtfully. I would have turned to see his face, but I loved the way his erection between my thighs teased me. I felt as if at any moment, he would ram it inside me.

"What is it?" he asked.

"Are you trying to figure out my particular daddy issues?"

Jamison snorted softly in my ear and then kissed the side of my neck. "No, that's not it."

His tenderness made me wetter. "You know how you carried my purse and briefcase?"

"Yeah…" he said as if he was trying to figure out why I'd mentioned that.

"No guy has ever done that for me before."

"No guy's ever carried your things for you? I'm sure your brothers have. Haven't they?"

I thought hard, trying to remember an instance. "I think my brothers wanted me to learn rugged individualism within an environment where servants were paid to make my life overly comfortable."

Jamison grunted thoughtfully, and I explained how Jasper had run the household in my father's constant absence. "He once told me, 'Bryn, I don't want you to get used to living this way just in case one day it's taken away from us.'"

"You're telling me Jasper Blackstone believed he could lose all the money your family has?"

I chuckled as I remembered what I was thinking when Jasper issued me the warning. "No… I don't think so. I don't even think what he said came from him."

"What do you mean?"

"His mother. My mother. Amelia…" I was on the verge of revealing something to a man who, by all indications, was my brother's foe. Making love to and falling for him was bad enough. "Forget it."

He moved my hair to kiss the back of my neck. "You can trust me, Bryn."

I fell silent. *Can I?* I wanted to trust him, but I knew all about deception. We had a once-in-a-life-time soul connection, but Jamison was still working for his father, which meant he hadn't given up on trying to please Boomer Cox.

"Have you read *The Dark Blackstones*?" I asked.

Jamison sniffed. "From cover to cover."

I chuckled. "Why did you read it?"

"I wanted to get to know you better."

I twisted around to see his face. "Then you read it after you met me?"

He planted a tender kiss on my lips, sending my heart racing to the moon. "Yes," he whispered.

His handsome face was so close to mine. We beamed at each other. "Well... you surely got to know me better," I said.

The breath from his long sigh wafted across my face. "How so?"

Striking like a viper with its prey, Jamison clutched my hip. I listened to myself release an unrestrained gasp as he shoved his thick, hard cock inside me.

Round Three.

JAMISON COX

I have two handfuls of her perfect cone-shaped breasts. Her hard nipples are against my palms. I want to bust right through her. My desire for Bryn Blackstone is beyond reason.

I suck on the back of her shoulder. She shudders and sighs. Her salty skin is soft as air against my tongue, and the warmth, slipperiness, and tension around my cock make me…

"Oh…" My voice shakes as I experience pleasure that's unlike any other.

But I'm not done. I put her on her back. I suck her pointy breasts. They're deep in my mouth. I bite a nipple. Not too hard, but I want her to feel it.

"Ah," she grunts.

Yes. I shove my fingers up her wetness, thumb against her clit. "Come for me, baby. Let me hear you come."

I work her clit. I eat her breasts. I finger her her until her walls tighten and she cries out, saying my name.

I WANTED HER TO GET SOME REST SO SHE COULD BE fresh for work at sunup, but I couldn't let her sleep. I was overdosing on Bryn Blackstone. I'd fantasized about what was happening between us thousands of times while masturbating.

"That wasn't supposed to happen," I whispered and pelted her back and the nape of her neck with kisses. "Umm…"

"Was it the book that inspired you to screw me?" Bryn's tone was somber, her body motionless.

I leaned over her shoulder to see her face. "Are you okay?" I asked, hoping I hadn't unintentionally offended her.

"I'm fine." Her smile let me know she meant what she said. "I just want to know if you were having sex with me or her."

"Who do you mean by 'her'?"

"Her—the Bryn Blackstone depicted in the book."

I pondered her question, recalling the evening I started reading the biography about her family. I'd had a long and taxing day at the San Francisco office. My father, who I hadn't heard from in weeks, had shown up and put himself in every major decision that had been mine to make. As usual, Boomer hadn't informed himself of the ins and outs of each situation, yet he insisted on interjecting himself and changing carefully set plans of action according to his gut.

His barging in and taking control had been getting worse as he'd gotten older, and he even liked to put me down while he built himself up in front of our staff. On the drive home, I thought of ways of talking my father into finally retiring and leaving the business to me. Ever since the Spencer Blackstone situation, we'd lost multiple accounts. Our candidate lost big in that race, and everyone knew why. We'd messed with the Blackstones, and no one wanted Jasper Blackstone on their bad side if they could help it. We could have helped it. I knew better. Jada Blackstone had requested my services. I told Boomer about it, and despite everything we knew about starting trouble with one of the most powerful families in the world, he saw an opportunity to play Patricia Forte against her son-in-law so our candidate could have a better shot at winning. I was never going to accept Jada's job offer. When I arrived at our meeting, my goal was to persuade her to convince her husband to drop out of the race. I had no doubt Spencer Blackstone was going to win —every poll showed it. I also knew, by chronicling every statement Spencer made publicly, that he didn't care about politics and was only in the race to beat his mother-in-law.

Then Bryn appeared at our table. She was a game changer. Boomer's plan remained the same, though—I was supposed to destroy Spencer's campaign from the inside. I was sort of okay with it because I knew he didn't want to win. If we'd left it at that, there never would have been any bad blood between the Coxes and the Blackstones. But losing to Michael Dunn angered Boomer. My dad was from a different generation. He'd learned that powerful meant being a mean asshole who had the right to bring a bazooka to a stick fight. Without my knowledge, Boomer had fired not one but two rockets at the Blackstones. Jasper had been making us pay for it ever since.

So the Blackstones, especially Bryn, had been on my mind that evening when I returned home, frustrated about my father's inability to learn a lesson about messing with the wrong people. I believed I'd lost Bryn for good, and soon I would be hearing about her marriage to some other lucky guy. My housekeeper had set the package containing the Blackstone family biography on top of a pile of mail on the desk in my home office. I ripped the package because I knew what was inside. Still standing, I read the first page. The language immediately sucked me in.

Unable to stop reading, I sat on the sofa, and hours later, near sunup, I was fighting sleep and upset with myself for not getting the rest I needed to get through a full day of work—I had to convince a handful of prospective clients to let me run their campaigns. But I couldn't put the book down.

At six o'clock in the morning, I called my secretary and asked her to reschedule my appointments for that day. I told her I was under the weather. I wasn't. Then I took the book to my bedroom. Lying on my bed, I read Holly Henderson Blackstone's depiction of Bryn twice. The book described how they met initially during college orientation and how Holly thought it was strange that Bryn whispered when she spoke. Then Holly went into an account of a bored heiress who was always up to no good. After the third time I read it, I seized my cock and fantasized about pounding the hell out of that bad girl as I masturbated.

After I came, I'd been embarrassed and thought, *What the hell was that?* I wasn't the sort of guy who used sex as power. I was still confused by why that had turned me on. I could still remember my favorite passage from the book.

I heard a finger snap. "Earth to Jamison."

I blinked myself back to the moment. She was smiling at me. Her face was angelic, but more importantly, so was her heart.

"I was just remembering my favorite part of the biography," I said.

Turning her head slightly, she narrowed an eye. "Oh yeah?"

I trailed a finger down the side of her soft face. "'Her hair was short, curly, and as soft as her practiced whispery tone. She reminded me of a blond flapper girl from the 1920s. Her skin was like delicate porcelain and her smirk as sensual as a red-lace bow. She was the embodiment of American perfection down to its mythical construction. But if you looked closely, paid attention, you would see the truth. Bryn Blackstone wasn't like the other girls, nor was she like me. She wasn't an angel or a devil, good or bad. Occasionally, I caught myself wondering if she truly existed. Bronwyn Henrietta Blackstone was an alien, and her upbringing was the planet that had made her.'"

Bryn's jaw had dropped. "You remember that?"

I smirked, feeling proud of myself, wanting her to know that was how into her I was. "Yeah."

"Wow." She propped herself up on her arm.

We stared into each other's eyes. *Damn.* I craved her so damn much. My cock was in down-boy mode for the rest of the night. I'd given her all I had, but I wanted to draw her under me, suck on her plump breasts, and taste my way down to her succulent peach, making her orgasm until I was able to slip inside her yet again.

Her lips were heading toward mine. They connected, and then her body was on top of me. We kissed, moving all over the bed until I was able to carry out my plan of sucking her breasts, tasting down to her clam, and making her climax repeatedly.

Nine

BRYN BLACKSTONE

y cell phone rang, and I opened one eye. The curtains were open, and the atmosphere was dank. It was snowing outside, and I had to get up, get dressed, and go out in the unfavorable weather conditions. Not only that, but I felt as if a freight truck had collided with my head on the one hand, while my body felt satiated on the other hand.

The phone kept ringing, and I slowly opened my eyes some more. Jamison was holding me firmly against him, which made my skin warm. I groaned and tried to scoot out of his embrace, but he pulled me closer, grinding his fresh erection against my ass.

"Where are you going?" he whispered.

"I had a call."

He chuckled. "It's already started, huh?"

I laughed, nestling deeper into his hard body. "And I have to get to work. I'm certain I'm late."

"Call off sick today," he said as he guided me on to my back. When he reached down to grab his package, I knew I should halt what was about to happen, but I didn't want to.

Jamison inserted himself securely between my thighs.

"But that was probably Eden who just called. She's wondering where…"

I gasped as his cock pushed through my heat, and then pumped in and out of me. Jamison sipped air deep into his throat. "You feel so damn good."

"So do you," I sighed.

I closed my eyes, letting my hips rise toward his stimulation, moaning, breathing, whimpering, and sighing his name.

Then, Jamison mumbled a string of curse-words as her shuddered against me, freeing himself inside me.

I'd already done the calendar counting. According to the start of my last period and my normal cycle, I wasn't in jeopardy of getting pregnant. But having a baby was the least of my worries.

"We should've used a condom. I mean, you have an entire box, and we've only used one." I waited for his response.

"I haven't been with anyone since you," he whispered and then carefully took himself out of me. Jamison rolled onto his back, never taking his eyes off me.

"No way. Really?"

"Yeah," he said with a sigh. "For real."

I was speechless. It was hard to believe a man as strapping and rich, who could merely glance at a woman and make her panties wet, hadn't had sex in over a year.

"Should I have kept that to myself?" Jamison said.

Throat tight and lips pursed, I shook my head. "Me neither," I whispered.

"You neither?"

"I haven't been with anyone since me and you either."

A slow smile formed on Jamison's mouth. His large fingers wrapped around my wrist. He was on the verge of guiding me under him again, but my cell phone rang.

"Damn it. I have to get to work, Jamison."

Then I saw Dale's face in my mind, and dread made me feel nauseated.

"Whoa. What's that look on your face about?"

"Dale, my ex. Remember I told you he was my client's boyfriend?"

"Yes, I remember."

"I think he's cooking something up. He's such a schemer. We both used to have that in common."

"My offer still stands," Jamison said.

"You were serious about that?"

"Of course. Let me be your assistant today."

I let out a laugh. "But you can't be my assistant. You're Jamison Cox, political strategist extraordinaire."

He finished the act of guiding me under him. Our noses nearly touched as we gazed deeply into each other's eyes. "Let me be with you today. I want to be wherever you are."

His lips and tongue engaged softly with mine. My heartbeat raced as our kissing intensified. We could have made out all morning and into the night. I could have kissed Jamison forever. But time had put constraints on how long we could indulge in each other's mouths, along with heavy petting and him skillfully finger-banging me.

"Okay," I said when our lips separated so we

could catch our breaths. "You can be my assistant. But we have to get out of bed now."

———

THE FIRST THING WE DID WAS SCARF DOWN breakfast. Jamison and I showered separately. I was late, and there was not a minute available to be used for more hanky-panky. While showering, I placed a quick call to my mother, Beth, putting her on speakerphone. Since she was a victim of Randolph's, my mom received enough restitution payment to never have to work again. Recently, she'd moved from Santa Monica to an olive grove in Paso Robles, California. She never realized how much she enjoyed growing and picking the olives and then processing fresh virgin olive oil. She'd made changes by leaps and bounds since I first laid eyes on her in that Nashville hotel.

But our conversation couldn't last long, being that I had to get to work and the contractor who was building the quaint general store on her property had arrived. Beth wanted to attract more tourists. She loved having conversations with strangers, telling them the parts of her life story she was comfortable with sharing. Plus, she made some of the best olive oil I'd ever tasted.

As I put on a pair of comfortable jeans and a fitted long-sleeved T-shirt and no bra—for Jamison's pleasure and because I wanted to be sexy for him, to my embarrassment—I called Kat.

"Ooh, who's the guy answering your phone?" she asked while on her way into her next seminar.

"Jamison."

"No way. *The* Jamison Cox?" she exclaimed. "The guy who shattered your heart?"

"The one and only."

Someone on her end excitedly greeted her. Kat returned the greeting with equal enthusiasm. "Bryn, let's talk later, okay?" she said.

"Okay. Love you."

"Love you too. Oh, and be careful, okay?"

I frowned. "Okay."

Our call ended. Her warning reminded me of how much I'd let my guard down when it came to Jamison Cox. *What's done is done. He and I had fun together.* But it was more than just fun, and I felt awful trivializing what we were experiencing together that way.

I hadn't much time to think about the next step for Jamison and me as I rushed to the mirror. It was just like Kat to bring sobriety into white-hot-passionate situations. I was two calls down. As I put serum on my face to give my skin that naturally dewy look and then pink-stain lipstick, I returned my twin brother Asher's call. I was not surprised to get his voicemail. He was always in surgery. I followed that up with a call to Pen to see if she knew what he wanted and reached her voicemail too. She was more than likely in surgery as well.

My final call before heading out was to Holly. I wanted to make sure she knew I still planned to fly into New York on Saturday to babysit Jane and my brand-new nephew, Oliver, that weekend while she and Jasper took a minibreak and went to Toronto. Holly, who was going into a meeting, confirmed that we were still on. I smiled from ear to ear as I put on my lace-up ankle boots. I couldn't wait to kiss Jane and Ollie.

Jamison was sitting on the sofa, arms extended across the top of the seat, when I dashed into the living room. He rose to his feet. "I love your style." His eyes sparkled and danced approvingly.

Whereas I was super casual and laid-back, he had a pair of heather-gray chinos, a navy blue cable-knit sweater, and dress shoes. I would have advised him to wear something less dressy, but I knew that what he had on was Jamison's version of casual.

"Same," I said, beaming back at him. And I meant it. The way his trousers cuddled his thighs and his package gave me shivers of desire that were not typical of me.

I stood immobilized as he walked toward me and wrapped me in his arms. I drifted into his embrace as his teeth gently seized my bottom lip before he softly sucked it into his mouth. It was a sensual start to a head-spinning kiss.

Then he looked down at my chest and flicked my nipple. "No bra?"

My lips formed a naughty smirk. "Uh-uh."

He inhaled sharply. "Come on. Let's stay in, baby."

I swallowed and took a moment to recover the strength in my legs and to let my mind find focus once again. "I can't," I whispered.

"Why not?"

"I'm on a tight schedule."

He wiggled his eyebrows. "An heiress with a tight work schedule. That's a new one."

I tilted my head to study his expression as I asked him, "How many heiresses do you know?"

Jamison tilted his head back to chuckle. "Not

many but enough to know you're different from the rest."

What am I looking for? Deception? Dishonesty? Cruelty? Vulgarity? All of the above? Those were traits I often suspected belonged to men who'd attempted to court me in the past. But I'd made a commitment to think differently so that I could open myself up to healthy new experiences when it came to love.

I kissed him quickly, deciding to not scurry up the path of questioning him about other heiresses he could be involved with until he had done something that proved he was a preppy playboy who banged more than one girl at a time. I took him by the hand. "Let's go, assistant. We're late."

Jamison tugged me against his barrel chest and tongued me long, hard, and deep. As usual, his kiss made my panties moisten, my head spin, and my body crave more.

"You're not playing fair," I whispered once our lips parted so that we could get air.

He raised his eyebrows. "Then it's working."

He was right, but I shook my head. "Nope." I tugged him toward the door. "Let's go."

I SIGHED. JAMISON WAS DRIVING AT A SNAIL'S PACE, but I knew it was because he was intent on keeping us safe. I remembered Dale driving us in the snow numerous times, speeding like he was possessed by the road-rage demon. When I asked him to slow down, he'd bark that he was from Michigan, so I shouldn't question how he drove in the snow. He'd totaled two very expensive cars and, by the grace of God, hadn't caused himself or anyone else serious bodily injury. So far, my observations were telling me Dale hadn't changed. For Eden's sake, I hoped I was wrong.

"And you really have no work to do today?" I asked Jamison.

"No, I'm recouping."

"Recouping from what?"

Glancing at me with a smile and displaying his killer dimples, Jamison winked. Just then, my cell phone rang, and I reached into my bag to answer it. The caller was Claudia, an artist who made custom light fixtures. I'd left her a message the previous day.

Claudia was emailing the tech team a catalog of her new light fixtures so that images could be processed and used with the app. "I call them wall crawlers," she said.

Then I asked how she was doing. Her parents were getting a divorce after forty years of marriage. Neither was involved with anyone else.

"My mom said we did our duty. It's time." Claudia's laugh was mixed with the gurgling sound that accompanied sobbing. "I don't know why I'm upset. They're seventy-five and always lived and spoke to each other like they were robots."

I glanced at Jamison. He smiled at me. If we were ever together for forty years, each day would be new and exciting. I just knew it.

Claudia and I agreed to talk about her parents and how she really felt about the divorce later, but first, I would call her if my client was interested in any of her pieces. We ended the call, but before I could put my cell phone away, it chimed again with a call from Alex. He and Alana would be boarding a flight to Denver that was sure to take off soon. When my phone beeped a third time, I turned to Jamison to apologize. I would have rather spent our time in the car talking about us. The state of our future together hung in the air. My phone rang a lot, but I remembered how Jamison's phone used to ring ten times more than mine had. I found it odd that a man who used to be so busy wasn't busy at all. I feared Jasper had done something to ruin his business.

"Sorry," I whispered, seeing that the caller was Jada, my sister-in-law.

Jamison raised a hand graciously and whispered, "No problem."

Jada spoke in a rush. She was home for the week and wanted to know if I cared if Jane and Ollie flew from New York to Montecito with Spencer that night, and I would spend the weekend with them all at the estate. There was no way I was going to turn down that deal. I would be able to visit my two nieces and nephew plus see Jada and Spencer at the same time.

As soon as I hung up, I could feel the tension in the air. It was a reminder of the animosity that existed between my family and Jamison's, and it was going to be a high hurdle to clear. We both chose to leave the obvious unspoken. Since I already knew Alana and Alex were on their way, I turned off my cell phone.

As soon as I put my device in my briefcase, Jamison took my hand and kissed my knuckles. "So, your ex-boyfriend... you don't talk about him much."

I groaned, rolling my eyes. Whenever I thought

about running into Dale, a knot formed in the pit of my stomach, which shouldn't have been the case. "I try not to linger in the negative. I mean, I hated him for a long time for being my first bad experience with love."

Jamison stretched his neck as he rubbed his jaw. I could tell he wanted to know more but was respecting my boundaries.

I sighed, choosing to open myself a little. "I never told anyone this, and it wasn't in the book but…" I smashed my lips together.

"You don't have to explain anything to me, babe," he said.

I inhaled sharply and held my breath. He'd referred to me as "babe." I meant something to him. I decided to take a chance and trust him. If he deceived me, my heart would shatter into a million pieces. I would be bitter and swear off love forever. But that was *if* he deceived me.

"I used to…" I sighed. What I was about to say seemed so horrible. "When I was younger, I wanted to be bad. I hated the rules. I hated people who followed the rules. My brother was a chemist, and he made a drug. I tried to manipulate him into making more so I could distribute it. He wouldn't.

So—I used my own chemist. Dale was the middleman."

Jamison cleared his throat. I could feel him growing tenser by how tight he was gripping my hand. I imagined he knew about the charge leveled against Asher when we were eighteen. Jamison's father had tried to use it against us. But I was confessing that my brother wasn't the criminal —I was.

"You know you can hurt me with this information," I said.

"I'm not going to hurt you, Bryn." He sighed. "And my father already tried."

I sniffed. "I know."

"Why did you tell me that, anyway?"

I took a deep breath. "Because you wanted to know about what drew me to a guy like Dale. At our core, we were similar. We liked being bad and breaking the rules and getting away with it."

Jamison kept a neutral look on his face. He pointed to Eden's gate, which was open. "The house is to the right?"

I coughed to clear the frog out of my throat. "Um, yeah."

I fixed my eyes on Jamison, trying to imagine what he was thinking. He turned into the driveway, and the gate starting closing behind us. Eden was expecting me.

"I have a question." He glanced at me with a sexy smirk. That was a good sign.

"Yeah?"

"Are you still bad?"

I shrugged. "I don't know. Being bad was about the angry, wounded girl sticking it to authority figures for disappointing me. So no, I'm not bad anymore. I guess I've grown the hell up."

He grunted thoughtfully.

I frowned. "Why the grunt?"

Jamison was still smirking. "I can mount an argument against your last claim."

"Against what part?"

"When you were talking to Jada, you never mentioned you were with me. We both know why. Also, I still believe you flout the rules, because you know the rules don't make us more mature—they're made to control individuality."

I could feel fire in my eyes as my sex throbbed. "The fact that you know that makes you twice as sexy."

Jamison stopped the car before I could instruct him to turn into the garage. We both leaned in for a hot and sensual kiss.

Ten

BRYN BLACKSTONE

Eden met us as soon as we entered the main floor from the garage. "Oh wow, oh wow," she said as if the sight of Jamison had caught her off guard.

I pointed my hands at Jamison as if I was presenting him to her. "Behold, our assistant for the day, Jamison Cox."

We both must have looked flushed. We'd made out in the staircase leading to the first floor. Jamison had shoved his hands down my pants, and his fingers made their way along the area above the crotch of my panties.

"Damn, you're dripping baby," he whispered as he rubbed me off until orgasm ignited inside me.

I tossed my head back against the wall and sighed. "Oh, Jamison…"

Fortunately, Eden hadn't heard me. But the sight of Jamison made her fan herself. "He's my assistant too? What can I tell him to do?"

Chuckling, I wagged my finger at her. "Not that."

"Well, then, welcome to the process, Jamison Cox," Eden crooned as she ran a hand through her long dark hair. The look in her eyes was noticeable. She would flirt with him as much as possible. But unlike with Dale, I wouldn't have to worry about Jamison sneaking off and screwing her when I wasn't looking. He was my first healthy pick, which meant he wasn't that kind of guy.

"She finally got here? It's kind of late," I heard Dale say. He turned a corner at the end of the hallway and walked toward us. His glare was fastened on Jamison, and Jamison's was locked on him. Dale stopped next to Eden. "And who are you?"

"He's our assistant," Eden replied.

"Who are you?" Jamison asked.

"I'm…"

We waited for Dale to answer. I was curious to know what he would refer to himself as. He reached out to shake Jamison's hand. "I'm Dale Rumor."

Jamison shook his hand. "I'm Jamison Cox."

The two men continued to appraise each other. The moment was just as horrific as I'd imagined. My past and present were colliding.

To put a stop to the awkwardness, I clapped my hands. "Okay, enough with the formalities. Let's get started."

UNLIKE THE DAY BEFORE, DALE LURKED AND EVEN offered his input. We started in the sunroom, where we tried out several of Claudia's light fixtures, which had been successfully loaded into the app. It had dawned on me, during our first day of work, that Eden's theme would be *Let there be light*. I shared that with her, and she loved it. I tried to avoid eye contact with Jamison. He kept staring at me as if the mere sight of me was making him hot.

Dale would ask me loads of stupid questions to get my attention. For example, he kept weighing the value versus the price of a fixture, as if he ever cared how much something costs. I wanted to yell at him to stop behaving like his father, Jim, who was a cheap asshole with a lot of money.

Eden was too distracted by our work and Jamison to notice what Dale was doing, or at least, that was how it seemed. She viewed the videoed version of the crawling lamp fixture, which was shaped like a spider with a thousand tentacles, each six feet long, that spread across the ceiling. "I think this is the one, Bryn. I mean, what do you think, Jamison?"

Dale pressed his lips together so firmly that they could have gotten stuck in a permanent frown.

"I like it," Jamison said.

"What the hell, Eden? And how much is that thing, anyway?" Dale asked.

Eden turned to me, waiting for me to answer the question.

"Eleven thousand dollars, but my customers receive a twenty-percent discount with this particular vendor."

"For a light?" Dale groused.

I shot Dale a look of warning. He didn't give a damn about interior design. He was merely there to make it hard for me.

Instead of piping down, he made his way across the room and knocked on a partition made of smooth black polished pebbles, which separated the floor-to-ceiling windows. "And what about this? Instead of an overpriced spider, maybe we should talk about what to do about this. It looks like something from the 1970s, and there's too much of it all around this house."

I opened my mouth to say that the home was newly built, and the rock wall was modern and chic, and Eden and I had decided to keep all of it, so he should just leave the room already. I wouldn't have said the last part of that, but I wanted to.

"Or do you not have the resources to make some real change around here? You say that you're part of BFE, but you seem mom-and-pop to me."

I was speechless. He was attacking my credibility. For some reason, tears pooled in my eyes.

"Enough already," Jamison boomed with authority.

Dale sneered at Jamison. "Aren't you the help?"

Eden gasped and shoved her hands on her hips. "Dale, what's wrong with you?"

I rolled my eyes, disappointed that it had taken her boyfriend insulting my... boyfriend, or whatever Jamison was to me, for her to address Dale's behavior.

"Nothing's wrong. I'm just asking a question," Dale said.

She crossed her arms. "Well, the wall is staying, so get over it."

"But you don't even like the wall. You told me that. You said it needs to go, and we can make it all glass. I agreed."

"Well, I changed my mind, Dale."

"Why?"

I frowned at Jamison and shook my head. Dale had finally melted down, and it was only day two. I wasn't surprised. The presence of my hunkier side-kick seemed to have set him off.

"Babe," Jamison said.

"Babe?" Dale and Eden said at the same time.

Her finger shifted between Jamison and me. "The two of you are a couple?"

Dale laughed with an edge.

Jamison maintained laser focus on me. His shoulders were back, posture steady. "Does she know?" he asked me.

I knew what he was asking me. I shook my head. "I don't think so."

He nodded sharply. "Tell her."

I chewed on my lower lip, contemplating what he was advising me to do.

131

Jamison glared at Dale as if he wanted to rip his head off. "Because this guy is milking the moment. And he's not going to stop until she knows. That's my expert advice, babe. Tell her."

"Until I know what?" Eden looked genuinely confused.

Dale's mouth fell open as he stared at me like a lost puppy. I wished he'd said something to her the night before. I wished he weren't so duplicitous. But I had tomorrow and then the next day and so on to come back and finish my job. The longer I waited to tell Eden the truth, the more I would be at Dale's mercy.

"Eden, we need to talk," I said.

"Okay," Dale said, shaking his hands with frustration. "I'll go. I'm leaving. Okay?"

I focused on Jamison, and he nodded, encouraging me to continue. I inhaled deeply and then slowly let it out. *You can do this, Bryn.* Jamison was right to lead me up the path to exposing the truth. It had to be done.

"Dale and I were in a long relationship together."

Eden's frown intensified. It was as though she were trying to process every syllable I had spoken. "Relationship?"

"I've known Dale since high school, and I was shocked to find him here. I'm sorry I didn't say something yesterday. It was just awkward, and him being here took me by surprise."

"Dale?" Eden said, pointing out of the room, and stomped off.

He sniffed at me and then followed her.

Jamison walked over and wrapped his arms around me. "Good job, babe. That was brave of you."

I gazed deep into his eyes. "Was it?" I said quietly.

Jamison planted a tender kiss on my parted lips. "Very."

That one soft kiss led to the next and then the next until we were engaging in a scintillating and hungry kiss. We'd lost our heads, forgetting we were in my client's house and I'd just informed her that her loser boyfriend used to be my loser boyfriend.

Eden cleared her throat. Jamison and I whipped our attention in her direction. She was grinning as if all was well in her world. "That was hot, by the way."

My eyebrows pulled. "Is everything okay? We can end the job, and you wouldn't have to pay for the work we've already done."

Her hand shot up. "No way. I've been waiting too long for this, so let's just…"

A cell phone rang. I knew it wasn't mine because the ringtone sounded like one of those old bulky landline telephones. Jamison jumped as he released our embrace and dug a phone out of his pocket. I tried to sneak a peek at the name of the person who was calling, but the way he held the device prevented me from seeing.

"I have to take this." He planted another quick kiss on my lips and then walked swiftly out of the room, leaving me and Eden alone. It was the moment I'd dreaded.

"I promise you, I didn't know the two of you were involved before I saw him here," I said.

"I believe you, Bryn."

I pressed my lips together, waiting for her to say something more about the talk she'd just had with Dale.

Eden swung her arms nonchalantly. "Should we get back to it?"

It was evident she was trying to hide her anxiety. I was never one to stuff my emotions, but after yesterday with Eden, I suspected she was that type. That was why I'd chosen *Let there be light* for her theme.

I figured she would never ask the questions she needed to about my relationship with Dale, and he would never tell her. I folded my arms and started from the beginning, telling her how Dale and I had met at a function in Washington, DC. We bonded over marijuana in a stall in the men's room. He asked me if I gave blow jobs, and I told him to go screw himself. He liked my answer, and I liked that he thought I was joking. I wasn't. I told her that the relationship had been on and off.

"Wait." Her mouth agape, she turned to gaze off down the hallway and then back at me. "He's your boyfriend in the book, *The Dark Blackstones*?"

I tried to hide my disappointment that she'd read the book. Of course she had. If I were her, I would have read the book too.

"Mm-hm." I cleared my throat.

She slapped a hand over her mouth and then grunted thoughtfully. If her response hadn't been about my relationship with Dale, I would have asked for an explanation for her reaction. But I didn't want to know.

"By the way, I didn't know either," she finally said.

It took a moment to remember what she was referring too. "Oh. I didn't think you did."

"And, um, I don't care if he was with you and you were with him. Actually, I think it's pretty hot, well, because you're pretty hot." Her eyes dipped down to my breasts. "And I'm into threesomes, just in case that's something you want to know."

I chuckled, shaking my head adamantly. "I'm not sharing Jamison, so…"

Eden swung her tightened fist. "No?"

I sniffed. "No way."

We laughed and then went back to work. When Jamison joined us, he seemed distracted for a while. But once Eden pitched her plan to him about us having a threesome, he laughed. I was learning something about Eden. She might be the woman to give Dale a taste of his own medicine.

WE MADE IT TO THE SECOND LEVEL OF THE HOME, finishing up what we'd started the previous day. Eden and I agreed that we should wait until my assistants arrived with swatches from vendors to move forward on ordering furniture. We finished earlier than we had the day before, and since it was a few minutes before four o'clock, she asked if we'd like to stay for an early dinner with lots of liquor.

Her eyes were fixed on Jamison when she made the offer. Dale hadn't made an appearance since I'd revealed our secret. I wasn't surprised. Whenever he was hurt and angry, he liked to go off somewhere and lick his wounds. There was no way he would want to sit down and have a meal with Jamison and me. It would just be Eden making moves on Jamison all night long.

"Not today," Jamison said, watching me closely. "We have other plans."

"Mmm," Eden said as if she was eating a delectable dessert. "And again, that sounded so hot."

"Oh my God, you've brought out a side of Eden I didn't know existed," I said, laughing, when we were back in the SUV.

Jamison sniffed while checking the rearview mirror as he backed out of the garage. "Oh yeah?"

"Yes. And she wanted to do me just so she could do you. She even eye mugged my breasts." I shook my head. "Women must throw themselves at you like that all the time. I sort of saw it when we worked together on Spence's campaign." I punched him lightly on his solid bicep. "The ladies love Jamison Cox."

Jamison pressed the brake and turned to dazzle me with his fiery brown eyes. "I only care about the love of one lady since the day we met."

His persistent eye contact, which he was very good at, took my breath away. "What a lucky girl."

"Woman," he said. "She's all woman. And I've been distracted by her breasts too."

I took a cursory glance at his magnificent bulge. My heart jumped into my throat, and need gripped my lady parts. Jamison delicately pinched my lower lip before leaning over to suck it into his moist and delicious mouth. Then he softly consumed my tongue. I moaned into his mouth before turning my face to cease our kissing. My desire for him was becoming more than I could bear.

"I can't be your assistant anymore," he whispered, his lips remaining near the side of my face. "It was hard not being able to kiss you whenever I wanted. And since we are an item, I can kiss you whenever I want, right?"

I smiled, and my head felt dizzy as I closed my eyes to consider what he'd just said. "We're an item?"

"It's what I want. Is it what you want?"

I nodded and turned back toward his mouth. "Mmm…" He smelled divine, and the warmth emanating from his skin put me in a daze. Like magnets, our mouths merged.

Knock, knock, knock.

I jumped and pressed my hand over my heart as we both looked to see Dale standing at Jamison's window. "What the hell's wrong with this guy?" Jamison muttered as he calmly rolled down the window. He turned to Dale. "What?"

Dale leaned to the side so that he could get a look at me, but Jamison shifted, blocking his view. "You have to drive out so I can close the gate," Dale said.

"That it?"

Dale remained quiet and leaned over far enough to where Jamison's shoulder would have hit the window if he'd tried to block Dale's view of me. "Bryn, I just wanted to say I'm sorry. That's all." He hustled away from Jamison's side of the vehicle.

Dale's apology caught us both off guard. He'd been such an A-hole earlier. Jamison and I stared at each other for several seconds and then laughed uncontrollably.

"What a day this has been," I said once we'd simmered down a bit.

"It's been unusual, that's for sure." He checked over his shoulder. "Let's get the hell off the property before Eden jumps in front of the car butt naked."

I could totally picture her doing that, which made me laugh all over again.

FINALLY, WE WERE ON THE ROAD AND HEADING BACK to the resort. Jamison had been caught in his own thoughts for a while. I wondered if he wanted to take back his affirmation of the two of us being an item. He appeared more sober with his eyes glued to the road. He was holding my hand while maneuvering the steering wheel with his other hand, but he was leaning away from me.

"How long were you with that guy again?" Jamison asked out of the blue.

I sighed with relief. At least I knew what had been on his mind. "A long time."

Jamison glanced at me then set his eyes back on the road. "How long is a long time?"

"I was sixteen when I met Dale. We had a strange off-and-on relationship. My father didn't approve of him."

"But what did Jasper think of him?"

I narrowed my eyes at him. "Why do you ask?"

"Isn't he the one who's always called the shots in your family?"

My frown deepened. "Did you learn that from the book?"

"Some, but everybody knows that. You don't mess with Jasper Blackstone. That's probably why, as wealthy as you are, you're able to fly commercial."

My neck jutted forward. "What does that mean?"

Jamison did a double take. "Come on, Bryn. You come from a gold mine. You never worry about being kidnapped for ransom?"

The thought of that made my heart bounce in my chest. "No. Why would you say that? I mean, I can't be afraid of anything like that. It takes my freedom away. And I need to be free." I was worked up into a frenzy.

Jamison squeezed my hand tighter. "Babe, I didn't mean to upset you that way. And you don't have to worry about that kind of danger, because everybody in the world knows your brother's vicious."

I gasped. "Jasper's not vicious." I had to come

to my brother's defense, although I knew Jasper could be brutal if pushed.

Jamison stretched his neck from side to side as if he was troubled about something.

"What is it?" I asked.

After a long pause, he shook his head. "How about we drop the conversation about your brother?" A smile came to his eyes first and then his lips as he let go of my hand to softly flick my chin. "I didn't mean to offend you, darling."

His tone was sweet and sincere. I knew he meant it. "And I didn't mean to be so fragile."

"You're not fragile. You have a strong commitment to your family. That's one thing I love about you."

I shook my head adamantly. "I meant freaking out over needing to be free. That was kind of"—I drew circles next to my ear—"cuckoo."

His sensual mouth smiled. "No, it wasn't."

I studied his steady gaze and strong posture. He wasn't merely trying to pacify me. *He means it.*

"You love me?" My voice sounded tiny, more vulnerable than I was used to.

"I do." He kissed my knuckles.

"And you're not going to run for the hills?"

Still smiling, Jamison shook his head. "Not unless you're coming with me."

I could have jumped his bones right then and there. That sort of devotion turned me the hell on. I was so hot for him my skin flashed with heat. It was as if I was having an out-of-body experience. "Pull over. Now."

I unbuttoned my pants and was pushing them over my feet as the vehicle made an abrupt turn. My panties came off next. We were still moving as I attacked Jamison's belt, button, then zipper.

He sucked a sharp intake of air between his teeth when my hand wrapped around his shaft. The layers of his manhood felt so damn erotic, soft skin surrounding impenetrable rigidness and thickness. I lowered my head. I had to have him in my mouth.

"OH!" JAMISON CRIES OUT AT FIRST SUCK.

The saltiness of his sweat and precum make me cream.

"Inside you," he mutters, lifting me by the arm and guiding me onto his lap.

I spread my thighs. He grasps his cock. I lift my lower body. Our eyes connect. His fingers go in and out of me and then around my clit.

"Ha…" *I whisper then swallow the extra saliva in my mouth.*

Ceremoniously, I lower my wet and throbbing sex over his erection. I'm so wet that he glides in like magic.

"Oh," *I cry and toss my head back as Jamison's eager hands clamp down on my hips, and he thrusts himself inside me.*

He does me hard and deep, and it feels so damn good. Skin beats against skin. The sound of him crashing into my wetness makes me wetter. Groping for something to hold onto, I reach for the roof and push against it.

"Look at me," *he orders.*

I force my lidded eyes open. We're watching each other.

"You're so damn beautiful," *he says as I shift up and down on his cock.*

And so is he.

I moan because he feels so damn good inside me. I lick my swollen lower lip and then bite it. Striking like a rattler, Jamison's mouth consumes mine. His silky tongue forges deeper into my mouth. Our lips brush, crush, and nibble at each other.

"No," *he whispers, and I know what that means.*

"Want to slow it down?" *I ask, slowly lifting and lowering myself over his length.*

Jamison nods. Our foreheads press against each other as

he waits. "I still can't believe I'm in Colorado, and my cock's inside you," he says.

I chuckle. "Me neither."

"I missed you."

"Me too.

Then, without warning, Jamison bounces me against him, swiftly, rapidly. He's in complete control. I hold onto his athletic shoulders, going along for the ride.

He whimpers and then shudders as he comes inside me.

We don't stop. We kiss wildly. I'm unable to merge into Jamison, although that's exactly what I want to do. We're playing with fire, but I don't care. I want whatever he can give me. I want to take him all for myself. I want Jamison Cox to be mine forever.

Eleven

BRYN BLACKSTONE

J amison and I kissed deeply at each stoplight. We made out against the car before heading into the resort, kissed feverishly in the elevator, and stopped to maul each other in the hallway. It was so odd. I couldn't get enough of him, and vice versa, apparently. Once we made it to my suite, we went directly to the bedroom and took off our clothes. Eyeing him seductively, I fell onto the bed. Jamison clutched my knees, spread my thighs, and was inside me yet again.

"Bryn," he said after thrusting his cock deeper in me and holding it there.

"Yes," I replied in a shaky voice.

"Has a man ever made you come?"

146

My eyes widened. The question made me feel embarrassed, and I knew why.

"When you went down on me, I had some pretty profound orgasms." I smiled shyly because I knew that wasn't what he meant.

"Not that way, babe."

I struggled to maintain eye contact with him. "Then in what way?"

"Inside you?"

I shook my head. "That's never happened. Even though I was once known as the bad-girl heiress, my sexual experience with guys who knew what the hell they were doing was meager."

Jamison snorted cockily. "Well, I think I have your body figured out."

"My body figured out?"

He smirked sexily as he resumed shifting his manhood in and out of me. "Lift your hips toward my cock," he whispered as if he was already experiencing whatever men felt down there that made them appear as if sex was God's gift to them only.

Eyes closed, focusing on the moment, I did as I was told. *Holy crap.* I could feel it beginning. My eyes expanded.

"You feel that?" he whispered.

I swallowed and nodded wildly.

"Follow that sensation, baby. Don't let go of it. It's yours."

My hips tilted up. He did more than go in and out of me. He slipped against my walls and pushed against my insides, making me...

There it is...

My mouth seemed to open on its own, and my voice trembled as I cried, "Woe!"

"Bryn? Is that you?" Alana called.

I gasped as I slapped my hand over my mouth, and the powerful sensation that made me want to pass out cooled.

"Who's that?" Jamison whispered.

Even though I couldn't see her, I knew she was watching us. Alana had a prime view of Jamison's ass between my thighs.

After a few beats, Alana said, "Sorry, sorry... hand over my eyes, closing the door. Sorry. The front door was open."

"That's my assistant," I whispered.

Jamison quietly chuckled as we remained completely still. I'd never been so embarrassed.

"Oh, and I'm glad you guys made it safely," I shouted, trying to sound as if I wasn't in the throes of passion. As soon as I said that, I realized I should have just stayed quiet.

Alana chuckled. "All righty, Bryn, and by the way, we're starving. Do you and whoever you're, um, screwing, want to grab some dinner?" She paused. "Is fifteen minutes long enough to finish?"

I raised my eyebrows at Jamison, and he did the same while nodding. Jamison shifted his cock in and out of me. His fullness felt so good.

"Okay. Meet you in the lobby." I sounded strained.

"Perfect, and enjoy! Oh, and thanks for our rooms. They're lovely, boss. Like the buttocks on that guy."

Alana chuckled, and Alex could be heard muttering, sounding as if he was chastising her, which he did when he thought she was being inappropriate. The front door slammed closed, and Jamison and I burst into laughter.

"Oh no, she heard me having a real orgasm," I said.

Jamison narrowed an eye. "How did you like it?"

I raised my eyebrows. "Oh my God, again, please."

Softly, our lips melded, lovemaking resumed, and we ended with a bang as he made me come a second time.

JAMISON AND I CHOSE TO DRESS FOR DINNER IN separate parts of the suite. We could hardly keep our hands off each other. I had to touch him, smell him, and have his muscles and skin against me. I was addicted to the taste of his mouth and the expanse of his cock stretching my womanhood. The sounds he made during sex, against my ear, made me cream like ice melted by fire.

After a quick shower, I debated wearing my black leather skinny pants with my black V-neck button-front sweater or something Jamison would find more accessible. It was cold enough to freeze my ass cheeks off outside. I had brought a long black cashmere trench coat, though.

"Warmth," I muttered.

I slipped into the leather pants and the black sweater—again, no bra. I gladly wore my black leather booties with the three-inch heels. Jamison was much taller than I was. I didn't have to worry about dwarfing him as I had when I'd gone out with Dale, who was only two inches taller than me. I was five feet eight inches tall. He was five ten.

I applied red matte lipstick and brushed out my hair to give it more volume. I added mascara and plucked my eyebrows just a little. After one more check in the mirror, I was ready to chase the night.

Jamison was waiting for me on the sofa as he'd done that morning. He whistled his approval and rose to his feet. "You are so beautiful, Bryn," he said as if my mere appearance had put him in a daze.

He looked scrumptious, too, in a pair of black pants, a gray silk shirt, and Italian leather loafers. He also had on his black cashmere duster. And his scent filled the room. *Damn*, he smelled so good. Jamison Cox was a hell of a sexy, well-dressed man —a woman's dream. I could hardly believe we were making a go at a real relationship. At some point, we would have to discuss strategy regarding my brothers—mainly Jasper—and his father. But not yet.

"We're late." Jamison wrapped his arms around me, drawing me against him.

"And this doesn't help." I said, smoothing one of his eyebrows and then the other. We laid soft, sensual kisses on each other, and I tasted the minty toothpaste in his mouth. "We should go."

Jamison nodded and took me by the hand, and together, we walked out into the hallway. We couldn't kiss in the elevator because a group of skiers was riding down with us. I felt distracted by my own craving for Jamison.

Again, what is this I'm feeling? I had to force myself to take a breath. Maybe Jamison had opened something within me that I'd never known existed before then. I used to force myself to want sex. But the first time Jamison and I made love, our togetherness had put a dent in my safety box made of steel wherein I'd hidden away my unbridled lust. Dale and I used to have a lot of vociferous headboard-banging, floor-shaking sex during which he would be the only one who got off. Frankly, I never enjoyed having sex with Dale. During therapy, I learned that it wasn't the act of sex that had turned me on—it was the string of actions that came before it that got me hot. I needed Dale to sneak into the mansion against Randolph's wishes. In defiance, I took Dale into my bed and gave him my body, knowing that I would never make a vow to the man my father wanted me to marry—Carter Valentine, who was still one of my dearest friends. Carter was strange, but I understood how he'd acquired his weird personality. He and I had always loved each other and forever would, but not in that way.

Carter remained stuck in my mind as the elevator doors opened, and Jamison and I walked out, holding hands. "What were you thinking about on the way down?" Jamison said in my ear.

I smiled. "An old friend. I'll introduce you to him one day."

He grunted, intrigued. "Competition?"

The question made me blurt a chuckle. "Ask me that after you meet him."

Jamison turned his head, eyeing me curiously. I winked at him.

Alana and Alex shot to their feet when they saw us.

"Those are your assistants?" Jamison asked.

I'd forgotten he wasn't able to see how tall and modelesque Alana was with her long dark hair, high, sharp cheekbones, and come-hither eyes. And Alex was the male version of Alana, only he had muscles.

"I promise, I didn't hire them because of the way they looked," I said in a rush.

I gave Alex his preferred side hug, but Alana and I embraced each other tightly. "We have to talk about what I heard in that bedroom," Alana whispered.

I dipped my chin as my face burned with embarrassment.

Then I squeezed Jamison's strong shoulder and

pointed a hand at Alana. "Jamison, this is Alana. She's my associate interior designer." My hand shifted to Alex. "And this is Alex, my craftsman. And Alana and Alex, this is Jamison Cox."

Alana tilted her head. "And he's your...?"

I glanced at Jamison. We'd already set what we were in stone. "He's my new love interest."

Alana laughed and rolled her eyes. Alex, who was generally a quiet person, smiled and reached out to shake Jamison's hand. "Jamison. Nice to meet you."

"Same here," Jamison replied.

Alana, who wasn't one for letting awkward moments linger, said there was a tavern in town that was supposed to have all the fattening food and drink a girl needed after two days of dealing with airport drama. Jamison offered to drive us in my rented SUV, so we left the hotel and piled into the car with Alana and Alex in the back seat.

"Oh gosh, now I remember," Alana said from the back seat. "Jamison Cox. You're a political analyst or something."

"Strategist. And she mentioned me before?" Jamison sounded excited.

"Oh, definitely so." Alana's tone didn't hint that whatever I'd said about Jamison was favorable. I couldn't even remember mentioning Jamison to her. However, I kept Alana on my staff not only for her impeccable design skills but also for her exceptional ability to listen and remember everything that she heard.

"And not in a good way?" Jamison sounded disappointed.

I cringed, praying Alana would use her impeccable communication skills to not make Jamison feel like the cruddy jerk who I'd probably made him out to be.

"Not in a bad way either. Just in a realistic way," Alana said, and I held in a sigh of relief. "And by the way, Bryn, Alex has a new girlfriend named Mia."

"Here we go," Alex said. I pictured him rolling his eyes.

"And Mia doesn't like to pick up her dog's poop because she says it's biodegradable and good for the earth. In New York City, the earth is concrete. She's gotta know that, right?"

"I picked it up, okay?" Alex groused.

"But it wasn't your dog. It's her dog. Her poop."

"But I picked it up."

"That's not the point, Alex. When you're not around to pick up her dog poop, she's letting her dog drop a deuce and leaving it on the sidewalk for someone to step in. I mean, like, who the hell does that? And you know what? We were supposed to walk our dogs with you and me, not with you, me, and her. And she talks too much. And her dog wants to eat Lilly. She's like a little woman with a big ol' pit bull. What's that about, Bryn? Daddy issues, right? Serious… her dad wanted a boy. Daddy issues."

Alex remained silent. I looked at Jamison with wide eyes. His wink told me he wasn't made uncomfortable by their bickering. I wanted to explain that it was normal for Alex and Alana to bicker that way. They were close. I'd always known they were attracted to each other, but Alex was from a small town in Ohio and Alana had grown up in Queens. I knew for a fact that he considered her one of the most beautiful women he'd ever seen, with her swan's neck, heart-shaped face, pouty lips, and mysterious eyes, but her rough edges intimidated him.

Alana had commented several times that Alex was good-looking, too, but soft. I'd seen several of her boyfriends, and none of them ever seemed tougher or manlier than Alex. So I had no idea what in the hell she meant by *soft*. I'd asked her once, and she blew me off, saying, "It's unexplainable. He just is."

Finally, Alex sighed. He usually took his time to come up with the right response for Alana. "Then I won't bring her anymore. But just don't bring what's his face to happy hour anymore."

"Who's what's his face?" Alana snapped.

"I don't know his name, but he's too loud."

"Rain?"

"Maybe. That's it. And who names their kid Rain?"

"Deal," Alana said. "No Mia from you. No Rain from me."

"Deal."

Awkward silence lingered until Jamison asked if either of them had ever been to Vail. Alex had, Alana hadn't, and Jamison and Alex shared their favorite ski spots in Colorado.

THE RESTAURANT LOOKED LIKE A WESTERN LODGE, with wooden walls, tacky old-West artwork, and no windows. Regardless of the unsightly decor, the restaurant was full. Conversation flowed easily during dinner, especially after Jamison asked each of my assistants what their first impression of me was.

"At first, I thought, *Oh, I might be bi?* Bryn's got this *Come hither* thing about her. Like, she's too hot to not crave. But now, screwing her would be like incest." She thumbed over at Alex beside her. "But Alex over here has had a crush on the boss from day one."

Alex grimaced at Alana. "Have you been day drinking again or something?"

She glanced at Jamison, embarrassed. "I don't day drink, and you know it."

"Then stop talking like you're smashed or something." Alex leaned toward me, waving his hand. "That's not true, Bryn. I've always had the utmost respect for you. Sure, you're beautiful. Any guy with eyes can see that. But that's it." He looked back at Alana. "Plus, she's down-to-earth. That's her best quality besides being wise—too wise for a dope like me."

Alana raised a finger. "I second that. I didn't even know she was a Blackstone until one of our clients mentioned it." Then she patted Alex on the back. "And, dude, you're not a dope. You're soft but not a dope."

Alex shook his hands in frustration. "You keep saying that. What in the hell does that mean?"

"I'm ready to hear that answer as well," I said.

After setting her gaze on me, Jamison, and then Alex, Alana huffed. "He doesn't go for the hard kill. He goes for the soft ones like Mia."

Alana and Alex maintained firm eye contact for a few seconds, and then Alana clapped her hands. "What other things do we love about Bryn? Let me count them all."

Alex cleared his throat as he readjusted in his seat. "She's kind."

I threw up my hands, my face warm with embarrassment. "Enough of the good stuff. Tell him the annoying stuff about me."

Alana and Alex grinned at each other, and Jamison stretched an arm across the back of my chair. I felt so claimed by him, and it made my heart go pitter-patter.

Alana turned her head slightly to examine me. "You really want me to spill the soup?"

"Sure," I said, waving my fingers in my direction. "Bring it."

"Well…" She shifted her attention to Jamison. "She's down-to-earth but way too down-to-earth.

Take the last few days, for instance." She closed her eyes and took a steadying breath. "All the misery of going to the airport and our flight being delayed and then canceled until further notice. And then we had to wait for our checked luggage because they couldn't hold it. And then we had to go back to the airport the next day and do it all over again, and by a nose, we were able to get a flight to Denver. All of that"—she said, gesturing emphatically—"Could've been avoided if she would just partake in the family jewels."

Jamison frowned, confused. "The family jewels?"

"She means the airplane," Alex said.

I was surprised he'd said something. Usually, he was okay toughing it out. Their airport experience must have been horrendous.

"Duly noted," I said and informed them that we would be using it for our vendor runs the following week.

They both expressed relief. Then the topic of conversation turned to airports and how miserable they could be and how the culture of each city was reflected in every terminal. We all laughed when Jamison remarked that the people in JFK often moved in their own world, like zombies, barely avoiding impact with each other.

Dinner was set before us. Alana and I had the buffalo chicken salad. Jamison and Alex ordered the steak with baked potato. We were on our second glass of wine when the conversation turned to all the politicians Jamison knew.

"Okay, I can tell you this—the president's a farter," Jamison said. We all erupted in laughter as Jamison waved his hand in front of his nose. "The guy's worse than a skunk."

Alana, Alex, and I were naming off politicians we knew, but Jamison wasn't as forthcoming as he'd been about the president. I was certain he'd revealed the detail about the gas by accident. All the laughter, food, and wine made him let down his guard. After that, instead of dishing the dirt, he would rotate his hand to one side or the other and say, "Eh." His tone would sound cheery if the person was good or dreary if the person wasn't his favorite.

"Well, hey there," said a jolly voice.

Everyone directed their attention to Eden, who was standing at the edge of our table, holding hands with Dale. She must have been wearing heels, because Dale was shorter than her, and that made me smile. The wine was making me revel in his *shortcomings*.

Twelve

BRYN BLACKSTONE

"Could you make room for two more?" Eden asked.

It seemed her eyes had trouble settling on Alex or Jamison. I really wanted to say no, since we were halfway through dinner. Before I could turn to Jamison, who was so good at reading my facial expressions, and show him that I'd rather Eden and Dale found their own table for dinner, Eden had called over the waitress and asked her to add a table to the end of ours and two extra chairs.

The waitstaff was pleased to make Eden Newell happy. She ended up sitting on my left and Dale across from her. I loathed having a view of his face. I decided to pretend as if Dale wasn't present as I introduced Eden to Alana and Alex and told her they would be joining me at her house in the morning.

"Alana and Alex? Are the two of you a couple?" Eden asked.

"No," they said simultaneously.

Then Alana smiled as she shot Alex a cursory glance. I was surprised at how flushed she looked as she forced herself to concentrate solely on Eden. "I can't wait to see your house, though. It looks lovely in pictures."

Dale flung himself forward and reached over to shake Alana's hand. "By the way, I'm Dale. Your boss forgot to introduce me. Dale Rumor."

I rolled my eyes as Alana studied him.

"Dale Rumor," she muttered. Her eyes widened. "Oh, Dale Rumor." She tilted her head when she looked at me. "Bryn? Do you have to go to the ladies' room? I have to go to the ladies' room."

I shook my head. "No, I'm fine."

"So, Bryn," Dale said extra loudly. "How are your brothers?"

I narrowed my eyes at him and wondered why he cared. Neither of my brothers liked him, not even Asher, who was prone to give anyone I wasn't fond of the benefit of the doubt.

I faked a smile. "They're fine."

Alana looked at me with puzzlement. She wasn't used to me being so curt with others.

Dale directed his attention to Jamison. "I thought I heard of you before. Didn't you run her brother's campaign? Is that how the two of you met?"

I could feel Eden grow rigid.

"Yes and yes," Jamison said.

I wished I could have signaled for him not to respond. Dale was like a fish in a bowl, who'd keep eating if you kept feeding it. Pay Dale too much attention and he'd keep being a jerk. I was certain he had an angle. I put my money on the theory that he'd spent the rest of the afternoon learning everything he could about Jamison Cox so that he could throw something salacious about my new boyfriend in my face. As for that fake apology he'd given me earlier that day, he could take it and shove it where the sun didn't shine.

Dale rubbed the back of his neck as he grinned. "But I heard it didn't end well."

Jamison nodded calmly. "It's all relative."

"Relative to what?" Dale shot back.

"Relative to the contract between me and my client."

I smiled. *Score one for Jamison.* His answer was enough to make Dale slouch in his chair and pout.

But I wanted to put the nail in Dale's coffin, so I crossed my arms and asked, "By the way, what are you doing these days, Dale? Are you employed?"

Dale sneered, which made me feel disappointed in myself for taking that jab. He got a kick out of making me behave that way. Also, it gave him hope. If I got scrappy with him, he would take it as me giving a damn about him. And I couldn't care less about who he banged or lied to or whatever new scheme he was cooking up and calling a job. I was certain that whatever he was doing with his life was making him very, very unhappy and was all the dopamine hits Dale needed to get through any day.

If that's the case, then why am I still so angry? What's that about?

"Well, glad you asked. My beautiful babe and I are writing and producing a movie. Not like the one we tried and failed at because, well... only one of us knew what we were doing," Dale said.

Bait. Bait. Don't take the bait.

Alana pointed her finger between Dale and me. "Whew. We've obviously got some bad blood here."

Eden turned to me and then Dale. "You know what? Maybe this was fate. Maybe we can resolve the bad blood between the two of you so we can work in peace together for the next three weeks."

The smug look on Dale's face was an indication that he was not ready for any resolution. And then it struck me. I was angry because I knew that he'd intentionally used Eden to get to me. I could guess how he'd done it because I knew how he operated. First, he convinced her to buy the property. She'd told me that a friend had talked her into purchasing it, and I would have bet it was Dale. Then he convinced her that she should look into hiring an interior designer. He showed her magazines that featured my work.

And as far as entering into a film project with him, I wanted to wave the red flag at her. The poor thing hadn't known he used to work for a slimy judge in Washington, DC, and was meanwhile using our relationship to learn as much as he could about my family. When his badly written and unauthorized screenplay was finally finished, he somehow wrangled a contact in Hollywood and set out to do what he'd always wanted to do—be famous. Since the story was based on my family, he talked me into signing on as one of the executive producers. *Executive producer. What a big title.* I hadn't known that me being executive producer meant I would invest more money than he did. Dale was the producer, which meant he could bed all the actresses.

However, the real reason he wanted me on the project was so that Jasper wouldn't destroy him. It took entirely too long for me to end our relationship, romantically and professionally, and after I got away from Dale Rumor, Jasper handled him accordingly. In the end, I let Dale go after grieving the fact that he was too narcissistic to be concerned about anyone besides himself. Because of my issues, I'd been drawn to him, but I could never depend on a man who took more from me emotionally than he gave. I didn't know if Dale had changed a little, a lot, or not at all, but as I took a moment to feel Jamison's presence beside me, I came to one conclusion—I no longer cared.

I shrugged and, in a gesture of good faith, reached out to shake Dale's hand. "We'll leave the past in the past."

He hesitated but then reached out to complete our handshake. He didn't say anything but slyly tickled the inside of my palm before letting go. Once again, he proved he hadn't changed at all.

FINALLY, I MADE THAT RUN TO THE LADY'S ROOM with Alana. She took me by the arms and guided me against the wall. "What the hell, Bryn? Your two exes are at our table. And you're screwing one of them, and the other's our client's hooptie?" She leaned in closer. "And did he give you an authentic orgasm? I thought I saw you climaxing from a real intravaginal orgasm."

She watched me with glossy eyes, waiting for my answer. It was hard to concentrate, since everyone who walked past us was watching us as if we were about to give them some hot girl-on-girl sex show. Finally, I nodded.

"You do know there are only a handful of men in the world who know how to do that." She shook a finger in my face. "And I guarantee you, none of them look like Jamison Cox. Those other guys are frogs, and they have to know how to do in expert fashion or they'll never get any. Your guy could have moderate skills and a less-than-average-sized penis and still land a ton of vagina."

I grimaced, wondering if she knew that what she said wasn't true in the least. I'd had conversations with all three of my sisters-in-law about sex, and they'd all confessed that my brothers gave them penis-to-vag orgasms. And my brothers were like walking, talking Greek gods. There was no use arguing with Alana that she was wrong. I figured one day she'd learn the pleasurable way that her theory was crap.

I dropped my hands onto her shoulders. "Alana?"

"Huh?" she said way too loudly. She'd had about three glasses of wine.

"I gotta go pee now." I kissed her on the cheek and walked into the ladies' room.

———

WHEN WE MADE IT BACK TO THE TABLE, EDEN WAS in my seat and talking to Jamison. Dale didn't seem bothered by all the attention she was giving my boyfriend. He scoped out the women in the room, including Alana, who he eye banged all the way until she sat down next to him. Eden hadn't seemed bothered by that either. She also didn't want to move back to her chair, but Jamison insisted she did.

Gosh, is he too good to be true?

The first thing Alana did when she sat down was ask Eden a barrage of questions about her sitcom and especially her good-looking costars,

Daniel Daring and Christ Potts. Dale continued staring at the females in the room, and the younger and needier they were, the more attention he gave them. I loved the fact that Jamison's eyes hadn't wandered once. I nuzzled up against my new beau, determined to go the distance with him for as long as possible and hopefully a lifetime.

It didn't take long to forget that Dale was at the table. Eden did a far better job ignoring his sulking than I would have when we were together. When Dale wasn't having a good time, he was like a joy sucker. I was starting to feel sorry for him.

Eden leaned forward so she could get a complete picture of Jamison. "What about this weekend? How about we do some horseback riding on Friday and skiing on Saturday?"

"Who wants to be on a horse when it's this damn cold outside?" Alana said.

Eden shot her a snide look. That question was for Jamison, not her.

"Plus, I'm going to California this weekend. I'm babysitting," I said.

"You are?" Jamison sounded surprised.

I looked into his whiskey eyes. "Yes. I'm spending time with my nieces and nephew at the Montecito estate."

Jamison nodded.

"But you'll be here, right?" Eden asked him.

He shook his head. "I'm going wherever she's going."

My eyebrows pulled. "Spencer's going to be there."

He nodded. "Okay."

"Okay?"

"Okay."

Then our lips became magnets, engaging in teasing kisses.

Alex cleared his throat. "I'm trying to eat over here."

Alana use both hands to wave us on. "No, by all means, continue."

Jamison and I laughed off our desire to sneak off somewhere quiet and bang. *But would that be enough? A wham-bam-thank-you-ma'am?* Our sex was like luxuriating in natural springs made of magical water with sprinkles of rainbows, fairy dust, and every beautiful myth humanity had conjured to make us mightier and take us away from reality. Up until that moment, our fast-moving relationship had felt like destiny, but it had also felt volatile.

"Okay, well, what about next weekend?" Eden asked Jamison.

Dale snorted bitterly as he threw his hands up. "Eden, I'm sitting over here. Can you give it a break already?"

She threw herself forward. "Could *you* give it a break?"

"Give what a break?" He clearly had no idea what she was talking about.

Eden looked at him, stunned. At least I then understood why she flirted so intensely with other men. It was her way of getting back at Dale for undressing other women with his eyes. I wanted to tell her that he wasn't aware that he did it. He was in a daze. He had issues that only a good therapist could help him resolve.

Eden turned to me. "So, are we on for the week after next?"

"I don't ski," I said.

Eden's jaw dropped. "No way. An heiress who doesn't adorn herself in a tight, sexy ski outfit and hit the slopes? Unheard of."

I laughed and snuggled closer against Jamison's body. He had his arm around me, and I was finishing my second glass of red wine, feeling woozily in love and, despite Eden and Dale's last spat, in good company. "I hated those people," I confessed.

"I can believe that," Alana said. "Bryn is the most un-heiress heiress I ever met."

Dale slumped in his seat and snorted. "If you had Randolph Blackstone for a father, you'd be an un-heiress heiress too."

"Hey," Jamison said in a booming voice. His body tightened—he was ready to stuff Dale in the bathroom toilet.

"Dale, stop acting out or go home!" Eden yelled.

Dale hardened his jaw and turned away from her. I knew what stage they were in. She was the one in control because he needed her for that production project he'd mentioned earlier. I was certain that if it weren't for that project, Dale would never have backed down so easily.

Jamison, glaring at him, shifted his position. I rubbed his thigh to calm him down and then faced him. He put his mouth next to my ear. "That guy brings out the worst in me."

I lifted my mouth to his ear. "He brings out the worst in everybody. He needs help."

"I love that about you, you know?"

"Love what?"

"He treats you with disrespect, and you have empathy for him."

"Whispering sweet nothings over there?" Alana said.

"Howdy. How's everyone doing tonight?" a woman's voice blared through the PA system.

Jamison and I looked away from Alana, who also turned toward the stage to see a blonde with two pigtails, probably in her early twenties. She was dressed in tight jeans, fur boots, and a checkered blouse tied in the front to show her midriff. Attention was what she wanted, and attention was what she was getting.

She announced that it was time for karaoke, and those who wanted their turn should come up front and sign up. Alana immediately pulled Alex out of his chair, and they made their way to the stage. The girl handling the list let them go first since Alex was so cute, which she mentioned three times before announcing them.

Dale jumped to his feet and narrowed his eyes at Eden. "I'm leaving. Are you coming?"

With their last argument, Eden had handed

Dale the victory. He'd managed to change her mood from happy to cruddy. She acceded to his wishes, said goodbye to me and Jamison, and asked that I tell Alana and Alex that she would see them in the morning. Dale didn't say goodbye to either of us.

Jamison and I were alone at the table at last. I smiled. "We made it."

"You handled the whole situation with grace, babe. I'm proud of you."

We gazed into each other's eyes and then kissed tenderly, keeping it PG, until the music started and Alana announced she and Alex would be singing "Wild Night," a song from the '90s by John Mellencamp and Meshell Ndegeocello. Jamison and I, still cozy, sat in amused anticipation as the music started. Alex and Alana held their microphones, and then the action started.

Their performances were coordinated, spirited, and, to my surprise—especially in Alex's case— entertaining and spicy. My jaw hit the floor as I watched Alana push her breasts against Alex while singing her lines. But Alex didn't keep his hands to himself either. He gripped her ass several times. And I swear he grew a boner that wouldn't shrink.

"They're having sex," Jamison said in my ear.

Unable to look away from the show, I nodded. "For sure."

THREE HOURS LATER

"What the hell was that?" Jamison asked after we closed ourselves into my suite. I fell back against the wall, laughing so hard I had to clutch my aching belly. The entire day was definitely one from the *Twilight Zone*.

It was late. The strangest thing had occurred. Patrons had enjoyed Alex and Alana's act so much that they kept shouting, "Another!" A new song was cued up, and my assistants sang while engaging in more heavy petting, gazing into each other's eyes and dirty dancing. A handful of performances later, after we each had one last drink, we headed back to the resort, and they ended up making out passionately in the back seat. Jamison and I were too shocked to speak over the moaning, slurping, smacking, and guttural grunts. Whenever they tried to break away from each other, the lustful haze they were trapped inside of would lead them to go back at it. It was as if we were not in the car with them.

When Jamison parked the vehicle in the spot reserved for my suite, he announced, "We're here!"

"Back at the resort," I added.

I allowed myself to catch a glimpse of what they were doing. Alex was unbuttoning Alana's pants, and their tongues were crammed down each other's throats. It was months of walled-off sexual tension finally set free. Alex must have understood what Alana meant by him being too soft. That night, for the first time, I got it too. I'd always thought that she avoided her attraction for him because he was too kind, not the sort who'd spit on the sidewalk or tell a stranger who was annoying him to shut up, but it was actually because he'd never made an assertive move on her.

"I'm pretty sure they're going to regret it in the morning," I said.

Jamison took me by the hand and tugged me against his taut chest. Our lips were ready to kiss as our rapid breaths collided. Electricity sparked in my body. Jamison was hard in all the right places.

"Now it's our turn," he said, his voice thick with craving.

Jamison claims my lips. Our tongues explore. He takes my sweater off. I unbutton his stiff shirt, and together, we finish taking it off. We stagger toward the bedroom. Next, pants off—mine and then his. We fall onto the bed. His fullness pushes against me and rubs.

Our moans are raw, fiery. Jamison snatches my panties off. I hear them rip.

I whimper and sigh, arching my back, overripe with lust as he practically tears his own underwear off. I need him inside me so much I'm about to burst into flames. Our gazes explore each other as he takes his cock in one hand and presses one of my thighs against the mattress. My breathing grows faster, louder as he stuffs his overgrown erection inside me.

"Ha!" The back of my head jabs the pillow.

"Oh… I've been waiting all night for this." His voice is raspy as he prods my sex like a man on a mission. I can tell by the way he's moving it that he wants me to come.

I want to come. Lifting my hips, I have to touch him. My fingers entwine with his hair then reach toward his chest, arms, and back. He feels so good inside me.

"I love you, Jamison," I say, eyes closed, chasing the orgasm. "I want you forever."

"Me too," he says before his mouth devours mine.

In and out.

"Oh," I croak against his mouth.

In and out.

The sensation is gathering, building, and becoming.
In and out. In and out. In and out. In…
"Oh, Jamison!" I scream at the top of my lungs.
He holds it right there.

I LET JAMISON DO ME DIRTY AFTER THAT. HE SET ME on my hands and knees and pumped into my sex from behind. He didn't pound me like Dale used to. He said he liked to go slow. He wanted to relish the feeling of being inside me. He wanted to know that it was me, Bryn Blackstone, he was making love to. And when he came, he wanted me to turn around so that he could see my face. He wanted to remember that it was I who had brought him to the highest point of pleasure.

Then we lay loose-limbed, letting our skin cool in the temperate room. "Did you mean that?" he said, still out of breath.

"Mean what?" I sighed.

"That you loved me and wanted me forever."

I smiled, because I felt no hesitation, no fear. "Mm-hm, I did." I turned to face him. He was looking up at the ceiling. "Did you mean it when you said, 'Me too'?"

After a moment, he faced me. He tried to hide it, but he looked worried. Then he smiled. "Yes. I did."

I believed him even though I knew why he'd looked concerned. I gently smoothed the wrinkle out of his eyebrow with my thumb. "We need to make peace between my brother and your father, don't we?"

"That's easier said than done."

We stared at each other for several seconds. When I pictured telling Jasper and Spencer that I was back with Jamison, I imagined that Spencer would be indifferent about it and Jasper would be overly cautious. My oldest brother, Jasper, could always be reached two ways. Firstly, I could reason with him. I would have to pitch an angle that he could accept. Secondly, I would have to ask him to trust me—no, beg him to. I hadn't known to what extent Jasper had hurt the Coxes, but I knew that when Boomer gave the first punch, Jasper struck back with a sword made of lightning.

"If you don't mind me asking, what has Jasper done to you?" I asked.

Jamison forced his eyes away from mine to refocus on the ceiling. "I don't want you involved."

My mouth slacked. "What?"

"I don't want you to think what we have between us has anything to do with your brother and my family's business."

I shifted to lie on my side, smoothing my hand over his chest then stopping over his heart to feel it beat against my palm. "Jamison?"

He closed his eyes to sigh and then looked at me.

"I'm the fastest way you're going to get him to stop whatever he's doing. So tell me, what has he done?"

"I don't want it that way, Bryn. I want him to stop because…" He pressed his lips together.

I propped myself up on my arm. "Jamison, please tell me what Jasper has done. I can promise you this, he won't stop until he believes you've gotten what he thinks you deserve. And…" I sighed.

"What's wrong with that guy, anyway? I read about the torture, and sympathize with him. But he's like a robot. You program him, and he administers the pain without feeling. My family built our business from the ground up. We didn't have billions of dollars passed down to us."

I sighed, took my hand off his chest, and flopped over onto my back. Jamison couldn't know that my father had wasted most of the inherited money. At the age of fifteen, Jasper had the where-withal to rebuild the family chest and maintain it. No one became that competent and in control by being a tyrant. Jasper could be reasoned with and influenced—and I was an expert at both.

"Sorry," he said, setting his moist hand on top of my belly. "I didn't mean to upset you by insulting your brother."

"You didn't upset me, Jamison. You have the right to have an opinion about my brother. I love Jasper as if he's my father, though, and in many ways, he's the one who raised me. But sure, from the outside looking in, he can be seen as…" I didn't want to say the one word that best described a vengeful Jasper.

"Ruthless," Jamison said. "He's ruthless."

"Did he bankrupt you?"

Jamison stayed silent.

"He did, didn't he?"

"Almost," he whispered.

I sighed into the darkness. "You don't have any clients. That's why you have time to be here."

Again, silence.

"I'm going to fix this, Jamison. I promise you. I give you my word."

He shook his head. "I don't need you to do that, Bryn. I don't want you to."

I quickly turned to press my finger over his lips. "This is about right and wrong, not about me fighting your battles."

His eyebrows pulled together. The creases between his eyes were deep and pronounced. I planted a soft kiss on his parted lips.

"Please?" I whispered then kissed him again. "Please?" I kept kissing and repeating my request until, full of explosive passion, his mouth claimed mine, and we were all over the bed.

Thirteen

BRYN BLACKSTONE

It wasn't the alarm that woke me up—it was Jamison's big fat erection grinding into the crack of my ass, requesting entrance to my warm passage. The night before, our skin-on-skin heavy petting and deep kissing had felt compulsive. We didn't stop rolling at all angles across the bed until our activity slowed. Then we clung to each other, wrapped our legs around each other's, and fell asleep. Throughout the night, whenever we lost contact, we would quickly find it again. Our bodies were asleep, but our souls were awake and in desperate need of each other's touch.

I'd given in to Jamison's beckoning. His heaviness was on top of me. He was between my legs.

My joints bore the weight of his six-foot, three-inch frame composed mostly of muscle.

Our warmed skin mushed together. He filled me up with his manhood. The room was hazy because it was snowy and gray outside…

"Um…"

"Hah…"

"Uh…"

Our sounds of lovemaking merged like a song of pure rapture until his "Oh" resonated, deep and guttural, as his body trembled.

"What does that feel like?" I asked after he rolled me over to lie on top of him. My cheek rested on his neck as we waited for our hearts to slow.

"What does what feel like?"

"When you have an orgasm. The way you tremble and grunt, it seems like the best thing since sliced bread."

Jamison chuckled. "You've been with a guy who blows. Don't we all do the same thing?"

I chuckled. "Yeah, but this is the first time I paid attention."

Jamison placed a kiss on my lips. "Yeah, it feels better than sliced bread, and even better because I'm with you."

I beamed down at him, but before we could kiss

again, my alarm chimed. It was time to get ready for work.

I tried to roll out of his arms, but he held me tighter. "Not yet, baby. It's your turn."

"My turn?" He'd already come. There was no way he could get it up that fast.

"Mm-hm," he said, smirking.

Jamison rolled me onto my back. His skillfully silky tongue sucked my right and then left breast deep into his balmy mouth. I moaned and wriggled as his teeth grazed my nipples, which sent strokes of pleasure through me. He indulgently licked and nibbled his way down my sternum, then stomach, and then...

I quickened, gasped, and dug into the sheets when his tongue first lapped my clit.

ONE HOUR LATER

I stared up at the elevator's ceiling, hands on my hips, tapping my foot. The thing wasn't moving fast enough. Jamison had given me multiple orgasms. He said he could eat me for breakfast with a cherry on top all day long if I'd play hooky and send Alana and Alex to Eden's for the day without me. His proposal was tempting, but I couldn't do anything to jeopardize spending the weekend with the kids. Alex and Alana wouldn't make much headway without me being there, at least not on that day.

"Tomorrow," I whispered. We were going to stay in all day and make love like horny Greek gods.

A slow smile came to my lips as I thought about our bodies against each other. It seemed unreal that I would have a normal, non–screwed-up boyfriend. Not that I'd had many screwed-up boyfriends. Dale had been my one and only boyfriend, and he was screwed-up enough for the ten I'd never had.

I wondered what he would be like that day. Maybe he would stay away from me, since he would be licking his wounds from the previous night. I hoped so.

As the doors slid open, I began to question my last thought about Jamison. Was he truly sane? Only time would tell.

"There she is," Alana said from across the room as she jumped to her feet. She and Alex were sitting on a sofa in the lobby, both messing with their cell phones.

I threw up a hand. "I'm sorry I'm late."

"Well, it's not like we don't know why," Alana

said, reaching down by the foot of the couch for her computer bag and purse.

Alex was holding the samples box. "I put everything else in the SUV already."

They seemed so distant from each other, which was strange given what had happened between them on the way home from dinner.

"So…" I said, grinning like a Cheshire cat. "Last night?" My curious gazed bounced between them.

They both looked at me as if they had no idea what I was talking about.

"You two were making out in the back seat. You don't remember that?"

Alex looked down at the floor as Alana shrugged. "Yeah, but we're processing that right now. So… let's just pretend it never happened," she said.

I grimaced, hoping the two weren't going back to square one, which would mean bickering and fighting their attraction for each other. However, I was certainly not one to force a conversation that no one else wanted to have. "Well, then, let's hit the road," I said.

And we all diligently and professionally headed off to work.

JAMISON COX

Bryn's alluring scent soaked the linens. I pulled the top sheet over my head and inhaled. *Damn*, her skin was so damn soft, warm, and flawless. She had a small brown mole on her shoulder. Pressing my tongue against it made me horny as hell. Being with her was making me lose my mind. She'd left for work, but wanting to be inside her gave me an aching erection.

Too bad she wasn't there. She'd left the room less than fifteen minutes before. I battled the urge to call her, ask her to pretend she'd left something behind. Bryn would return to our room, then to our bed, and I could make love to her once more.

I tossed the sheet off me and grabbed my cock again. "Get ahold of yourself, dude," I whispered.

The thought of her curves, round ass, and soft clit against my tongue made me shift my cock as I remembered all the ways in which I'd taken her.

Ring. Ring. Ring.

I jumped and looked toward the house phone sitting on the nightstand and then scrambled to answer, thinking it was her. "Yeah," I said.

"Is this Mr. Jamison Cox?"

The woman's formal tone concerned me, especially hearing it that early in the morning. "Yeah. What can I do for you?" I made my tone brisk on purpose.

"There's a Miss Bree Lovell here to see you. She asked me to ask you to meet her in the lobby within five minutes, or else she'll follow Miss Blackstone and her team to the jobsite."

I scrambled to sit on the side of the bed. "Is this a joke?" I asked, rubbing the inside corners of my eyes.

"Sorry, sir?"

No. It wasn't a joke. "Forget it. Tell her okay."

I slammed the phone back on the base and covered my face with my hands, sighing into my palms. It wasn't that I couldn't believe what was happening, because I could. It was the story of my life. When things were going well, I could expect my father to blow my contentment to pieces. Bree being downstairs was his doing.

I dropped my hands from my face and punched the mattress. "Damn it!" I shouted at the top of my lungs.

The truth about what couldn't be avoided forced me to take a long, deep whiff of the sheets.

Bryn had eased into my nostrils, expanded in my chest, and sat there. I couldn't take her with me. I couldn't linger either. I got up, dressed, packed what little I brought in my overnight bag, and walked out the door, refusing to look behind me. I couldn't. It hurt too much.

———

When I made it downstairs, I stopped to notice Bree standing near the front entrance, arms folded, staring out the glass doors. She looked the same— tight skirt that stretched to her calves, snug jacket, and high heels. I could smell her perfume from where I stood. I didn't know if my nose had picked up her scent or I was experiencing olfactory memory. Nothing about her settled me. There was a rumor she was sleeping with my father. I knew for certain that it wasn't just hearsay. But Boomer banged many women. My parents had a strange relationship, one that I was hell-bent on never emulating.

Bree twisted her body around to see me before I could walk toward her. Her expressionless face reminded me of that video Bryn had showed me two days before.

Bryn...

I had a choice. I could tell Bree to go straight to hell and take my father with her, but then I'd lose more than I already had. I had to be smart about the next move I made.

Think, Jamison. Think.

Bree strolled toward me. I liked the idea of her coming to me and not the other way around. It convinced me that I hadn't chosen her.

"We have a flight to catch," she softly said.

I thrust my chin upward. "How did you know where to find me?"

"Your father found you."

"Then why are you here?"

Her stare was emotionless. "You know why I'm here."

I sighed sharply, rubbing my eyes. When I'd run into Bryn at the airport that weekend, she had me pegged. I had gone to Newport, Rhode Island, to be with a woman—Bree. The situation was complicated, though, and I hadn't made any promises or commitments.

I shoved a hand toward the door. "After you."

She turned and strolled forward, having no doubt that I would follow. She shouldn't have been so confident. Me leaving with her wasn't yet set in stone. I would be fine without my family's money, and my mother would always love me no matter what. And truthfully, I was perfectly content with cutting ties with my father, both professionally and emotionally.

But Boomer had warned me on many occasions that he had enough insurance on me that if crossed, he could send me to jail for a long time.

"Like what?" I had asked.

He'd winked. "Try me, and you'll find out."

What kind of thing is that for a father to say to his son?

If I told him to take his failing business and screw off, he would use whatever evidence against me he'd acquired over the years to take me down. One thing was for certain—I knew his threats weren't empty. And even though he was my father, he wouldn't hesitate to send me straight to jail if I turned on him. Not only had my instincts warned me about that fact, but so had my intellect.

But more than ever, I wanted to be with Bryn Blackstone. I wanted to have her and to hold her until death did us part. I'd given her up once, but I wouldn't do it twice. And for that reason, I followed Bree Lovell to the parked sedan to be driven to the airport.

———

Bree and I sat in the back seat. She gazed straight ahead, keeping her posture straight and chin up as if she were a department-store mannequin. She liked me. I knew she was hiding the fact that she was happy as hell our parents wanted us to get married. I'd kissed her once just to try her on. I didn't like the smell of her skin or the taste of her mouth. Her cold heart made her lips icy. But I had to get her talking so I could learn more about what was going on.

"All right. I get on the airplane, and then what?" I asked.

She continued facing forward. "It's not for me to decide what's next."

"Then why the hell are you here?"

Finally, she turned to look at me. Behind the coldness, I saw hope in her eyes. "You're not happy to see me?"

Be careful, Jamison.

I shrugged. "I don't know. Should I be?"

Bree grunted and shook her head. She knew I was trying to soften her up, make her hopeful enough to drop her guard.

She faced forward. "I'm not talking to you like this."

I glared at her profile. There was no use in trying to play her. She was too shrewd for her own good. Like a cat tossed off the roof, she knew how to land on her feet. It hadn't benefitted her to reveal why she'd shown up to collect me. Plus, her allegiance would be toward my father, since she saw him as the dominant figure in our father–son duo. Also, as far as Bree was concerned, marriage wasn't about love, and had nothing to do with pleasure.

Power. Control. The rules. That was what sex and marriage were about. She wanted a man like me to sex her and validate her. I was a prize to Bree Lovell. And Boomer was going to hand me to her on a silver platter while dipping his cock in her whenever he wanted. Therefore, the time had surely come to accept all of that as glaring fact so that I could find my balls and fight for what I wanted. I had to be on my guard, keep my wits about me, and be ready for the battle of my life. I repeated that to myself as the car stopped next to a private airplane.

Just because I loathed Bree didn't mean I'd forgotten my manners. I invited her to walk up the ramp first. I went up behind her. When I stepped into the cabin, I stopped. There he sat, Boomer Cox. My father's thin lips were molded into the permanent frown he always greeted me with, and he glared at me with eyes dulled by the bitterness that ate him up from the inside. It hadn't always been so contentious between us. He loved me, I was sure of it, when I was a boy. Then one day, I came to the realization that I could never please him, not even if I was doing something the way he asked me to. I had friends who were carbon copies of their fathers. They'd repeat whatever their fathers would say as if their words were gospel. That was never me. I was born a thinker and a watcher. I saw what no one else was paying attention to. I was very young when I saw my father clearly. I'd observed whatever conditions and matters caused him to hesitate. I was able to see the parts of Boomer he couldn't see for himself. I knew what made him want to fight. And in the airplane, I knew by the way Boomer was looking at me that he was at war with me.

"Did you enjoy your piece of ass?" he asked. That was his first shot—to cheapen a beautiful and rare specimen like Bryn Blackstone and make it seem as if she wasn't worthy of me or him, when in fact she was better than the both of us.

Bree sat in the seat next to Boomer. She crossed her legs, casually pulled a laptop out of the side pocket, and opened it. She was good at behaving as if she was alone and calm in a room that was on fire.

"What are you doing here?" I asked. "And how did you find me?"

"If you don't want to be found, then you shouldn't use my resources to get around." He pointed at the seat directly across from him. "Sit."

My insides cringed. I had to fight the urge to do the opposite of what he ordered. This wasn't about my ego or my broken heart. I wanted to stand strong and brave and show Boomer he would have to go some hard rounds with me to win. But that would be a losing move.

Expelling a loud breath, I gazed longingly out the exit just as the crew closed the door.

"Sit," he barked.

I quickly put my focus on him again. Shoulders back, I followed his orders.

"Buckle up. You're not going anywhere," he said.

Calmly, I did that too. Bree was typing on her computer as if the air was light and cheerful. Looking at her, even for a second, I knew there was no way I could do what my father had been trying to convince me to do.

"Okay, so what the hell is this about?" I asked, deciding to show a little resistance. If I gave him both my balls, Boomer wouldn't believe my performance for long. He was used to me defying him in my own way. That was why I was in Vail. And deep down, I believed Boomer liked my defiance, because it was the part of me that was like him.

"We're going to Washington to meet with Alice Templeton. We have a new client," he said.

I tilted my head, feigning interest. I was done working with Cox and Cox. I was dead set on striking out on my own. But that wasn't the moment to let him know it. "Who?"

He turned his lips up in a fierce grin. "You."

I jerked my head back. "Me?"

"You." He rubbed Bree's thigh, his hand coming mighty close to her crotch. "And this here beautiful, proper woman is going to be your first lady."

Fourteen

BRYN BLACKSTONE

When we arrived at the house, Dale was out of sight and out of mind, and I was happy about that. Eden had asked about Jamison's whereabouts, and I informed her that as of the previous night, he'd been fired as my assistant.

"But he was so good at standing there, all strapping and striking and feeding a girl's wildest dreams."

I frowned because I'd sort of had enough of her lusting so openly over my guy. Her behavior was disrespectful, and I knew if Jamison was the type to fall into her clutches, she would have banged him by then.

"What about Dale?" I asked. "Aren't you two in love?"

She glanced at Alex as he helped Alana place the textiles that we were going to use in that room in position.

"I don't think anyone can be with Dale because of love. I mean, did you used to love him?"

My eyes widened. I was shocked by her answer. "I thought I did."

"Well, I guess I know I don't. We're together right now at least, but who knows what tomorrow will bring." Her eyes smoldered as she pointed her chin at Alex. "What's his story, anyway?"

Nausea bubbled in my stomach. Eden wasn't the first client to salivate over Alex, but I feared she would be the first to make a serious effort to bed him.

I stepped in front of her, blocking her view of Alex. When I had her complete attention, I folded my arms. "Eden?"

She shook her head. "Yeah?"

"I want you to stop sexually harassing the men that work for me and my boyfriend. Got it?"

Her mouth fell open as if not only had I offended her, but she also had no idea what I was talking about. That was fine. I didn't care. However, my warning was real, and we both knew that I didn't need to finish her house. There were more than a hundred clients clamoring to take her spot.

"Fine," she finally said. "I'm sorry."

I nodded sharply. "I accept your apology."

From that moment onward, we got down to some serious business and made remarkable headway. Alex made a lunch run to the same sandwich shop where Dale had bought the hero sandwich for me the other day. However, I had Alex get me the roasted turkey on toasted rye with Dijon mustard. We ate as we worked.

We made it to the third floor, and as we packed to leave, I went to the toilet. I was finished and washing my hands when I heard the doorknob turn. Stiffening, I watched in horror as Dale slipped into the bathroom.

TIME STOOD STILL AS WE STARED AT EACH OTHER. His cloudy gray eyes were glossed over, his skin was patchy red, and he was staring at me as if he wanted to eat me alive.

"Finally, we're alone," he said.

I wondered what had changed. The others must

have moved downstairs, leaving me alone upstairs. I'd avoided putting distance between me and Eden. I knew Dale like the back of my hand. He wouldn't try to make a move on me if she was near.

"What do you want, Dale?" I heard myself ask. It was as if I was having an out-of-body experience.

"Is this really how we're going to end things, Bryn? I still love you, you know."

I was speechless as so many words were forging a traffic jam in my head. "Why are you here?" I finally asked.

"Because I wanted to talk to you alone."

I shook my head. "No. Why are you in Vail at this house with Eden? How did that come to be?"

The longer he stared at me, the more his eyes narrowed. I snorted, knowing he was trying to conjure an answer.

"Could you be honest for once?" I asked, throwing up a finger emphatically.

His Adam's apple bobbed as he swallowed. "You're so sexy, baby. Could we just… one more time for old time's sake?"

He was blocking the door. I glanced at his cock —it was swollen. In the past, that would be the moment I would give in. He wanted me. Someone wanted me. I would let him have me. But as I stood there, I felt stronger than ever. My brokenness had been fixed.

"No," I said, shaking my head adamantly. "I'm over you. And you probably should get some help or something. I see you're still eye banging other women while sitting across from your current girl-friend. And now you're in here trying to do me." I folded my arms, raising my chest high. "Can you see that you have a big problem, Dale? Huge, glaring issues."

That glossed-over look hadn't left his eyes. "What do you want from me, Bryn? Whatever you want, I'll do it. Just… I miss you. And I don't like that guy for you."

He was moving toward me.

I shot an arm out. "Do not come closer."

Dale stopped in his tracks. I knew he would. Suddenly, I was struck by déjà vu. We'd been in the same situation on many occasions.

I snapped my fingers. "Earth to Dale. Come out of it."

He blinked hard until his eyes had softened. We were staring at each other. He inhaled audibly.

"I'm not going to make you feel ashamed, Dale. But it's time you got help."

His nostrils flared, and his face tightened. "Forget you."

I remained motionless as he turned his back on me and slithered out of the bathroom just as inconspicuously as he'd slipped in.

WHEN I MADE IT BACK DOWNSTAIRS, I LEARNED that my suspicions were true—Alex and Alana had carried all the textiles, including the modules, back to the SUV. Eden had hired a personal chef for the remainder of her stay, a hot, young guy with a winning smile, and was in the kitchen with him, going over menu ideas. She paid very little attention to me when I waved goodbye. For certain, she was upset that I'd set boundaries with her. But I didn't care.

I made it to the stairwell leading to the garage, finally alone, and stopped and checked my messages. When we'd arrived at Eden's house that morning, I'd sent Jamison a cute *I love you and can't wait to see you later* message. At a certain point, I stopped listening for his reply, and as I saw, he hadn't answered.

His lack of a response wasn't a cause for

concern, though. Jamison hadn't used his cell phone a lot in recent days. I suspected he was avoiding Boomer. I would see him soon, and I debated telling him what had happened between Dale and me. His protectiveness reminded me a lot of my brothers. Jamison would probably have zero tolerance for Dale from that point on. He would insist on accompanying me to the jobsite in the morning so that he could officially set a line that Dale would not dare cross.

"Why so quiet, Bryn?" Alana asked as we rode back to the resort.

Alana and Alex had been going back and forth about whether we should go out to a restaurant, eat at the grill on the premises, or just go back to our rooms, relax, and order room service. She was also overprotective and always ready for a fight with someone like Dale. After a moment of contemplation, I decided to keep what had happened in the bathroom from Alex and Alana too.

"Nothing. Just tired. The day was long, and so was last night."

"Oh, right. Too much great sex."

I smiled, happy that she'd opened the door to that discussion. "And what about you? Remember what you said last night about good-looking men and orgasms?"

"What?"

"We were on our way to the toilets and…"

"Oh yeah." She chuckled. "I remember."

"Good-looking guys and orgasms?" Alex said, keeping his eyes on the road.

"Were you proven wrong last night?" I asked.

Alana looked at Alex, who stole a glance at her.

"Mm-hmm," she said. "Most definitely."

I nudged Alex in the shoulder. "Good for you."

"What's good for me?" He seemed annoyed to be so lost about what we were talking about.

"I'm sure Alana will explain it to you when we each"—I cleared my throat—"go back to our own rooms and order room service, and you two go to sleep in your own beds. Right?"

"Oh…" Alex finally said and then smirked as he grunted. I caught him winking at Alana through the rearview mirror.

WHEN WE ARRIVED AT THE RESORT, I WENT straight to my suite. "Jamison," I called as soon as I entered.

The eerie, cold feeling of emptiness gave me the chills, and I folded my arms as I walked from one end of the suite to the other, calling Jamison's name. On my next walk-through, I noticed something else —his bag and all his toiletries were gone. My heart turned to granite, and my breathing became labored.

Tears filling my eyes. "Jamison?" I called, walking through the apartment again.

He'd mentioned going downstairs to the gym before I left that morning, which seemed like another rational reason none of his things were in the room. Maybe he'd taken a shower in the locker room. I could have critically analyzed that possibility until it made no sense at all, but I decided to check into it.

Once I made it to the gym on the first floor, I searched every corner of the space.

"Can I help you?" a grinning, overly muscular man asked.

"Have you seen a guy, tall, whiskey eyes, dimples, um… early thirties? You won't be able to miss him."

At first, he seemed confused by my description. Then he smirked flirtatiously. "Sounds like me."

My frown intensified. "Then you haven't seen

him?"

He kept grinning. "No, beautiful, I haven't seen him."

"Thank you," I said in a rush and turned my back on him.

As I power walked to the front desk, I thought about Jamison not answering my text message. Also, it wouldn't be like him to not send me loads of messages throughout the day, telling me how much he couldn't wait until I was back and he was inside me. We were in that can't-keep-our-hands-off-each-other stage. My body had been missing him all day.

When I made it to the desk, I was happy to see Kara on duty. I waited anxiously behind two guys who looked as if they skied way too much. They both stole looks at me. I swore the people around there were always looking for a hookup.

Fortunately, another front-desk clerk opened her station and called the two guys to her. Kara seemed disappointed by that. I was happy when she stopped gazing longingly at the two boys and smiled at me.

"Hi, Miss Blackstone. How can I help you?"

I could feel the guys' eyes on me as soon as she spoke my name. There weren't very many Black-stones on the planet. I was positive they had recognized me as the heiress to the Blackstone fortune.

"Hi, Kara. Remember the guy from two days ago?"

"Jamison Hot?" she asked.

The other girl chuckled.

"Yeah, Jamison Hot," I said, deciding to go along with it.

"I heard he left this morning with a woman."

"A woman?" I asked.

She went on to say that she was a pretty brunette in a suit. They were going to the airport. According to the message that was conveyed to Jamison, he was to come down and see her or she would meet him at my jobsite. That sounded like a threat to me.

Brunette. Suit.

"How did she sound?" I asked.

Kara shrugged. "I don't know." She turned to her friend. "That woman that came for Jamison Hot. How did she sound?"

"Weird. Like… OMG, that agent on that show. Um…Um…"

"*Twin Peaks*," the two ski bros and I said at the same time.

"Yes," the other clerk said. "Agent Tammy Preston."

Fifteen

BRYN BLACKSTONE

I felt dizzy while riding up in the elevator on my way back to my room. Fortunately, I had no copassengers, but that didn't stop me from fighting back tears. Holding them in felt as if I was blocking the crushing downpour of Niagara Falls. However, it was imperative that I keep my heartbreak a secret. If I gave in, the door could slide open, and someone would see me wet faced, red eyed, and crying my heart out. I was most concerned about Alana or Alex seeing me that way. I didn't want to have to explain why I truly believed Jamison had left with Bree "Slinky and Snaky" Lovell. Plus, I could still be wrong. All of my sadness and tears could be for nothing. I could return to my suite, dart into the living room, and find Jamison sitting on the sofa, waiting for me in his usual casual way.

But all the evidence pointed to the worst-case scenario. The Lovell estate was in Jamestown, Rhode Island. Jamison being involved with Bree would explain why I'd run into him at the airport in Providence. I wished I'd asked the front desk clerk if Jamison and Bree had appeared intimate. But would it have made a difference? He was with her, and that was all that mattered.

The elevator doors slid open, and I scurried out of the box and up the hallway. It took forever to take my room key out of my back pocket and unlock the door. As soon as I stepped inside and stood under the light in the foyer, there was no need to call for Jamison. The emptiness reached through my chest and squeezed my heart. He wasn't there. I decided to accept that he'd left like a thief in the morning and didn't have enough concern or respect to at least leave a message. Dale had been my first real pick when it came to allowing a man into my life, and Jamison had been my second. In both instances, I'd chosen lemons.

As I dragged myself to my bedroom, I reminded myself to take responsibility for my mistakes. There were good guys out there. I had merely picked the wrong ones.

———————

EVERYTHING WEIGHED HEAVILY ON ME—THE comforter, the sheets, and the air. As the minutes turned to hours and time stacked like blocks, I tossed and turned, trying to make sense of what had happened between Jamison and me. My mind wouldn't let me simply dismiss him as a bad choice.

Did I read everything wrong? I played back every moment we spent together, including the dinner we'd had, the first night we made love, and our last kiss before I left for work. Nothing. Jamison had given me no sign that he wasn't serious about giving our relationship a chance. Maybe he was a good liar. Dale was a liar, but he'd never been that great at it. Jamison, on the other hand, must have been a master manipulator.

But what was the purpose for the lies and for coming on so strong? I would have had sex with him anyway. Maybe he was one of those dreadful guys, after all, who felt he needed to dupe women into believing he was serious husband material so we'd part our thighs and let him in. I could have comforted myself by believing Jamison was that way, but I knew he wasn't. He'd left because of Boomer. That made the most sense. Bree had shown up at the resort, threatening to appear at my jobsite if Jamison didn't comply. That wasn't what a brokenhearted girlfriend would do. I imagined she slunk in and, using her breathy voice, issued Boomer's warning and then slithered out with Jamison in tow. All evidence pointed to the fact that Jamison wasn't with me because his father had put an end to our red-hot love affair. But it still hurt that Jamison wasn't strong enough to tell Boomer to go to hell.

When I became certain that Jamison wasn't in love with Bree Lovell, I was finally able to fall asleep. It felt as if my alarm chimed as soon as I closed my eyes. I hadn't moved a muscle. The cadence played, and I kept the covers pulled up to my neck while blinking at the ceiling. I wanted to stay in bed the whole day. My body missed his touch, and my soul missed his presence. But I couldn't lie in bed and lick my wounds. I had a big job to finish as fast as I could. First, Dale—who was just as slimy as Bree—was slithering around the worksite. Second, the weather wasn't getting better, and storms were in the forecast, which would delay crucial deliveries.

For those reasons, I inhaled deeply and jumped to my feet on the exhalation. I stood with my eyes closed, allowing my dizziness to resolve itself. "You have a job to do, Bryn," I whispered, coaching myself to not regress by crawling back under the covers.

What will I tell Alana? Dale would get a kick out of learning that Jamison had left me. I couldn't say anything, at least not yet. Resolved to pretend all was well, I dragged my heavy arms, legs, feet, and head to the bathroom to get ready to start my day.

SMILE.

Smile.

Smile.

I would have practiced doing it, making sure it was convincing enough, but I wasn't riding down to the lobby alone. Three guys rode with me. I remembered them from two days earlier, when Jamison had been with me. The one with long blond hair said good morning to me. I envied his smile and glassy eyes. I wished I was as unburdened as he was.

"Hi," I said, using the moment for practice.

"Are you hitting the slopes?"

Smile... I shook my head.

"If you need a ski buddy, I'm always available," he said.

The elevator stopped, and the doors slid open. Stifled by his offer, I walked out without a reply. He was obviously flirting, even though he'd seen Jamison and me together. *Can everyone sense that the man I love has abandoned me?*

The guys walked past me again when I joined Alana and Alex at the circular sectional sofas in the middle of the lobby. "My offer still stands," the guy shouted before heading out into the cold day. When I looked at him, he had his thumb up.

"Is he talking to you?" Alana asked, frowning at him.

I shook my head. "I think so."

"What offer did he make?"

Hold it together. Don't cry.

"I don't know. Something about skiing."

"Humph," she said, studying me with one eye narrowed.

I showed her my practiced smile, and I knew it worked when hers matched mine.

"So, where's that dashingly handsome beau of yours?" she asked, rubbing her hands together.

My smile still felt perfect. "Asleep!" I exclaimed.

At least that was what I guessed. Whether he was in Rhode Island or California, I suspected he'd be asleep.

"Did you get the message from Eden?" Alana asked.

"No. What message?"

"Her boy-toy chef is making breakfast. I'm starving, and so is Alex, so let's go eat."

Alana's eyes danced when she looked at Alex, and he blushed. Not only were they definitely doing it, but they also reminded me of the way Jamison and I used to look at each other.

Snap out of it, Bryn.

"Bryn, is everything okay?" Alana asked.

I realized I was continuously shaking my head, so I stopped doing that. "Yes. I'm fine." My fake smile reigned supreme. I pointed toward the glass doors. "Let's go gorge ourselves." I rubbed my belly. "I'm starving too."

ON THE WAY TO EDEN'S, I THOUGHT IT WISE TO keep the conversation about work. We all agreed we had to work faster than usual, hopefully finishing the project in a week and a half. I suggested we fly in Danika, Glory, and Ross to help us get it done.

"I think we should buy as much as we can from one furniture store. Highpoint has just about everything we need, and if we buy in bulk, they'll give us a good deal," Alana said.

We'd just driven past the spot where Jamison had veered off the main road so that we could ravish each other. I rubbed my chest, over my heavy heart, as I worked on looking and sounding present. "I like that idea, Alana. And since we're flying in more people, I think it's time we stay at the Blackstone estate. It'll actually be more cost-effective and less of a hassle than the resort." Plus, we would travel a different route to get to Eden's house, so I'd never again have to look down that private road where Jamison and I had sex. Also, the resort, my suite, held too many memories of a love gone wrong.

"Yes, I like that," Alex enthusiastically said.

"Great job, Bryn. It's about time we get to use the family goodies," Alana added. "Will Jamison be staying with us?"

My throat felt as if it had suddenly expanded as I stared at my lap.

"Uh-oh… what happened?" Alana asked.

I quickly lifted my head. "Nothing," I sang optimistically. "Of course, he'll come too. Of course."

The cab of the car fell silent, but I wouldn't let the quiet linger. I asked Alex what he'd heard from the local construction company we'd hired to install all the flooring, demolish old walls, and put in new ones.

"He's starting on the first floor as soon as this afternoon. He suggests we pay to double his crew. He has the same concern about bad weather kicking up soon."

I sighed. Deep down, I knew it was the worst time of the year to do renovations in the high mountains. When I'd scheduled Eden's interior design, I hadn't thought it through. There was still a lot I had to learn about my new business. We should have only taken on projects in warmer climates during the winter and started Eden's vacation home in the spring. But if I'd waited, then I would never have run into Jamison at the airport, because I would probably have flown from Providence to LAX on Monday instead of to Denver on Sunday.

"We'll get through it as best we can," I said.

"That's all we can do," Alex said.

When we made it to Eden's, she escorted us to the dining room, which held a breakfast spread fit for royalty. Dale joined us at the table. I avoided eye contact with him as I explained to Eden that due to weather concerns, we would be working faster to complete the job and bringing in more people.

"That means our house is going to be a disaster zone for the next couple of weeks," she said.

"Two weeks, hopefully less," I said.

I could feel Dale staring a hole into my face, but I refused to acknowledge him. After I made the announcement, no one minded that I busied myself sending texts to the travel coordinator for MIND by Bryn Blackstone, asking her to arrange a chartered flight for the extra help being flown in from California. I also sent an email to Jasper's assistant, who handled family affairs, and asked if she could have the Vail estate prepared for later that afternoon. I tried hard to remain tuned out of their conversation. Eden didn't mind. She, Alana, and Alex were discussing where in the master bathroom to put her claw-foot soaker tub and what sorts of windows would provide the most privacy. I ate as fast as I could so that we didn't linger. The longer I sat, the more apt Eden was to ask about Jamison.

"You're eating fast," Dale said, his voice rising above the others. I knew he was talking about me.

The table grew quiet. When I looked up from my cell phone, all eyes were on me. My cell phone miraculously chimed and vibrated in my hands. Kat was calling.

"I have to take this," I said as I shot to my feet.

"Tell Jamison we miss him," Eden said.

My gaze passed over her and then Dale, who was watching me with narrowed eyes. He knew something was wrong.

I held up a finger, excused myself, and said, "By the way, I'm done with breakfast. We should get to work soon," and went off to answer Kat's call.

I tried to get as far away as possible from everyone. I headed toward the living room just as the doorbell chimed. I knew it was the construc- tion crew—they'd called Alex while we were getting out of the vehicle and asked if they could get an early start—so I told Kat to hold on as I ran up two floors and hid in one of the six guest rooms.

"What are you doing?" Kat asked.

My problems were ready to come gushing out of my mouth, but I waited until after I closed the door and walked onto the balcony to tell her all about the last three days with Jamison and how he'd left me without leaving a word.

"Oh, I'm sorry to hear that, Bryn. You rarely open yourself up to love in that way and... Hey, I have someone I want you to meet. He's handsome, kind, and a premier surgeon."

I jerked my head back. "Is this a setup? Are you trying to set me up?"

Kat laughed. "Well yeah. You're the perfect woman. It's damn well time that you fall in love with the perfect man. His name is Dr. Edward Grey, and I am certain he's the one for you. Hell, all the women in the hospital want him—patients, doctors, nurses, the lady who sells coffee from the cart. If you think about a romance-novel-hero guy, Dr. Grey's it."

My smile was lopsided and cynical. "Something's fishy about that name."

"He's not fishy, Bryn." She went on to say that she'd told him all about me, and he was in Houston for the conference. "Take a break and fly out on one of those private jets and have dinner with us."

I smashed my lips together, and anxiety fizzled throughout my body. I wasn't shocked that Kat believed one man could be so easily replaced by another. She wasn't in my shoes. She stood on the outside, looking at my heart. That was the norm. She was only trying to make me happy because she loved me.

"Thanks so much, sis, but I'm fine. I have to get over Jamison first. And then…"

"You have to get over Jamison?"

I leaned over the balcony, and there was Dale, looking up at me.

Sixteen

BRYN BLACKSTONE

"Damn it," I muttered and told Kat I had to call her back.

"Quick, are you coming?" she asked.

"No. I'm babysitting the kids this weekend," I said in a rush. "Sorry, I have to go. Bye."

I waited until she said goodbye. Then I looked down at Dale again, who was grinning up at me as if he'd just discovered he had winning lottery tickets.

I shook my head. "What the hell are you doing down there?"

"I live here. Then you're no longer screwing that poser?"

Anger made my eyes burn. What gonads he had

to refer to Jamison as a poser when Dale was the biggest phony I'd ever met. There was no use reacting to him, though. If he outed me to everyone else, then so be it. I was ready to tell the truth, anyway, but only if I had to.

So without another word, I turned my back on Dale and walked back into the house. I practically ran down three flights of stairs to rejoin my team, who were already working. Dale hadn't beat me to them, and that was a relief. With my huge practiced smile and amiable disposition, I joined the gang, and we began placing orders for the new stone counters, Miele appliances, and kitchen furniture.

SURPRISINGLY, DALE HADN'T RUBBED MY MISERY IN my face. However, he remained close. But unlike two days earlier, he offered no opinions. If I looked, I would catch him staring at me as if he was trying to telepathically let me know how much he wanted to bang my brains out. But I kept my mind on whatever task was at hand, not allowing my mind to wander to the place it wanted to go, which was Jamison Cox. I worked efficiently and joylessly.

Alana made a funny comment about the

current beam in the theater room resembling a sex tunnel. "All it needs are feathers, furs, and flashing red lights," she said with a laugh.

"Ooh, I like the sound of that," Eden crooned.

I realized there was a mood I needed to capture if I wanted to pretend everything was okay with me, but I couldn't attain it. And the fight to be jovial had suddenly made tears roll out of my eyes.

"Bryn? What's wrong?" Alana hurried over and took me by the shoulders. "What's going on?"

I closed my eyes, and my chin quivered as I shook my head. When Alana initiated our hug, and I embraced her back, I broke down crying.

"Eden, could we have a moment, please?" Alana asked.

"Um… sure." Eden sounded worried.

After a few seconds, Alana told me we were alone. "Is this about Jamison?" Her tone was sympathetic but demanded that I, for once, tell her the truth about my heartache.

I sniffed. "He's gone. He left without even telling me."

WE SAT ON THE FLOOR, FACING EACH OTHER WITH our legs crossed. "Damn it," she spat. "I thought he was one of the good ones." Alana narrowed an eye. "Are you sure? Because he was totally into you. I would have bet everything I owned on that."

I bit down on my back teeth to stop my chin from quivering again.

"Breathe, Bryn." Alana took my hands in hers.

I squeezed my eyes shut.

"Take your time to breathe. Relax. It's okay." She sounded as if she were taking me through a meditation session.

I inhaled deeply and then slowly released the breath. That felt better. I did it three more times before I opened my eyes and smiled faintly.

She raised her eyebrows.

I nodded. "It's complicated."

Alana studied me. "You're the most perceptive person that I know, so when you say it's complicated, then I have to believe that it's really complicated. But how is it complicated?"

I took another deep breath. "I think it's his father, Boomer."

"Boomer?"

I snorted a chuckle. "Precisely."

"With a father named Boomer, it sounds like

you dodged a torpedo." We chortled together. "Okay, then, what next?" she asked.

I shook my head. "Nothing. It's over."

"It's really over?"

"It's over." I sighed.

"Is your heart going to make it through the rest of the day? Because I can handle this if you want to go back to bed."

"I think so," I whispered.

She turned her head slightly. "Think?"

I smiled. "I know I can." The longer we stared at each other, the better I felt. I had some good people in my life, and Alana, my best friend, was at the top of the list. "Sorry I've been such a serious and intense killjoy today."

"That's not how I saw you at all. I mean, serious and intense, yes, but killjoy? Never."

I simpered. "Thanks." I never wanted to think about being disappointed by Jamison again, at least not if I could help it. So I patted Alana on the knee. "By the way, what's going on between you and Alex?"

Her eyes were alight as she smirked. "A lot. A whole lot."

Suddenly, Alex bolted into the room. "Hey," he said, looking at me. "How are you?"

My mouth fell open. Eden must have told him that I was having a breakdown in the theater room.

Alana dipped her head as she looked up at me. "You *are* fine?"

I winked at her. "I'm fine."

She beamed at Alex. "She's fine."

Seventeen

JAMISON COX

"She said she was fine," Alex said.

"Fine?"

My voice echoed, so I checked over both shoulders. The hallway, which looked like a setting from *The Shining*, was empty. I held the phone closer to my ear. "Is that what you saw when you looked at her? That she was fine?"

"No, that's not what I saw, but that's what she said. Look, Jamison, I don't know why you did what you did, but it doesn't feel right, you asking me how she's doing. And I'm talking to you, and you're the one who hurt her. You should be saying something to her, not me. She thinks you've blown her off. Why can't you just tell her what's going on?"

I loosened my collar and ran a hand through

my hair. I was in Washington, DC, about to meet with James Rally, one of the billionaire brothers of the notorious Rally Fund, which they used to pay an army of lobbyists to look out for their business interests. The other brother was John Rally. I'd long considered them both rapacious old assholes who'd always been at the top of my list of people to never work with. However, that had never stopped James from approaching me on several occasions, imploring me to manage the campaign of one of his political tools. Rule one in my business was to never let them know that you thought they were scum. I always gave an excuse for why I couldn't take them on as clients. Not even after Jasper had dried our well did I take them on. But James had come knocking again.

"Damn it," I whispered, closing my eyes.

I suddenly remembered that I had told James I was taking on Pedro Santiago as a client. He, along with Boomer, must have figured out a way to convince Pedro not to do business with me.

Boomer had managed a candidate for the Rallys on his own, though. I refused to get involved. Their guy had run for governor of Maryland. The Rallys wanted to stop the state from banning fracking. Their candidate lost big on the one hand, but on the other hand, they learned decisively that my father wasn't the reason Cox and Cox was successful—I was the one who'd put us on the map.

"What is it?" Alex asked after I cursed the air for remembering that I'd told James about Pedro.

"Nothing. It's just, I can't say anything to her right now. I'm working things out." I needed my old man to believe I was shaking in my boots. He'd said he had me in checkmate. James was supposed to enlighten me.

Alex's sigh was loud, but then he paused. "Okay, but hurry up. I don't like seeing her this way. She's such a great person, you know."

I knew he would understand. Our fathers were cut from the same cloth. I could set the world on fire, and Boomer would only point out what he thought I'd done wrong.

"I know," I said.

"And I don't like lying to her either."

I loathed having to go about doing what needed to be done in such a stealthy manner, but I had no other choice. "How about we cut off all communication until I'm in a better place?"

"Yeah, that sounds like the right thing to do," he replied without pausing.

I said goodbye to my last lifeline to the woman I

loved. My strong legs weakened, and I leaned against the wainscoting. The heater made the air too hot, and it was hard to breathe. I glanced up and down the hallway. There was no way out. Boomer couldn't make the meeting with James Rally. For a man with Rally's kind of wealth and prosperity, having an office two stories beneath the ground floor said a lot about his character. Under any other circumstances, I would've turned around and gone back the way I came, but instead, I pulled my shoulders back, checked the time on my watch, and knocked on the door.

"Get in here."

My shoulders tensed up. It was James, but he sounded like Boomer. As I put my hand on the knob, I knew for certain that I was done dealing with men like them. They felt like winners, but they weren't. They were bullies, willing to use their advantages to get whatever the hell they wanted.

I opened the door. James, with his light-blue eyes, white hair, and permanent frown built from decades of bitterness, scowled at me. "What the hell were you doing out there in the hallway all that time?"

My eyebrows pulled. I'd checked for cameras

before I made the call to Alex. I hadn't seen any. "You heard me?"

"Barely. Sit," he snapped as if I'd already done something to piss him off.

I knew his demeanor was his first power play. He was setting the tone, letting me know I was the whipping boy and he was the man with the strap.

There were four chairs spread in front of his desk, though. I sat in the one directly across from him and hunched my shoulders, making myself appear vulnerable. I couldn't say anything. I had to let him go first. I knew I wouldn't have to wait long, though.

"So…" His right eye narrowed to a slit. "You're going to be our next president?"

I readjusted in my seat. There was no chance in hell that was going to happen. "Apparently."

"'Apparently' is a weak answer for the most powerful man on earth."

"What Boomer wants——"

He interrupted with a loud snort and then studied me for a few seconds. James's chair creaked as he leaned back. His old furniture and stuffy office made him seem like a normal asshole who, even though he had more money than God, was still slogging through crap to make ends meet. He was the kind of person who penny-pinched on the crap that mattered and spent elaborately on toys and cunt that didn't belong to his wife.

He steepled his fingers against his chest. "Forget about Richard. You're the one with the plan. I want to hear it."

"It's too early for that. I just learned about all of this yesterday."

"You don't have a lot of time to get moving, though."

He was right. They were cramming their plan through, ensuring I didn't have too much space to change my mind. The messed-up part was they were squarely counting on me to orchestrate my own funeral.

James tapped the top of the table. He was nervous, probably wondering if Boomer actually had the juice to make me pull off a victory.

"Give me a few preliminaries, something to chew on," he said.

"There hasn't been an unmarried president since James Buchanan."

"You're marrying the Lovell girl." He threw his hands up. "At least she's a hot piece of ass. Getting her to part her thighs might be hard. But sex is cheap for guys like us."

There was no use in telling him that Bree had tried to have sex with me on several occasions. Just last weekend, when I was staying at the Lovell estate in Jamestown, she had snuck into my bed, straddled me while I slept, and rubbed my cock. I almost succumbed to the temptation. It had been a long time since I'd had sex. My cock to engage with her vagina. But a man didn't sink his junk into a woman like Bree Lovell without a condom, period. She'd make it mean more than casual sex. She'd blow up my phone twenty-four seven and spread lies about how I told her I loved her, along with getting herself pregnant and saying I was the father. She was insane, and there was no way in hell I was going to marry her.

"Right," I said passively. "Also, I look too opportunistic. I'm the guy who's been getting others elected to office."

"You don't think I already know that? I don't like that you're telling me what I already know."

I pressed my lips together. It took every ounce of energy to remain seated. "Because that hurdle is huge, James."

He thrust himself forward. "I don't want to hear problems. What's the solution?"

Stay calm and lie. "There is no solution. I need to

win despite my two disadvantages. I'll be newly married to a Lovell and my job."

"Solutions," he reiterated.

"I'm working on them. It won't be overnight, so you guys can hold your horses."

James's laughter slowly built. Once his bitter laugh reached its crescendo, his eyebrows pulled close together, creating deep creases in his forehead. "You think I was born yesterday? I know about you and the Blackstone girl." When he smirked, a lustful glow gripped his eyes. It was the sort of look that made me want to punch him for thinking of Bryn that way. "That's grade A twat for you. One dive into that, and you lose all your common sense, all your survival instincts." James calmly opened the top desk drawer, took out a manila folder, and tossed it in front of me. "Read it."

Finally, we were getting somewhere. James and I stared at each other. I was waiting for him to show me why he had the upper hand. When his smirk finally appeared, I frowned as if in distress and lifted the folder. I'd been waiting a long time for the moment when I'd find out what Boomer would use against me to keep me in line. I read the top page, then the one beneath it, and then the next and the next. When I was done, I calmly closed the folder and glared at James.

He hadn't stopped smirking. "I'll ask you again, what's your plan? And stop the BS. We have a meeting in…" Just as he checked his gold watch with diamonds around the face, there was a knock on the door. "Come in," James barked like a grumpy pitbull.

The door opened, and in walked Bree, Alice Templeton, and Boomer. Boomer whacked me twice on the shoulder. "Did you get him all softened up for us?"

"He's tenderized and ready to broil," James boasted.

"Oh, be nice to him," Alice said. "After all, he's going to be our next president of the United States of America."

Considering what I'd just read, I couldn't run away. If I was going to win the war, I would have to convince them I was willing to move fast to reach their goal and then move even faster to obtain mine.

"The Saturday after next," I said.

The silence held their curiosity.

"Bree and I will get married the Saturday after next."

Eighteen

BRYN BLACKSTONE

The designing was moving along at a good pace. Eden kept randomly asking if I was okay and then offering her version of words of encouragement.

"Screw him. Screw him and the white horse he rode in on," she said while Alana and I hung window-curtain samples.

"Eden, with all due respect, talking about Jamison doesn't help me forget him. So could we just pretend he never existed?" I asked.

"Oh. Sure."

And that was the last time we mentioned Jamison Cox. For the rest of the day, I let Alana show Eden some design choices that I'd never thought of. Then, by late afternoon, three of Claudia's light fixtures had arrived, and we agreed that they looked lovelier in real life. Eden had become such a new fan of Claudia's work that we decided to fly to Southern California later next week so that we could look at some of her custom-designed headboards and other light installations that could be used for wall features. We also shopped for more of the special touches, like lamps, trinkets, rugs, and other essentials. By the end of the day, I was wiped and still ignoring all the long gazes Dale was throwing my way as he tried to obtain my attention. I was disappointed in the old me for always giving in to his flirting, even when he'd done it in front of his new girlfriend. The old me had been satisfied to know that it didn't matter whether Dale was with someone else—he would always be mine. However, the new me was proud to be repulsed by his behavior.

When Alana, Alex, and I piled into the SUV, I announced that we would be moving to the Blackstone estate that evening. Our rooms had been readied, and a private chef was already preparing dinner. "And Alana..." I said, my voice more vulnerable than I wanted it to sound.

I had given her the front seat, so she turned to face me. "What is it, Bryn?"

"I think I should fly out to California in the morning." I had to get out of town and let some serious family time wipe away my happy memories with Jamison by replacing them with new ones of my nieces and nephew.

"Absolutely. I think you should too," she said before I could ask if she could handle all the tasks we had planned for Friday alone. "Danika, Glory, and Ross are flying in from LA tomorrow, so we'll have plenty of muscle." She reached for my hand, and I gave it to her. "Plus, with Dale gawking at you that way, maybe you should just take next week off too."

"I wanted to punch the guy in the face," Alex said.

So they'd noticed, which meant I wasn't imagining things. I'd been giving the job at Eden's a lot of thought. Eden had blindsided me with Dale. If I'd known he would be there, I would have done one of two things—asked that he not be there or cancelled our appointment.

"I think it's time to make the healthiest decision for myself and let you take the lead on the rest of the project, Alana, even the shopping."

She smiled and kissed the back of my hand. "Good job, Bryn. Of course, I'll take the lead. Plus, for the most part, we're set. We already know where we're going. From this point onward, it's mostly project management and tweaking, and I can call you whenever I need your input and guidance."

"Thank you," I whispered. The back of my throat was too tight to say much more than that.

WE ARRIVED AT THE SPA AND PACKED OUR THINGS. Before vacating the suite, I stood in the living room, arms folded and eyes closed. I couldn't stop my soul from searching for remnants of whatever energy Jamison had left behind. The thing was, I truly loved him, and that couldn't go away so easily. Also, my affection for him hadn't developed in a span of three days. Our love for each other began at that restaurant in Santa Barbara. My sister-in-law had passed out, and he raced me to the hospital as fast as he could as we followed the ambulance. I could feel myself fighting my attraction for him as we sat in the car together. He asked me a boatload of questions, like where I'd been, what I did, what I liked, and if I'd ever seen this or that. The more I talked, the more I rejected him. I kept telling myself that he was too straitlaced. The truth was, I was afraid that he wasn't crazy and damaged enough. I would have had to take Jamison Cox seriously. When we began working together, we would have still, quiet moments and occasionally share a chuckle. Then I would get away from him as fast as possible. Then one night, his persistent chase resulted in him catching me. *Wow, what an amazing night we spent together.* In the morning, I'd known Jamison Cox was the one I'd never suspected existed.

I opened my eyes. The empty, cold suite was still and hollow. Maybe I'd fooled myself back then. Maybe I should have given Kat's doctor friend a fair shot. A doctor was a man who had his act together. I was no longer afraid of that kind of guy.

"I'll do it," I whispered. I would take a stab at dating another guy who was the opposite of Dale Rumor.

There was a knock on the door, and I was satisfied with my decision when I let the bellman in to take my luggage downstairs to the SUV. Yes, I loved Jamison, but it was best that I make a vow to leave our love, if that was what it was, in the room where we'd last been together. No more—Jamison would never have another opportunity to hurt me again. *Never.*

"Look at this goddamn place," Alana said as we arrived at the gates of the estate. "It's almost as large as the resort we just left."

The Blackstone mansion in Vail looked like a summer castle made for royalty. I'd never stayed in it, and as the gates rolled open, I realized why. I had a lot of excuses for choosing to lodge at the resort rather than the mansion. My gaze took in the eaves, chimneys, and nicely placed windows. I narrowed my eyes at the glass facade and conjured a picture of Randolph standing under the chandelier, looking out the window. He wore a crow mask and a black tuxedo. I felt I'd seen him in that getup, but I couldn't place where or when. However, I knew he'd been engaged in some kind of licentious behavior. All the family properties held his dark secrets.

If only the air could talk. If only the stairs and doors and secret hallways could record history. I fought the urge to hyperventilate. My body shook as Alex drove up the curving road toward the big house.

"Have you been here before, Bryn?" Alana

asked. Fortunately, she seemed clueless about what was going on inside me.

"Never," I said as normally as possible.

"The estate is fantastic."

The closer we got, the more activity we saw. A white van was parked in front of a side door, and people were carrying crates of food into the building. We made it to the three-level parking structure, which had enclosed glass walls. A number of cars were already there.

"Who's here?" Alana asked, examining our surroundings in awe.

"More than likely the house staff."

"What the—" she whispered. "I counted sixteen cars." She turned to face me. "That many people?"

I nodded. "Mm-hmm."

Alana narrowed her eyes. "Are you okay, Bryn?"

I was tired of saying I was fine when I wasn't. Being there, after everything else that had happened to me recently, reminded me that I was still in recovery, and in order to not relapse, I had to start using my tools and telling the truth, the whole truth, and nothing but the truth.

"I'm scared. You both read the book about my family. Well, this place has seen a lot of Randolph's sins. If it were up to me, I would've had the entire estate demolished and rebuilt before I stayed here. But we're here now, and it's a go. So just bear with me." I took a deep breath.

"Damn, I never thought about that," she said.

"Me neither," Alex added.

I put a hand on both their shoulders. "I'll get through it. One step at a time, heh?"

Alana put her hand on top of mine. "We're here with you."

I wanted to say thank you, but instead, I yawned and then slapped my hand over my mouth. "Sorry. I just want to go to bed." Lack of sleep, after nights of making love to Jamison, was catching up to me.

"Well, ladies, let's get the show on the road," Alex said.

Alana beamed at him. He was taking charge of a difficult moment, and I suspected she found that sexy enough to make her want to bang his brains out.

INSIDE, THE MANSION WASN'T AS BAD AS I THOUGHT. The temperature was perfect, and the decor, which was modern and homey, made the place comfortable. I was surprised the furniture wasn't gaudy. Randolph had been into that old-world baroque decor. Heaviness. He liked everything heavy, even the air.

"Bronwyn, how are you, my dear?"

I stiffened once I recognized the voice and then quickly turned around. I covered my mouth with both hands and gasped. I wanted to say his name. But instead, my feet automatically walked me over to William, our family butler from the former Newport estate, and I gave him a tight hug. We'd grown up with him, and next to Jasper, he'd been our main caretaker.

"What are you doing here?" I exclaimed, feeling more relaxed. "I thought you retired."

He said Jasper had asked him to train two new butlers, and since I was spending upward of two weeks at the estate, they decided Vail was the best place to do it. We met the trainees, Leon and Gregory. They both appeared to be in their early fifties, and knowing Jasper, they'd been well vetted. Leon showed Alana and Alex to their room. They'd stopped trying to convince me that they weren't sharing a bed.

Then William showed me to my room. "Have you ever lodged in the estate before today?"

I yawned. "Never." My eyelids were so heavy.

"Hmm," he said thoughtfully. "Notice the decor."

"I have," I said as we walked in front of the glass wall on the left side of the hallway. It was growing darker, but well-placed lights brightened the grounds below, and the snow glowed on a nearby ski slope. The view was majestic.

"Randolph never visited this particular estate, although many of his famous friends had. This is where he chose to wine and dine and impress guests."

My mouth fell open. "No parties with underage girls or body parts cemented into the walls?"

"Not here, my darling."

I instantly relaxed, as if every cell in my body took an enormous sigh of relief. The air was clean, and there would be no evil spirits calling in the night, choking me in my sleep and making me feel paranoid. We walked in thoughtful silence until we reached a large, beautiful room with a king-sized bed, which had a lit accent built-in wall feature made of raw crystal rock, behind the smooth royal-orange leather headboard.

"Wow," I said. Suddenly, I was in sensory over-load as I took in the teardrop chandeliers above two royal-blue velvet chaises with white leather backs, both facing the foot of the bed. "I would've totally bought those for this space."

"Yes, I was told that the room was designed with you in mind."

My mouth remained open as I admired the white faux fur rug on top of light wood floors. Those, too, would have been my design choices. "Tell me there are no secret passages." If there were, that would ruin everything.

"Jasper had them merged into the main house four years ago. The work was done on all twenty-three Blackstone properties around the world."

Suddenly, my insides felt as if the sun had risen over my heart. "Jasper designed this house?"

"Yes."

"But he never told me."

William chuckled in his very contained manner. "We both know your brother will never say so unless asked."

"True."

I gave the space a second and third once-over. It was easy to see that my brother knew me well. "Thanks, William."

He bowed then asked me to call him on the extension if I needed anything else. I requested dinner in my bedroom with water and hot tea service. I was too drained to sit at the dining room table and make conversation.

AFTER EATING, I DROPPED MY ROBE, CRAWLED INTO bed naked, and didn't wake up until my alarm blared. I hadn't slept well since a week before my brother's wedding. I'd taken on the task of planning the ceremony, since the bride and groom had graciously agreed to hold it at the renovated Newport estate. I'd worried myself to death, making sure everything was perfect.

My alarm woke me up at eight forty-five in the morning. Alana and Alex would have left for Eden's house forty-five minutes earlier. My flight to Santa Barbara left at ten o'clock that morning. I was taking the family airplane, so I felt no pressure to make it to the airport two hours before boarding call.

I stretched and yawned and then picked up my phone to call Eden. I wanted to personally let her know that Alana would be taking over as project manager. But then I saw that I had a missed call and a text message alert from Asher. He'd called and texted me an hour before. I must have been too deep in sleep to hear either. I quickly returned his call, and he answered on the first ring.

"Bryn," he said, gasping as if his life depended on me hearing whatever he had to say.

Dread suddenly overcame me. "What is it?"

"It's Gina. Since you're in Colorado, I need you to go to her."

"Gina? Our Gina?"

"Our Gina, yes."

I shook my head. "What's wrong with her?" The last I'd heard, she was a swim coach and was training girls to compete in the Olympics.

"Damn it," he said under his breath. "I have to go, but I'll text you the address. Thank you, Bryn. Thank you." He hung up, leaving me with my mouth caught open, listening to silence.

Nineteen

BRYN BLACKSTONE

S peaking to Asher had officially marked the end of relaxation mode. With one call, I was back to moving fast and being pressed for time. I showered, blow-dried my hair, and dressed warmly, since I wasn't going straight to California, where it was eighty degrees that day. While packing for my weekend with the family, I scarfed down the most delicious roasted vegetable omelet I'd ever tasted. I expected to find Gina in good condition though. She often practiced getting Asher all worked up just to prove to herself that he still cared about her. I used to resent her for that, but as I matured, I understood why she did it and, in turn, developed a lot of empathy for her. She needed to know that Asher still loved her, especially since he'd gotten married.

While being driven to the airport by one of the hired cars that came with the estate, I called the BFE travel department and asked if my flight to California could go to Denver first. The coordinator put me on hold and, after about three minutes, let me know that my flight and grounded services in both cities had already been changed.

"Already been made?" I asked.

"Yes, Miss Blackstone."

"By who?"

"The arrangements have been made by Angela Williams."

"Jasper's assistant?"

"Yes, Miss Blackstone."

I grunted thoughtfully. If Jasper was involved, then something really could be wrong with Gina. When I considered that, I was more worried than I'd been before. But then, maybe still, things weren't so bad. I would have to wait and see.

The car stopped near the airplane's ramp, and all I had to do was climb up while the driver handled my bags. The stewardess served me a cup of coffee, and not long after I settled into my seat, we were up, up, and away. When I closed my eyes and focused on relaxing and the fun weekend I would have with Jada and the kids, I smiled, realizing I hadn't thought about Jamison since before bed the previous night. I wanted to stay with that trend of not giving him a second thought, so I focused on Gina.

Months before, I'd debated whether it was appropriate to invite Gina to Asher's wedding. My brother was an expert at being mindfully ignorant of the realities he didn't want to deal with. Here was the truth: Gina had always loved Asher more than Spencer. Asher would debate me on that point, but I knew it for a fact. Asher was her safe place. He was the one who'd found her wounded. She'd been so used and abused by Randolph that she hadn't been able to escape the secret tunnels in the former Blackstone family mansion. Asher had found her and cared for her as if she were a wounded animal. He loved her, too, but not in the passionate and fiery way that he loved Pen, his wife. He'd craved Gina that way once upon a time, though, when they were teenagers, and they'd acted on their new sexual attraction for each other. I had no idea if it was because she was having sex with

Spencer, too, or because Randolph was still pimping her out to his wealthiest associates every now and then, but the feelings of romantic love Asher had held for Gina gradually diminished. However, I'd still invited Gina to the wedding. I put her name on the guest list so that she could receive a paper invitation, but I phoned her as well. Gina didn't answer and never returned my call. She didn't RSVP either. Regardless, I held a spot for her just in case she found the strength to support Asher on his big day. She never came.

I'd been so busy after the ceremony, what with running into Jamison, losing my phone, and then losing Jamison again, that I hadn't called to check up on her. Frankly, I was used to Gina not taking most of my calls. On the rare occasion that she did answer, her tone was usually brisk, and she would try to end the call as soon as possible.

But our relationship had always been complicated. Growing up, I'd simultaneously hated her and loved her. She was the other Blackstone sister, and like most young people, we had our sibling rivalry. Regrettably, I believed I was better than her. I didn't know any better. The truth was, we were both victims tethered to one man, Randolph Blackstone. After many stints in rehab and then finally finding the right therapist, I was able to forgive myself for looking down on Gina, and I asked her for forgiveness. That was two years ago.

She'd fallen out of contact with Asher and Spencer, and I hadn't spoken to her since Randolph died. Holly, Jasper's wife, had kept tabs on Gina when we all scattered to find ourselves and landed her a job as a swim coach. When I was ready to ask Gina for forgiveness, Holly was the one who gave me her phone number.

"So, you're saying this to me over the phone?" Gina asked snidely.

I thought back then that she had a point. A large part of my recovery was to always be emotionally honest with myself. "I'm sorry. I was too chicken to say this to you face-to-face. I was afraid you would reject me. I've been such a bitch to you for so many years."

"Yes, you have been a bitch. But you treat me better than most people. So goddamn you, Bryn, you don't need to apologize to me."

I twisted my mouth in anguish, feeling uneasy about her acceptance of my apology.

"Is that all?" she snapped.

I wanted to say no. I wanted to magically inject her with happiness and health. She needed to drink from the same well of recovery that had transformed me. But Gina hadn't even dipped her pinkie toe into the healing pools of recovery.

"That's all," I finally said.

"Then I have to go."

She waited for me to say goodbye. That was a good sign. If she wanted to dismiss me and never have anything to do with me, then she would have hung up in my face.

"Okay. Hopefully, we can talk soon."

She snorted. "Right."

"Goodbye, Gina," I said.

"Bye," she snapped.

And that was it. We'd spoken a handful of times in the past three years. I had to be the one that called her, though. Our conversations were always short and to the point. *I'm fine. You're fine. Do you need anything? No. Talk soon.* Once, I told her that I really loved her, and she went quiet for a long time before saying she had to go.

I did love Gina. I cared about her. It would kill me if anyone ever hurt her or if she hurt herself.

I tried to call Asher back just before landing, but

my call went straight to his voicemail. He must have gone into surgery or a meeting or something. I hadn't thought to follow up with a call to Pen to ask if she knew anything about what was going on with Gina until the airplane had landed, but since I was in the back seat of a big black SUV driven by a frowning, burly man in a black suit, I decided against it. The man said his name was Nick, and despite the sun being hidden behind thick clouds, he had on a pair of black sunglasses. I found myself wishing Nick had a sunnier personality. For some reason, I felt the gray day and his dreary disposition were the beginnings of what was to be a gloomy future. I hoped I was wrong, but when the blinker clicked and the vehicle made a right into a parking lot of an establishment that looked like a dilapi- dated motor hotel, my dread intensified.

I leaned forward so the driver could hear me clearly. "Are you sure this is the address?"

"Yes it is, ma'am. I've been instructed to stay near you while you are on the premises."

I tilted my head, intrigued by that revelation. So Jasper knew the place wasn't somewhere I should be alone. And the driver wasn't a tank of a man for no reason. I was about to ask if the property was a hotel, but then I saw the sign for the Cedar Pine Apartments.

"What in the hell…" I muttered.

"Excuse me. I'm sorry," he said.

I shook my head. "Nothing. I'm just surprised this is the place."

I thought Gina had gotten paid well for being a coach, and in addition to her salary, she received thousands of dollars of month from being one of Randolph's many victims, plus she had access to all Blackstone properties, aircrafts, yachts, and automobiles. Basically, not in a million years did she have to live that way.

I gasped when a slender man covered in tattoos up to his neck stepped outside, smoking a cigarette. Snow was pushed up against the side of the road and lay on sidewalks and the ground between the trees across the street. However, the guy wore a tank top and shorts. The heater had made it nice and warm in the car, but the cold draft sneaking in through the crevices of the door chilled the side of my face. I'd done enough drugs to know that he had to be high enough to not feel his ass freezing off.

"I can do an address check again if you want," the driver said. I quickly read him the address that

Asher had sent me, and he confirmed that we were there. "Unit 208."

My heart felt as if it stopped beating as I squinted at the numbers on the doors of the unit. I prayed to God that Gina wasn't turning tricks again and that the sickly-looking tweaker wasn't one of her low-grade clients. I sighed in relief when I saw that he had walked out of unit 212, which was far enough from where I was supposed to find Gina.

I was tired of delaying the inevitable. "I'm ready," I said as I opened my door.

The driver opened his door too.

THE SMOKER WATCHED LIKE A HAWK AS NICK AND I walked up the stairs, as if defending his territory. I felt confident that Nick could easily take him in a fistfight, though. He had to know I didn't belong there. Gina had always looked more pampered and delicate than I had. I wondered what he'd done when he realized she was living in her unit alone. Then he stopped staring at me, and his eyes widened at Nick. I turned back to glance at what had made him so suddenly grow tense. My driver had taken off his shades and was scowling at the man as if ready to douse him with ketchup and have him for lunch.

I stopped in front of unit 208 and knocked. I still held out hope that we had the wrong address.

"That woman ain't in there," the guy said. He was smiling and missing most of his front teeth. I was right—he was a meth addict.

I was about to ask if he could describe the tenant for me when someone said, "What do you want with her?"

I snapped my attention in the opposite direction. A middle-aged woman, whose face bore a lot of worry, eyed Nick and me. Her head was sticking out the door, but her body was still inside her unit.

"I'm here to see Gina," I said.

"I can see that. But who are you?"

My mouth fell open. Saying that I was a friend didn't seem powerful enough to get the job done. "Gina's my sister." That wasn't a lie. I could always mount a strong case that she and I were family.

The woman's glower ran from my head to my feet and then landed on my face again. "Give me a second." She slammed her door.

The skinny guy gazed out over the tree-covered field across the street from the complex, pretending he wasn't closely following our activity. I raised my eyebrows at Nick as I sighed. He answered with a shrug. At least he, too, found the entire situation strange as hell.

The woman came out in a long, thick, black wool coat while carrying a key. "Get inside, Wayne. It's cold out here," she said, scowling at the skinny guy.

Instinctively I moved out of her way.

"Damn, Nan, can I have a cigarette?"

"Not without a coat, you nitwit. It's freezing out here." She finished opening Gina's door. "I checked on her yesterday. She was in bed, sleeping and crying about something."

I pressed my hand over my heart. "Crying?"

"She says she has depression and I shouldn't worry. I was going to check on her later. Will you let me know how she's doing?"

Nan had a warmness in her eyes that I only noticed when I really looked at her. At least I knew how Gina could live in the complex in peace. It appeared that Nan was the person in charge, and she would let no harm come to the vulnerable.

"I will," I said.

Nan nodded sharply and looked at the skinny guy again. "Didn't I tell you to get inside? It is cold out here. You can't feel it because you're high, so get indoors before you get frostbite or something."

I didn't look at the guy again, but he muttered something unintelligible, and then Gina's window banged as he slammed his door, disappearing into his unit. The place was made so cheaply that it seemed like one kick would send the whole complex tumbling down.

Why couldn't Gina have stayed in her penthouse in New Orleans? Asher hadn't sold it, even though he'd threatened to. Not only that, but Gina had luxury condos in Miami and Manhattan too. *Why in the world did she choose to nest here?*

Nick insisted on entering before I did. He brandished a weapon and then ordered me to stand by the door as he checked out the apartment.

My eyes grew wide. "You have a gun?"

"I used to be a police officer. Now I'm licensed to carry as security."

With that said, I did as I was told. While I waited, my attention fell on the worn-out sofa and the dried wood coffee table. The carpet was trampled on and needed to be vacuumed and steam cleaned. There wasn't a television in the living room. I looked toward the small kitchen. Cleaned plates, cups, and silverware were stacked in a dish rack, and a cup filled with water sat on the counter. If I'd had to guess, I would have put my money on Nan coming in to make sure the dishes were washed and Gina was eating and drinking.

"Damn it!" I heard Nick shout.

I ran into the bedroom to see what had caused such an exclamation from that towering mass of a man.

Twenty

BRYN BLACKSTONE

"Gina, open your eyes," Nick said loudly as he shined a small light in each of her eyes. "Her pupils are not overdilated. That's a good sign."

I picked up two of the pill bottles next to her bed. One was a prescription of oxycodone, and the other was Vicodin.

"Her skin is warm." Nick's large palm was pressed against Gina's forehead. "Gina, could I get you to sit up?"

"Leave me, leave me," a groggy Gina kept repeating.

"Gina, it's me, Bryn," I said loudly.

Suddenly her face contorted as if she was in

pain, and she started crying. "No, Bryn. No... you see me this way... no..." She tried to fling her body away from me and failed.

I sighed with dread and turned to Nick. "Could you give us a moment alone, please?"

His eyes narrowed as if he was thinking about whether that was really the best course of action.

"She's high, not overdosed," I said.

His stony eyes studied Gina again. She was whining "No" as tears streamed from her eyes.

He nodded. "I'll be out there."

I watched him walk out of the room, and then I softly closed the door behind him. "Gina," I called as I took my coat off and laid it at the foot of the bed.

She'd gotten a good enough grip on the blanket to pull it up to her neck. She was trying to cover her head but didn't have enough strength to take it that far. I finished taking my shoes off and then climbed up into the full-sized bed next to her.

"Gina." I wrapped my arms around her. "I know it hurts, but this is not the way to make the pain go away."

Her cries grew louder, harder.

"I know," I repeated, raking my fingers through

her disheveled hair, which was oily and smelled unwashed. "Gina, will you let me help you, please?"

"Why?" she whimpered, squirming as if no position could bring her comfort.

"Why what?"

"He married her. Why?"

I closed my eyes and sighed. Her emotional breakdown was indeed about Asher. My eyes landed on the bottles of pills sitting on the nightstand. "Gina, do you remember how many pills you took?"

"Make it…" she muttered, turning away from me. "Hurts…"

I swung my legs over the side of the bed and darted over to count how many pills were supposed to be in each bottle and how many were left, and I noticed that the prescription for oxycodone was for someone named Lyle Conway. The Vicodin belonged to someone named Ruben Johnson. Each bottle contained fourteen pills, and there were only three left in one and two in the other. The dates of the prescriptions were from over a year before, which was normal when it came to illegal drugs. However, I couldn't be positive the drugs in the bottle were what was on the labels.

Shaking my head, I exhaled sharply. "Nick," I called and then went over to tap Gina on the face, attempting to wake her up as much as I could. "Gina, I'm calling an ambulance."

"No," she moaned, shaking her head.

"How much of this have you taken?"

Gina tried to take a deep breath and ended up coughing. "I—fine."

"No you're not."

"Do not call." With what little strength Gina had, she hoisted herself into the sitting position and pressed her back against the wall. "I'm up, see?" She struggled to keep her eyelids open.

"Will you come with me, please?"

"Where?" she asked.

"The same place that helped me. It's time to get help, don't you think, Gina?"

When she tried to breathe, she grimaced as if her whole body ached.

"You want me to call that ambulance?" Nick asked.

Gina groaned louder. It was her way to voice an objection to calling for help. "My job," she barely said.

I held up a hand to stop him from saying

another word and squatted beside the bed. "Gina, those drugs on your nightstand are illegal and expired. I can't be certain you've taken what was in the bottle. Also, Asher getting married shouldn't make you want to hurt yourself. But it does, and taking drugs or even working at your job harder isn't going to change the deeper problems here. Gina?"

Her heavy eyelids blinked rapidly as she tried to focus on me.

"Gina, you see that man in the room?"

She forced her eyes to focus on Nick.

"That's Nick. He used to be a cop. He's a good guy, hired to protect us. So I'm going to say this in front of him. You understand?"

"Say what?" she murmured.

"When Asher found you in the tunnel, your legs had been broken by someone who abused you to the point where you were bleeding and—"

"No," she whined, squeezing her eyes shut.

I rose to my feet and leaned close to her. My nose was near her cheek. "All of it, Gina. It will always have power over you—make you feel cheap and slutty and unworthy, until you beat its ass. Come on. I'll be there for you every step of the way. Let's beat them together."

"Beat who?"

"The past. Randolph's and those like him."

It took her a few seconds to post her focus on me. Then she nodded softly.

I sighed with relief. *Thank God.*

Twenty-One

BRYN BLACKSTONE

THREE HOURS LATER

First, I helped Gina into the shower. The warm water and steam helped her recover some. Not much, though. Then I got her into a pair of jeans and a sweater. She let me put socks and shoes on her feet. Every so often, she would break down in tears and then slowly pull herself back together. Not only was her heart in pain, but her soul was too.

We packed a small bag that included underwear and another change of clothes. That was all she needed. As soon as Nick opened the door and I stepped outside with my arm around Gina's waist, Nan came outside too.

"Are you okay, honey?" Nan asked Gina.

Gina swallowed. "Um, yes," she said in a small voice.

I could tell she was trying to smile to convince Nan that her claim was true, but her mouth wouldn't let her form one. Nick locked the door and slipped the key into his pocket. I let Nan know we were going to keep the key because Nick told me that someone would be there soon to pack Gina's things and close down the unit. He also confirmed that he was taking orders from Nestor, who was Jasper's special investigator.

On the way to the airport, she huddled against the door and fell asleep. Every so often, she groaned and readjusted her position. Since she'd been up and moving around before then, Nick and I surmised that we didn't have to take her to the hospital before our flight. I called Asher and let him know what I'd found. When I informed him that we were on our way to the Lantern of Life Recovery Center and I would call my therapist, Dr. Taylor Parker, he insisted on having Dr. Mita Sharma involved.

"I'd been conferring with her about Gina for a while. We were waiting for Gina to agree to recovery. Mita works with Lantern of Life, too, so I'll have her meet you there in the morning."

I sighed hard. I really hadn't wanted to get into the battle of the therapists with my brother. Dr. Parker had helped me tremendously. But Gina's recovery wasn't about me, so I said okay and let Asher handle all the details.

When my brother fell silent, I knew he had more to say. "Was it because of me?" he asked.

I groaned as I raised my eyebrows.

"I knew it," he said. "Could we talk about it later?"

I looked at Gina, who had just shifted positions. "Mm-hm."

"Thanks, Bryn. I know you have a long weekend planned with the kids, but you'll see her all the way through, won't you?"

"Yes, definitely. Plus, I have thousands of weekends to spend with the kids."

We said goodbye, and then I called Jada and informed her that since I was on my way to Malibu with Gina, I didn't know if I would make it to Montecito until late Saturday or Sunday morning.

"I know. I heard." She explained how Spencer was happy that Mita would finally be treating Gina. "They all love her, you know."

I swallowed, choking up. "I know."

"And you love her too."

"I do."

"So… hey, how about I bring the kids out to Malibu?" she asked.

I could have broken down and cried. Of course Jada would do that for me. She was an extension of my brother, his better half. They had the same heart and concern for others. Giving and caring were never too hard for her or him.

"Yes, that'll be… heaven-sent."

My final call was to Alana. I explained how I'd been redirected to Denver. I made the call to her simply because she was my best friend. I let her know that I wanted to come back and help finish up but wouldn't know when that would be.

"As I said before, don't worry," Alana said. "I love having you around, but I kind of think Eden is relieved you're not here to tempt her scoundrel of a boyfriend."

We both chuckled at that.

By the time we reached the aircraft, all my important calls had been made. Nick followed behind us, carrying Gina's bag, as I assisted her up the ramp. He put her bag in an upper bin as I buckled her up in the seat across from mine. The two stewardesses, Carrie and Ronnelle, couldn't take their eyes off Nick, maybe because of his size or maybe because he wasn't so bad on the eyes.

He grimaced at Gina as I stood facing him. "Listen," he said and then set his eyes on my face. "I've seen a lot in my days on the job. I've known a lot of people who are paid to do what you did back there. You, Bryn Blackstone—you're the real deal." He observed Gina again. Her eyes were closed, but tears streamed out of the corners. "Could you let me know how she does? I feel like I'm invested here."

I pressed my lips into a firm and sober smile as I nodded. "Yes, I know. And for sure, I'll give you an update."

WE'D BEEN FLYING FOR THE BETTER PART OF TWO hours. It was just after four in the afternoon, but it felt later than that. During the flight, I'd answered a number of emails, including one from Alana. The spider lamp had been hung in the den, and Eden thought the fixture was too heavy for the space. I asked if she could remove some of the legs, and if that didn't work, I advised her to pack it up and send it back. I sent Alana a catalog from three more artists who did light fixtures, just in case thinning out the legs didn't work.

"Bryn," Gina said.

I ripped my eyes off my computer and set them on her. She'd been asleep up until then. Gina's eyes were fully open, and that was a good sign.

"Hey," I said, smiling.

"Where are we going?"

"You've agreed to go to rehab," I said, keeping my tone tender.

I could see the fear in her eyes. "They can't help me. No one can."

I carefully set my computer on the seat beside me. "What do you mean?"

She closed her eyes as she rolled her shoulders, wincing. "I'm dirty all the time, and you're telling me that can go away, and I'm telling you it can't."

I liked that she said that. I took it as a sign that she wanted to talk and was really willing to give recovery a chance. I closed my laptop. "It's a process. And…" I smiled at her. "You look better. Would you like anything to eat?"

"I'm not hungry," she said with a sigh.

I nodded.

"You're frowning," she said. "What is it you want to say to me, Bryn?"

I twisted my mouth thoughtfully. The moment was delicate, and I didn't want to say the wrong thing. However, I knew Gina was like a little bird, looking for love in every place. When we were younger, I used to use that to my advantage. I played push-pull with my affection for her, being nice one moment and a raging bitch the next. From what I knew about my own experience of being wounded, Gina still saw me the same way she'd seen me back then. That was why I wanted to tread delicately. I didn't want her to feel as if she had to perform for me to receive my love.

"It's nothing," I finally said.

"Bryn. What?" Her tone was sharp, demanding.

I rubbed the back of my neck nervously. "Um, what happened with your job?"

Her lips started to tremble.

I shook my head. "You don't have to tell me." I pressed my hand over my heart. "Listen, I always knew that job wasn't the cure-all."

"I couldn't look them in the eyes anymore," she said. I felt as if I'd forgotten to breathe, and my back was attached to the leather seat as I waited for her to say more. "I couldn't get into the swimming pool with them anymore. I felt like I tainted the water."

I closed my eyes so I could truly reply from my heart. "I can't talk you out of seeing yourself that way, Gina. And I know there's nothing I can say to change your mind." I opened my eyes. She was watching as if chomping on my every word, looking for more of them to cling to but unable to get a grasp on them. "Those same things you're saying about yourself, I used to say about myself. I can't tell you how it happened, but with help, I just stopped believing that awful lie."

She shook her head adamantly. "You're not like me."

"But I am. I am like you. Do you know what Randolph did to my mother? What he did to Amelia? We were all his victims. You in one way, and me in another."

"But you had Jasper," she retorted.

"You did too. He kept you safe, as much as you would let him. He kept Randolph from using you more than he would've if Jasper hadn't stepped in."

"Really?"

"Yes. Jasper was never going to force you to stop doing anything, but they knew he'd better not hear about any of them hurting a hair on your head or else."

Her jaw dropped as she gazed off thoughtfully.

"I want you to understand that Jasper loves you too. You're unable to recognize his kind of love because it comes with protection and without control."

She watched me with watery eyes and then turned to stare out the small round window. "I heard you on the phone with him."

I knew who she meant. "Ash?"

She nodded. "I used to dream of our wedding day, but deep down, I knew it was only a dream."

"Gina…" I waited for her to look at me again. After a few beats, her eyes were on me. "He could never marry you. Your heart loves him as a brother. You're so beautiful. You've always only wanted to be loved. You've been sweet, kind. You have a severe defense mechanism that comes with a bite, but once your walls are down, you give your whole heart. And that part of you is not a weakness. It's your strength. You'll see."

Tears streamed freely out of her eyes. Then Gina cleared her throat. "You promise?" she asked, barely audible.

I unbuckled my seat belt and got up to sit beside

her. Then I made sure we maintained solid eye contact. "I promise." I held my palm up for her to take my hand. "You don't have to take it if you don't want. You have every right to be angry at me for the way I treated you when we were younger. So you owe me nothing. You can reject me, and I will still love you, be here for you. Understand?"

"I've never been angry at you, Bryn. I've always loved you too." She set her hand on top of mine. "Didn't like you…"

We both chuckled.

"But I loved you," she reiterated.

We interlaced our fingers. I smiled at her, and Gina freely laid her head on my shoulder. She soon fell asleep, and shortly thereafter, so did I. Neither of us woke up until our airplane landed at LAX.

Twenty-Two

JAMISON COX

On Friday night, I could hardly sleep. I tossed and turned, trying to think of a better way to fight my father's plan to control the country through me. I had to admit, as far as tactics went, Boomer's was brilliant. He would be the puppeteer dishing out favors, gaining power by having me on a string. And I could win an election. I had no doubt about that. However, my chances of a victory would increase tenfold if I could marry Bronwyn Henrietta Blackstone instead of Bree Lovell. But that was not why I finally got my ass out of bed and made a phone call, which was the hardest one I ever had to make.

I planned on leaving a message, but after a ring, Spencer Blackstone answered, saying, "Who's this?"

I had called the number that was reserved for family and friends. It sounded as if he wasn't too happy to see an unknown number.

"This is Jamison Cox."

He fell quiet. "What do you want?"

I couldn't let his tone make me hesitate. Every second counted. "I want to talk to you about my father and his plan to make me the president."

I thought Spencer would laugh mockingly—I would have if I were him. But then I remembered that Spencer Blackstone never took anything lightly. As soon as I told him what I wanted to discuss, he believed the outcome was possible and was wondering what that meant for him and his family.

"I'm listening," he said.

And I told him everything, starting with my weekend with the Lovells, skipping my days with his sister, and ending with my meeting at James Rally's office, listing all the participants.

"Alice Templeton?" he said.

"She was there too."

He snorted bitterly. "She never stops, does she?" He seemed to be asking himself that question. "With all of that said, why are you calling me, though?"

I kept my sigh of relief to myself. I'd been

hoping he'd ask me that question. "You and I worked together. I think you know me better than Jasper does. You know it wasn't me. None of it was. Your family will have a lot to worry about if my father is able to wield that kind of power, though."

"You'll be the president, not him. Unless…"

I gave Spencer a few seconds to put one and one together.

"What does he have on you?" Spencer asked.

"A couple of years ago, you read off names on a list at a fundraiser. Remember that?"

This time, when he snorted, I knew he was smirking proudly. "I remember it well. That was fun."

"I could be tied to some of those transactions. I made them while blindly following Boomer's orders and signing documents without paying close attention. He kept records of all of it."

Spencer grunted thoughtfully. "What are you doing tomorrow?"

I shook my fist victoriously and, in a calm voice —not indicating how ecstatic I was to hear him ask that—I said, "Whatever you have in mind."

When Spencer said he would be in Montecito alone that weekend so I could come up, I was slightly disappointed. I almost asked what had happened to Bryn being there, but I needed to focus. Also, I didn't want to give any indication that I was capable of using my love for his sister as a bargaining chip. I missed the hell out of her, though. He did say that his wife was in Malibu with the kids. I put it all together and concluded that Spencer and Jada only had one kid, so more than one kid meant Jasper's kids were with Jada in Malibu, and Bryn was with them too.

Spencer and I made a plan to meet at his estate at two o'clock Saturday afternoon. That gave me all Friday to figure out how to slip out of DC without Boomer's knowledge. I'd already bought myself several burner phones after ditching the one that I used regularly. I walked it down to the hotel's lost and found and paid the manager to have the attendants keep the device charged but allow all calls to go to voicemail for at least a week. After that, they could do whatever the hell they wanted with the mobile phone. I figured out that Boomer had tracked me to Vail through my device. I'd carried the thing while I was supposed to be hiding out, but I wouldn't make that mistake twice.

I didn't take our flight charter service either. Instead, I booked an economical flight to California, traveling on one of those cozy airplanes where passengers were stuffed into the cabin like sardines in a can. I flew into San Francisco, and instead of taking my car, I rented one at the airport and drove down to Santa Barbara. I spent the night at a quaint hotel in a small neighborhood. It had farm-style rooms with free breakfast on bone china. I knew Bryn would love the place, and as soon as we were back together again, I vowed to spend a few nights there with her. We would be back together again, even if I had to crawl back on my knees, begging for another chance.

At the Blackstone estate, I gave my name to the guard manning the gate. He scowled at me as if he already knew what I looked like and then let me through. They had more security than I remembered, and it made sense. They had a famous name and a kid to protect. I parked next to the curb of the circular driveway, directly in front of the stairs leading to the front entrance. I'd been trying to keep my nervousness at bay, but looking at the door made me tug at my collar, loosening it to feel cool air on my neck.

I stared at the front door, which was made of

decorative iron surrounding frosted-glass panels. Once I walked inside, there'd be no turning back. My blood turned to stone. I would be taking a shot at my father. That went against everything Boomer had ever taught me. He was supposed to take the shots, and I was supposed to absorb the bullets.

I scrubbed my palms against my face. Then I took out my phone and made a call. I needed to hear her voice.

One ring.

Two rings.

Three rings.

"Hello," Bryn sang in a lovely tone.

I closed my eyes and absorbed her second "Hello. Anyone there?" A woman said something, and Bryn answered, "It's no one." The line went dead.

After that, I was ready to go inside and prepare to slay the dragon.

THE BUTLER ESCORTED ME TO A ROOM WITH A VIEW of mountains and ocean. I'd seen it before. I believed they called it the south-facing parlor. On the drive over, sitting in the car, I hadn't noticed how perfect the sunlight was. The view and the soft instrumental music playing in the background put me at ease. While waiting, I ran through what I was ready to say to Spencer.

I couldn't reveal too much without getting much back. If I was lucky, he'd be my brother-in-law one day. I knew Bryn Blackstone enough to know that no man got more than a second chance with her. There wasn't a third. But I hadn't said goodbye to her. We hadn't broken up. As far as I was concerned, we were on hiatus.

"But you're playing it wrong," I whispered.

"Playing what wrong?" Spencer's voice boomed from behind me.

I whipped myself around to face him. Then I jerked my head back. I was shocked by what he wore. He had on a pair of athletic pants and a gray Adidas T-shirt with running shoes. His hair was wet too. I wore a suit, the attire men put on when they were slated to have a serious business meeting.

I cleared my throat, wondering if he was prepared to take me seriously. "Love life," I said with a sigh.

His grunt was merely a way to pass on any conversation regarding my love life, which was what I expected of him.

"Sorry I was late. I went for a run, and I had to shower before we sat down together. Hungry?" His tone was easy, as if we didn't have difficult items to discuss.

I hadn't eaten in roughly two days. The mention of food reminded me that I was starving. But I shoved my hands into my pockets, keeping it cool. "Sure."

He pointed his head toward the way out. "This way, then."

I followed Spencer Blackstone down the spacious terra-cotta-tiled hallway. I only noticed the warm tones because of how relaxed everything made me feel. Even Spencer himself had aided in taking the edge off.

"Other than the topic at hand, how have you been, Jamison?"

Small talk. "I've been well. And you?"

"I can't complain. The foundation's taking off in new directions. We have new ventures in every field."

We walked into a sunroom, which had arched windows, two large open bay doors that allowed the ocean breeze to cool the room to the perfect temperature, and an attached patio showcasing a small round swimming pool with blue Mediterranean porcelain tile on the walls, floor, and around the edges.

Spencer directed me to sit at one of the two white porcelain place settings on a large farm-style table. I sat down opposite him. He graciously gave me the seat with the view. I took it as a good sign, but the gesture likely hadn't meant much to Spencer. He wasn't the type who was always thinking about hierarchies and power plays, which was why he would have made a terrible politician but a great leader.

As soon as our asses hit the chairs, a server wheeled in plates topped with stainless steel covers. "For lunch, you have filet mignon with wild mushroom and garlic sauce on top of garlic risotto and lemon-herb asparagus."

"Thanks, Rick," Spencer said.

"You're welcome, Spencer." Rick's tone was a lot more casual than the one he'd used to announce the food.

Spencer picked up his knife and fork and started digging in. I did the same.

"I looked at what you emailed me and did some research..." Spencer snorted. "The way it stands, you're screwed."

Interesting he chose to start there. "I wouldn't disagree."

"I'm not surprised, though. Boomer would eat his young if it kept him from starving."

I nodded resolutely. "He'd douse me with hot sauce for a lesser reason than that."

Spencer snorted. "I'm sure he would." He put down his utensils and sat back in his seat. The shrewd version of him was about to speak. "The best course of action I can take to make it all go away is lose all transactions. But that'll put my ass on the line, since the Lovells are already being investigated by federal prosecutors. They've seen the evidence. They know I have it. But first, I want to ask, did you make those transactions?"

I sighed gravely. "I did."

He nodded thoughtfully. "You followed Boomer's orders without question."

I sigh. "I did."

He stared at me for several seconds. "Then you willfully dispersed the cash that the Lovells received from foreign entities who have US political interests?"

My lips fought the urge to answer. I checked over both shoulders and then around the room. Spencer remained composed while waiting for me to say something. One answer could sink me, and Spencer knew it.

Is he testing me? He had asked the sort of question a federal prosecutor would ask. If I answered in the affirmative, I would admit my guilt, which came with a lengthy prison sentence. My instincts warned me that I could be walking into a monumental setup, and that was what his casualness was all about—he wanted to knock me off my guard and then pounce. Maybe...

The chance of that being his motive was fifty-fifty—a fifty percent possibility that he still saw me as the enemy and was looking to hang me out to dry and a fifty percent possibility that he was testing me, seeing if he could trust me. It was a gamble that I had to make, a bet I had to force.

I swallowed to moisten my dry throat. "Yes."

Shoulders back, I had to force myself to stand tall under Spencer's scrutiny. I'd already handed him my balls on a silver platter by telling him exactly what he wanted to hear.

He folded his arms. "Why should I help you?"

I was glad he asked me that question. Also, his body language said a lot about the sort of man he was. Boomer would have been scarfing down his steak, which would have been porterhouse, instead of filet mignon, and bloody. His eyes would have conveyed the message that I was on that plate and he was eating me alive.

Spencer, on the other hand, was carefully negotiating a partnership, feeling me out while deciding how trustworthy I was. I'd screwed him over in the past. When I replied yes to his last question, I was sure he had me on audio or video, confessing to a crime. I had no problem with that. I was going down either way. Elephants would start flying before I waited at the end of the aisle for Bree Lovell.

"Because you don't want Boomer anywhere near the Oval Office," I answered.

He raised an eyebrow. "Boomer's not our primary concern."

"James and John are?" I asked.

Eyes narrowed, he nodded subtly. "Power games. We'll be playing them until the day we die." He said that more to himself than to me. "Here's what I want to hear from you. Are you truly ready to be free of Boomer? You're going to be his enemy. He'll never speak to you again. He'll be destroyed, though, so he can't wound you. But he will be wounded, and even licking his sores won't make them heal. Are you ready for that?"

I jerked my back against the seat and rubbed my neck. I hated that I hesitated, but the moment of truth had come. Up until then, throwing my father under the bus had felt like a piece of cake. I was doing to him what he'd done to me a million times over. After all, Boomer was all bravado and entitlement. He relied on surging into the room like mighty thunder and counted on his foes to shake in their boots rather than contest him. Men and women who played by those rules were rapidly becoming a dying breed. The Blackstone brothers were the new power players. They were savvy, patient, and shrewd. They played power games for survival, not simply to win. They didn't have to win. Therefore, when I maintained eye contact with Spencer, I saw myself. We were the same. We were the future, and the future was then.

"I should've never signed on to manage your campaign. Boomer wanted me to infiltrate you. I wasn't going to do it until…" I took a deep breath. He was waiting patiently for me to finish. "Bryn showed up."

"Bryn?" His tone was flat.

I threw my hands up as I shrugged. "I know it makes me look weak…"

He grunted. "No. That doesn't make you

appear weak. Bringing in Bree Lovell, who lied about her identity—that was weak."

"Agreed."

"Attempting to sabotage my interview on *New Day America* was pretty weak too," he said with a cold laugh.

"Yeah," I barely said, resisting the urge to shake my head. Things were swiftly moving in the wrong direction.

He unfolded his arms and put his palms down on the table. "But I'm not going to sit here and act holier than thou. I had my own Boomer, and I've done a lot of wrong in the name of pleasing the unpleasing and unpleasable."

I snorted. His humor had taken the edge off.

"Your father has provable crimes that are a mile long. Getting him off your ass will be as easy as swatting a gnat," he said. Once again, as he'd done several times, he studied me as if he could read my mind.

"What is it?" I said more snappishly than I wanted.

"You don't think we know you were with our sister earlier this week? Were you ever going to mention that?"

I rubbed my chest and coughed after I lost my breath.

Spencer pointed his steak knife at me before cutting his meat. "This game of chess... we need it to end. One day, we won't have to play. But we don't want to wait that long. We're going to need a candidate for you to make a winner."

I stopped before I was able to put my first bite of risotto in my mouth. "You want your own puppet?"

"Not puppets. Virtue. One president, one hundred senators, and at least four hundred US representatives who can't be bought. We want to get legislation through to keep lobbyists out of Washington and make term limits indestructible."

"But as Blackstones, you can benefit from the way things are."

He snorted bitterly. "Nobody benefits from the way things are, not even those who are benefitting."

His cell phone rang, and Spencer took it out of his pants pocket. He glared at the screen and then lifted a finger, asking me to give him a moment to take the call.

I nodded as I processed the sheer scope of the job he wanted me to do. *It's virtually impossible. Or is it? It is.*

There would be a midterm election next year and then the big one two years after that. *Five hundred congressional candidates, plus a president.* I didn't even know that many people who wanted to run for office.

I was able to piece together that Spencer was speaking to his wife. My mind was pulling double duty, trying to process the offer Spencer had made me and figure out if I could hear any information about Bryn. Jada must have said that the kids were enjoying themselves. Spencer asked about someone named Gina. He tried not to look at me when he spoke about Bryn. I pieced together that Bryn had spent the morning at a rehab center with Gina but had returned to the house and was at the beach with the kids.

Spencer, who'd been grinning the whole time, chortled. "She is good at handling the brood." He laughed. Then he said he loved her too and would see her soon. I wondered what he meant by *soon* but wasn't going to ask.

Spencer set his cell phone on the table and put the full force of his attention back on me. "So, what do you say?"

I nodded as Bryn's face and the faces of possible candidates shuffled through my mind. "I'm all about leveling the playing field. Which political party are we favoring here?"

"None. It's fifty-fifty."

My eyebrows flitted up and stayed there. "Okay. That makes it easier. But thanks to you and your brother, nobody will touch us."

"You're striking out on your own."

I scoffed.

"Don't worry about Boomer," he said. "He'll receive a package soon. And don't worry about Templeton or the Rally brothers either. Everybody's got skeletons they're terrified will fall out of the closet, and well… we've already located the bones."

My frown did nothing to ease the throbbing in my head. I'd been managing campaigns since I graduated from an Ivy League college with a degree in political science. I used to sit in class with guys who were there because of who their parents were. Those bozos had the biggest egos and did the least to get by. But they were the minority. Most of us dug, scratched, and clawed to be at the top of the class. We competed with each other, sometimes dining at our professors' feet, sometimes questioning their standpoints, but many times testing our own beliefs, finding our own perspectives. I was part of that group. But right off the bat, after graduation, I'd had a real-world lesson with the first candidate I managed for Cox and Cox. The opposition didn't care that I was newly out of college. They saw it as a sign of weakness. I was an idealist who'd entered a dirty business. And over the years, I had learned one thing for sure—nobody gave something for nothing. For some reason, my gut was telling me that the Blackstones were different, and my head was saying the opposite. If the Blackstones were different, then indeed, they would be an anomaly. Only time would tell the truth about them, and I was willing to take the chance of living in the clouds.

So I extended my hand across the table. "Deal."

Spencer completed the gesture, and we shook on it.

"Now what?" I asked.

He pointed at my plate. "First, we finish eating."

"And then?"

"We get your new business up and running." He clapped his hands and then rubbed his palms together as he leaned back in his seat. "Now. Are you up for dessert?"

"Absolutely," I said, grinning like a Cheshire cat. "Absolutely."

Twenty-Three

BRYN BLACKSTONE

MONDAY AFTERNOON

I'd just concluded one of the longest weekends of my life. After our flight landed late Friday afternoon, a car drove us to my house on Mulholland Drive. Gina, who still hadn't developed an appetite, went straight to bed. I ordered a grocery delivery, enough to make scallops and brussels sprouts for dinner and breakfast the next day. After eating, I went to bed too.

In the morning, I made us oatmeal with apples sautéed in dark chocolate and honey with walnuts. It used to be Gina's favorite breakfast when we were kids. That morning, she ate two bowls of it.

Before we left, I ordered a car to take us to the

rehab facility in Malibu. Since I knew everyone who worked there, I remained at Gina's side throughout the intake process. She shook and clung to me like a frightened kitten as we sat in the examination room and she had her full physical. Gina was wearing a gown and booties. She said that she'd never received a Pap smear or any form of examination of her female parts.

"Everything is wrong with me down there," she said as we sat in front of the examination table.

"No, it isn't," I said, even though I knew she wasn't able to believe that yet.

She hugged herself tighter. "And all I want to do is get the hell out of here. I want to run as far away from here as I possibly can, but where would I go? What will happen to me?"

I rubbed her gently on the back. "I understand. I felt the same way every time I came back here."

"How many times?"

I turned to look at her. The other day, lying in bed, she'd looked so sickly. Gina always maintained overprocessed blond hair and wore mounds of makeup, both of which aged her at least twenty years. But at that moment, she seemed younger and innocent.

"Four," I said.

She grimaced.

"And I can assure you that this place works, because I'm not as haughty as I used to be," I said.

For the first time since we'd arrived, Gina chuckled. "You weren't haughty, Bryn. You were just mean and pretty awful."

I blurted a chuckle. "I was definitely both of those things. And I'm so…"

She softly elbowed me. "Don't you dare apologize again."

"No?"

"No," she said with great certainty. "Especially with all you're doing for me now."

We smiled at each other. I was glad our brief exchange had put her at ease.

Then Gina squeezed her eyes shut. "Let's talk about something else, something lighter. How's your love life?"

My mouth fell open, and I nearly choked on saliva going down my windpipe. I coughed until I recovered.

"That bad?" she asked.

I shook my head. I meant to nod, but it hurt too much to do that. "My last relationship just didn't work."

"Why not?"

I shrugged. "I don't know. Maybe I never knew him it all. Or maybe my picker is still off."

"What went wrong?"

I didn't want to talk about Jamison, but Gina's life was on the line, so if discussing my love life or lack thereof would put her at ease, then I was all for it.

"I don't know. We had a passionate two days of sex and made all sorts of declarations of love."

The expression on her face dropped. "Sex?"

I crumpled in my seat. "Yeah." I sighed.

"How many dates did you go on before sex?"

"Zero, I guess."

She groaned as she rolled her eyes. "With a lot of the men I… you know… I thought I loved them. I thought they loved me too. Maybe I just don't know what love is, but I know sex can be beguiling."

My posture perked up as curiosity rushed through me. However, Dr. Melissa Clark, accompanied by Gina's primary therapist, Dr. Mita Sharma, had entered the room. I was asked to step out while Gina received her examination, and we never got an opportunity to continue our conversation. After the exam, Dr. Sharma made Gina feel comfortable enough to complete her check-in without me. So Gina and I hugged goodbye, and I promised I'd be back on her first visitors' day.

However, as I rode to the Malibu beach house, I couldn't get what Gina had said about sex out of my mind. *Is it beguiling?* Maybe the power of sex had made me and Jamison think we were in love during the moments we were together. But I'd never wanted to jump any man's bones as much as I had Jamison's. Maybe our body chemistries matched more than our lives did. It wasn't as if I hadn't known there were barriers to our making a successful go at being together forever.

By the time I was playing with the kids on the beach, I'd settled myself with the belief that Jamison and I had shared some thrilling and fun times together, but that was over. The girls and I built a sandcastle. Ollie couldn't help because whenever he had sand in his hands, all he wanted to do was eat it, so I let Jane and Allie bury my legs in the sand, and then I put on a puppet show with my toes. September—Ollie and Jane's nanny—stood with Ollie as the ocean water rolled up against his feet. I splashed in the waves with the girls, careful not to go too far into the water.

In the evening, we went swimming in the pool. Jada's half brother, Stefan, came to visit with his girlfriend, Anisha. He put steaks and burgers on the grill. Then Jada's friend Hope stopped by for dinner with her husband. We all had a great time bonding and getting to know each other. The kids might have stayed up too late, which was why after breakfast on Sunday morning, they slept during the hour drive back to Montecito and didn't wake up until late that afternoon. They woke up groggy and irritable, but I was the queen of changing their mood. We ate lunch in the theater room and played an interactive movie about space exploration and deep-sea diving. They were out like three little lambs before the second video ended. None of the kids made it to the table for dinner, and neither did Spencer, who said he had to work. Jada, September, and I ate dinner alone and engaged in stimulating conversation.

I learned that September loved children and was in college, studying early childhood development. She wanted to open her own day care. We also landed on the subject about how I'd convinced Gina to finally get help.

"I liked being there for her, you know?" I said. "I love making Gina feel comfortable and knowing she's going to get the help she's been needing for a long time."

"You ever thought of being a therapist?" Jada asked. "If so, you'll always have a job with the foundation. We run support groups and hire our own qualified therapists for those who want it. You'd be a great addition."

I'd always known their foundation had a psychological health component, but I'd never thought I could be one of the healthcare providers. "I'll consider it," I said.

"You should," Jada replied.

Before the sun rose, September and I boarded a flight back to Manhattan with Ollie and Jane. When our flight landed, Holly was waiting for us in the private terminal. I jokingly reminded her that Ollie and Jane had only been away from her for the weekend, not for a year. Holly rolled her eyes, and then we hugged. Dressed for work in a skirt suit and heels, she took the kids to the office with her like she normally did.

I had decided to push back my flight to Vail and hired a car to take me to Jasper's Lower Manhattan office. Regardless of being hurt by Jamison, I wanted to make good on the promise I'd made to him and convince Jasper to stop harming Jamison's business. I also wanted to speak to Karen Diploe, my head of business operations, about making some changes.

I wasn't one for going all out fast. I'd slept on the idea of going back to school to become a therapist. However, MIND by Bryn Blackstone was new and thriving. Interior design would never remain in BFE's profile if I didn't make the decision to keep it flourishing. That was why I was thinking about Alana when I received a text from her.

Check this out, she wrote and added a link to a gossip column, which ran a Who's Marrying Whom section. I clicked on the story. Jamison Arlington Cox was listed as being engaged to Breana Leandra Lovell. I wanted to simultaneously burst into tears and punch the back of the seat in front of me. But instead, I stared out the window, not seeing anything at all and trying to not feel the emotions that wanted to devour me from the inside out.

Screw him, my anger shouted at the top of her lungs. *Let his business burn.*

I closed my eyes and shook my head. I couldn't do that. A promise made was a promise kept. Tears streamed out of my eyes, and I didn't attempt to stop them until right before the car drove into the porte cochere of the building where the BFE offices were housed.

I picked two tissues out of the compartment against the back of the front seat, blew my nose, and then took several deep breaths to compose myself.

"Are you ready, Miss Blackstone?" the driver asked.

"Yes. Thank you," I replied in a small but gracious voice. There was no doubt about it—my heart was broken all over again.

It was extra cold out by the Hudson River, but I was dressed in jeans, boots, a sweater, and my ankle-length gray cashmere coat with a multicolored knit scarf. I wrapped my scarf around my neck as I walked quickly into the lobby. Each step toward the private elevator that led to Jasper's office felt as if I was carrying ten extra pounds around each ankle. *How could Jamison do that to me?*

Don't cry, Bryn.

I felt so pained that my heart actually hurt. Fortunately, all I had to say was "good morning" as I waved to those who worked in reception. Everyone knew me, and since I walked fast, no one tried to engage me in small talk.

I closed my eyes, forcing the tears back down as I waited for the elevator. *Pull it together.* I inhaled deeply. *Pull it together.* I exhaled. *Pull it together.*

Ding.

There—I was ready to present a strong front to my brother. The doors slid open. Stunned whiskey eyes were staring into my baby blues. I covered my mouth with the palm of my hand, and then I pressed it against my chest.

In a strained voice, I asked, "What are you doing here?"

Twenty-Four

BRYN BLACKSTONE

J amison lowered his raised eyebrows and then coughed into his balled fist to clear his throat. I waited for him to say something, but apparently, like me, he was too shocked to speak. The elevator began to close on us, and he extended an arm to reopen it.

Be nice, Bryn.

Be kind, Bryn.

No need to willfully hurt those who hurt you.

"Jamison Cox. Thanks, buddy," a heavy voice said from behind.

I spun around to see who the man with the cavalier and confident voice was and ended up locking gazes with a hunky guy with sea-green eyes that danced with curiosity. Like Jamison, he was wearing the sort of black suit that connoted power. I quickly took note of the elevator number. I hadn't made a mistake. The elevator car was the express ride that led directly to the reception area outside Jasper's office. Normally, I would have taken the express elevator that led to the inside of his office, but I was visiting my brother without an appointment.

The stranger stopped behind me and held out an outstretched hand, ushering me to join Jamison. "After you, Miss…?"

He was fishing for a name.

"Creed, you're on time," Jamison said.

I pointed over my shoulder. "I'll just go that way. I see my brother's busy this morning."

"Oh," Creed said, throwing up his hands. "I knew I'd seen your face before. You're the lovely Bryn Blackstone."

My forehead tightened as my eyes narrowed to slits. *Is he flirting with me?* He wasn't an average-looking guy. His sneer was mischievous and his facial features chiseled, reminding me of modern-day Clark Gable. I considered him handsome and just clean-cut enough to come off as nonthreatening to the status quo. On any other given Monday, I probably would have fallen for his electrifying charm, but unfortunately, the man with the sultry whiskey eyes still held my heart in the palm of his hand.

"Creed, get in. We're late," Jamison snapped. His face was drained of blood.

Creed didn't move a muscle. "If you're going up, then you might as well join us. We don't mind the company, do we, Jamison?"

Beep.

Jamison's scowl made him appear as if he was chewing on lemons. "Bryn, come in. I'm not going to bite."

I inhaled deeply. First, I ran into Jamison at the airport the previous week, and then I ran into him at the BFE building. *Why can't I shake that guy? And why is he going to Jasper's office in the first place?* On my exhalation, I stepped into the elevator and situated myself as far away from Jamison as possible. However, as fast as lightening, he shifted to stand beside me. My jaw dropped as Creed stood on the opposite side of Jamison.

"Then the two of you already know each other?" Creed asked. I stared at Jamison's reflection in the gold panel in front of us. Creed was leaning forward and looking at me.

Smiling tightly, I looked down at my feet, deciding to leave it up to Jamison to answer that one.

"Yes, we do, and we're working things out," Jamison said.

I snapped my head up. "Ha! And by the way, congratulations, Jamison. And please give Bree my regards."

"What?" Jamison asked, appearing authentically confused.

"Bree?" Cree asked. "Bree Lovell?"

Jamison lowered his mouth next to my ear. "Bryn, how about we talk in private?"

Feeling his energy against the side of my face made my nipples tingle. I hated that Jamison could so easily trigger my erogenous zones. Fortunately, my tits were well packed behind all the layers of clothing I wore.

But I suspected all Jamison wanted to do was lessen the blow. The Who's Marrying Whom column had never gotten it wrong. Jamison and Bree were definitely getting married, and the date was set for the weekend after next.

"We have nothing to say to each other," I said.

"Plus, I'm busy anyway." I took a side-glance at Creed. It felt weird airing our dirty laundry in front of a stranger.

"Please be reasonable about this, Bryn. Let's talk," Jamison said.

Eyes closed, I shook my head. "There's nothing left to say. Our business has concluded." I opened my eyes, forcing myself to look at him with a warm smile. "And I forgive you, because bitterness will only tear me up from the inside out."

I was going to behave like an adult no matter what. The unhinged, infantile Bryn who felt entitled to rage at anyone who hurt her had been banished back to her age group—even if she was knocking on my brain, begging to occupy space. But I was embarrassed that Creed had gotten a front-row seat to the fatal end of Jamison's and my short-but-hot love affair.

The elevator stopped, and I prayed for the doors to open faster. My tears were about to betray me. I didn't want to cry in front of the two men.

Creed stepped out into the vestibule and extended his long arm to hold the doors open.

"Miss Blackstone, I would love to grab dinner sometime soon."

It was as if his voice was a million miles away.

"Sorry, I have a meeting." I shot out of the elevator like an arrow. "Have a nice meeting with my brother. I'll catch up with him later." I walked through the area outside my brother's office so fast I left wind in my wake.

Angela and Lois, Jasper's first and second executive assistants, appeared confused by the intense rush of people entering their space at once.

"Bryn, good morning," Angela said, shocked.

Am I smiling? I think I am. "Good morning, ladies. Off to a meeting with Karen Diploe."

I successfully made it past their desks. But Jamison was on my heels, and I knew he'd caught up when his strong hand wrapped around my biceps.

"Bryn." He sounded desperate.

"Jamison, let go of me," I said, baring my teeth.

Right away, Jamison released his grip, but he stepped in front of me to block my path. "There's an explanation."

I nodded spastically. "I know… I know." There was always an explanation. Dale used to have thousands of them.

"You know?"

"Yes. As I said, I forgive you, Jamison, but you don't get another chance with me."

I was ready to step around him when I heard, "Bryn? I thought I heard you out here."

There was no quick escape then. I turned to see Jasper standing in the doorway of his office. My brother had the best poker face on the planet. He wasn't looking at me. His eyes were fixed on Creed. He looked surprised to see him.

"Yeah, I'm just going to see Karen," I said.

"Right," Jasper said. Then I hurried over to him, and we gave each other a hug and a kiss and said we'd talk later.

Jamison stared at me longingly as I whipped past him. The next thing I heard him say was, "Jasper, I wanted to introduce you to Creed—"

"Yes, Creed Hammerstone," Jasper replied.

My legs managed to get me to the dark alcove, where I opened the door that led to the stairwell with steps leading up to the roof terrace—which had a full bar and lounge space—or down to the break room, which had a coffee bar, sandwich shop, and breakfast grill. I sniffed my tears, dried both eyes with the back of my hand, and walked downstairs, knowing that as soon as I was back in a public space, there would be people I knew, and I didn't want them to sense my distress. But still, I could hardly believe I'd basically told Jamison to go to hell. I hated that my body was beating me up for it. It still wanted to be near him. It wanted him inside me. And oh, so badly, my lips craved his kiss.

The sliding doors opened. There were people everywhere. Someone noticed me. I smiled. It was time to fake it.

Twenty-Five

JAMISON COX

I hadn't intended to present Creed to Jasper that way. Spencer informed me that he wanted a viable candidate who could win, and as far as I was concerned, Creed was one of those guys. I sat on the firm black leather sofa with enough space between me and Creed. I'd wanted to give Creed a few pointers before walking into Jasper's office. First, *Sit the hell up straight and show a kernel of humility*. Instead, his ankle was pitched on top of his knee, and his arm lounged, outstretched, across the back of the sofa.

Jasper sat in an armchair across from us. It was our first time ever meeting each other. Everything I'd ever heard about the guy had been from study, rumors, and viable information passed down from those who knew him. I relied on facial cues to get a read on my clients and the people I interacted with, and Jasper hadn't shown me one expression that revealed what he was thinking—not a grin, smirk, grimace, or anything in between. He gave nothing away.

He'd just asked Creed why he believed he'd lost his last two election bids for a district seat in the House. It was a question I hadn't expected Jasper to ask.

"I don't know. I could've done better. We can always do better," Creed replied.

I wanted to slap him upside the head and tell him to never give Jasper Blackstone a nonanswer.

I shifted in my seat to steal Jasper's attention away from Creed. It worked. "Then there was the fact that his wife lost her battle with breast cancer. I'm sure that took a toll on his campaign runs," I said.

Again, Jasper showed no facial expressions.

Damn, what is this guy made of?

"I see," he said.

Finally, Creed must have found a few nuggets of common sense, because he removed his arm, put both feet on the floor, and sat up straight. He was easy to read. Jasper's lack of reaction had given

Jasper total control, and Creed had figured out that his demeanor was too easygoing. The largest-man-in-the-room act wasn't working.

"We were married for nine years, right out of high school, and I've been without her for five years," Creed said.

"Grieving," I added. *Damn.* I came off as too desperate.

"I'm surprised you're here," Jasper said. He talked with his hands. That was something—a narrow tunnel into his mind.

"I decided to take the initiative. I informed Creed that the Blackstones were looking for a presidential candidate you could back and I could manage."

Jasper steepled his hands in front of him and tapped his index fingers together. "You're not married," he said as if making that comment to himself.

"He's a widower of five years. He doesn't need a wife," I replied regardless.

Creed shifted abruptly and leaned toward Jasper. "But a wife wouldn't hurt. I'd like to take your sister out to dinner if you can arrange it."

The sneaky snake.

Jasper's expressionless gaze passed over me

before landing back on Creed. "I'm not involved in my sister's romantic endeavors."

Creed smirked smugly. "But it wouldn't hurt if she says yes to having dinner with me. Something special happens between us, then I'll have a wife with class, style, grace, and beauty—the perfect first lady."

"Anything's possible, but as I said, I'm not involved in making choices of that nature for my sister. Jamison?"

Although I wanted to wring Creed's neck, I piped up and tried not to show my anger. "Yes?"

"I need to speak to you alone."

Creed looked at me with his mouth agape. Jasper speaking to me in private was not a good sign for either of us. I shrugged at Creed.

"Is everything okay?" he asked Jasper. The guy sounded too desperate.

"Yes. Step out, please," Jasper replied, tilting his head toward the door.

Creed hesitated and then rose to his feet. He opened his mouth as if he wanted to say something, but the lack of expression on Jasper's face must have made him change his mind.

Once we were alone, Jasper set his complete focus on me. I never knew the guy had blue eyes. It

Z. L. ARKADIE

was as though they could shoot fire and ice and obliterate me.

"Why did you bring him here?" Jasper's tone was even.

"Thought I'd demonstrate some initiative." I fought the urge to squirm under the power of his stare.

"This weekend, we were able to get JAC Consulting approved."

"That fast?"

"Yes. We're ready for the first phase, and there's no need for you to go fishing for candidates. We have them for you."

My posture stiffened. "All five hundred that Spencer and I discussed?"

"Five thirty-six."

"All of Congress and the presidency?"

"Yes."

"Wow." I coughed to clear the lump out of my throat and maintained my strong posture. "How the hell were you able to do that?"

"As you know, not all of them are rotten apples. Actually, most of them aren't. They've been waiting for somebody like us to be on their side. And here we are."

I nodded, liking the sound of that and pretty

proud to be part of the effort. Then my father's face came to mind, and he didn't look happy.

"But I'm still not out of Boomer's crosshairs. Not only that, but I still have to figure out how to divest from Cox and Cox." The thought made my neck tight, so I had to stretch it from side to side.

Jasper's eyebrows wrinkled. *Finally, a facial expression.*

"Have you ever verified your partnership in Cox and Cox?"

My eyebrows pulled together. "I didn't think I had to. I'm a Cox, and my father's a Cox."

"Your mother's a Cox too."

A knot formed in my chest. "But she has nothing to do with the business."

"Your mother is the second partner in Cox and Cox, not you." His tone was too blunt for the explosion that was going off inside me.

I couldn't get comfortable. "That can't be true." I couldn't stop shaking my head. "Did she know?"

"No. I don't believe she did, and I'll tell you why."

When Jasper said that I was given power of attorney to sign for my mother, it was as if he was speaking to me from a million miles away. But the signature on the request for power of attorney didn't belong to my mother but to Carl Baker—Boomer's business manager.

I did everything I could to sit tall and strong as I pictured my father watching me from behind his oversized desk, wearing that I-got-one-over-on-you smirk of his. "I have—had—three friends with fathers like mine," I said.

Jasper remained silent, and I gathered he was giving me a moment to complete my thoughts. I had to get them out, or I would burst.

"They all killed themselves," I said. "One drank and drugged himself to death. One put a revolver to his head. One purposely crashed his father's favorite jet. His suicide note said he believed it would be a poetic way to go. His father replaced the jet in a matter of days. The new one was more expensive, better. Then he married a woman half his age. She's now pregnant with another son for him to screw up."

"But here you sit," Jasper said.

I set my focus on him again. "Yeah... here I sit."

"It's not easy to stop trying to win your old man's approval. With someone like Richard, that's a wasted effort. If he was going to change, he would've done so by now. You know what happens to men who have fathers like ours if we don't dig deep and free ourselves. I'm glad you reached out, because you're one of the few, Jamison." He shook his finger at me. "My actions against Cox and Cox were never about you."

I still had a lot to process. *I'm not an owner in Cox and Cox.* I rubbed my temples, recalling the instances Carl had brought me documentation to sign because I was one of the partners. I considered Carl and all the jerks I wanted to fire. Boomer had fought tooth and nail to keep them in their jobs. I had no real power or ability to fire them, and they all knew it.

I sighed and scratched the back of my neck. Surprisingly, I felt a lot lighter. "So what did you do to get my father off my back?"

"Cox and Cox was a high-performing firm but not very lucrative. Did you know that?"

I scratched the back of my neck again. I didn't want to look as if I was an incompetent businessman in Jasper's eyes, especially since I'd just started a new company at his behest. "I didn't." It was hard for me to say that.

"Have you ever heard of White Star Investment Group?"

I shook my head. "Never."

"Richard owns it. It's a Ponzi scheme, and he floats cash into Cox and Cox."

Deep breath… "Damn." I rubbed my chest to keep myself from hyperventilating.

"Do you need a moment?" Jasper asked.

Do I?

I shook my head. "I'm fine. Let's continue."

He nodded sharply. "Regarding Creed Hammerstone, he's not the kind of candidate I'm willing to endorse."

I blinked hard, forcing myself into the moment. "All right. Could you tell me why? For future reference."

"He's too susceptible."

"Susceptible to what?"

"Everything. Mike Dunn will be your presidential candidate." He shot to his feet, walked over to his desk, and retrieved a flash drive. "All the candidates, with their profiles, are on here. Angela will text you the access code. Don't lose this. Another thing…"

I remembered to sit up straight. "Yes, what is it?" I was still spastic after learning all that new information about Cox and Cox. I couldn't even celebrate the fact that I was about to manage the presidential campaign for a candidate of Mike

Black's caliber. He was ten times more of a winner than Creed.

"Are you still interested in my sister?" he asked.

My heart pounded like a bass drum, and I coughed to clear the emotion that the mention of Bryn sent through me. "Yes, very much so." The words were strained.

"Then I advise you to convince her to trust you again, because you opened up Pandora's box when you brought Creed here. He was more worried about landing my sister than impressing me. He's not a bad guy. I know my sister, though. Over the course of time, he's capable of wearing her down."

My neck felt tense again, but I didn't want to massage it. I'd done it too many times already. My meeting with Jasper Blackstone had taken turns I never saw coming, and that had been stressful as hell. I rolled my shoulders to expel some of the tightness. It didn't work.

"Got it," I said in a tight voice.

"Any other questions?" Jasper asked.

I swallowed, nervous about the one last question I had to ask him. The way he narrowed his eyes said he was waiting to hear it.

"You call my father Richard, not Boomer."

"Right," he said curtly.

"Why is that?"

"Because that's his name."

"But Boomer's his reputation."

His smirk and snarl were back. "Yeah. I know." His lips clamped together, indicating that was all he had to say on the matter. But I understood him perfectly. Jasper was letting me know that to him, my father was merely a tap, not a boom. For a second, I felt like a traitor. However, I immediately recalled Boomer's threat and that look in his eyes when he knew he had me in checkmate.

I tapped the breast pocket of my jacket. "Thanks for this."

Jasper nodded politely. "By the way…" He pointed at the spot where I kept the flash drive. "You have a great team of employees to hire. Their names and CVs are on that disk too. They've all been vetted. None of them are on our payroll, and none of them are susceptible to being on anyone's payroll other than yours."

I thanked him for handing me my future on a platinum platter. But more than that, even though I'd discovered what sort of criminal Boomer was, I was free of him.

When I walked out of Jasper's office, I'd learned a huge lesson. Real strong men didn't wear the boom on their chests. It was hidden, tucked in a reputation. Even when you met the bruiser face-to-face, it was unnoticeable. But you knew it was there, sitting in the middle of the table, and you'd better not tempt him to lower it. That was Jasper and Spencer Blackstone in a nutshell.

"What the hell happened in there?" Creed asked.

I'd forgotten he was sitting in the waiting area. I faced him just in time to see him rising to his feet. He was red-faced. He must have been sitting out there, stewing in distress. I didn't feel sorry for him, though. I gave Creed a chance to impress Jasper Blackstone, and he blew it by coming off too cocky and trying to find an easy route to getting into Bryn Blackstone's—my woman's—pants. *So screw him.*

I patted him on the shoulder. "Sorry to waste your time like this. Mr. Blackstone thanks you for coming in to see him, but he's choosing to go in a different direction."

Creed's mouth and eyes widened. "Damn," he groused and then stared longingly at Jasper's door. Then he glared at the space where we last saw Bryn. Jasper was right—the guy was going to make a play for her. However, one factor I could cling to was that Jasper, the man who'd told Creed he didn't get involved in his sister's love life, had encouraged me to go get her.

I cracked a smile and patted Creed on the shoulder again. "Listen, buddy, you win some and you lose some." And he would lose again if he tried to get between Bryn and me.

Twenty-Six

BRYN BLACKSTONE

I met with Karen Diploe, but we ended our meeting fast. I hadn't wanted to run into Jamison or Creed Hammerstone, who had come off as sort of creepy. I sat in the back of the car, heading to Teterboro to catch my flight back to Vail. However, I couldn't fight the feeling that I was leaving something very important behind. Karen and I had discussed presenting Alana with an offer to be the new chief designer of MIND, which was my position. When I sat down at the table in a private conference room with Karen, I'd already made my decision. I wanted to give becoming a therapist a shot. I was quite aware that I would have to work hard at my degree. I'd already obtained a

BA through an online university, but for my PhD, I wanted to sit in actual classrooms.

Grinning, I knew I was ready for the challenge. I'd already made up my mind to apply to Redmond College. During the one year I studied there, I'd created such a ruckus that I was positive I would have to beg the administration to let me back in. But I was willing to do that.

My cell phone chimed, and I checked the screen before answering it. I sort of hoped it was Jamison, but it was the flight service.

"This is Bryn," I said.

"Miss Blackstone, this is Jonathan with the BFE charter."

"Hi, Jonathan. How can I help you?"

"I'm sorry to inform you, but your flight into Vail, Colorado, has been canceled. A severe storm has moved into the area, and no flights are flying in or out."

I bent over, holding the phone closer to my ear, hardly able to believe I'd heard him correctly. "Are you sure?"

"Yes, Miss Blackstone. I'm sorry. We can book your flight for tomorrow afternoon. The weather report indicates that the storm will clear out by six p.m. tomorrow. Would you like to do that?"

I was on the verge of asking about flying into Denver instead, but I was sure the city would also be grappling with the storm. I wanted to run away from Jamison, but there was no use in forcing it. "Yes. Book me for six p.m. tomorrow," I said and thanked him. Then I asked the driver to take me to my apartment on the Upper West Side.

THREE HOURS LATER

Traffic had been a nightmare. At one point, we sat in the car, not moving an inch, for thirty minutes straight. The upside was I was able to call Alana and listen to her complain about the storm.

"It wasn't smart to start this job in the winter, Bryn."

"I know," I said.

"It's been tough getting the floor work done, too, moving trucks in and out of the snow."

"Maybe we should just pull the plug for now."

She hummed thoughtfully. "We've done so much work, though—a lot over the weekend. And Eden and Dale have flown back to Hollywood for a few days. They have a meeting that just came up with a few big-time producers. I was going to deliver that bit of good news to you after we finished the accent wall in the master bedroom."

"Alana," I said softly.

She turned silent. "Uh-oh. What's wrong?"

Then I told her about the offer that was coming her way and my plan to make my biggest and newest career change.

"Oh my God, really? Me?" she exclaimed.

I smiled, happy that she was happy. "No one's better than you. I'm not even better than you."

"You're pretty good, Bryn. And for a newbie, you can go head-to-head with me and win a whole lot of rounds."

I chuckled. She was right. "Thanks, love, but the truth is, I'm more passionate about becoming a therapist than remaining a designer."

"And you always kind of merged the two, anyway."

My smile intensified. I was glad she was able to pick up on that.

"Well, good for you, Bryn. We only have one life, right?"

"Yes, one life is all we have."

I hummed as good vibes enveloped me. I was going to miss spending weeks on a worksite with

Alana, who had become my best friend. I let her know that I'd be back to finish up with Eden and do proper handoffs of all the clients who'd booked me to design their spaces. But since she was snowed in, and it wasn't noon yet, I promised to go shopping in White Plains to look for a few pieces for Eden's guest bedrooms.

Once we ended our call, I speed-dialed people and had quick conversations with my mother and then Kat, who still wanted me to meet her doctor friend. She was excited to hear that I was back in New York. She and the dashing prince of a doctor were also in New York.

I smashed my lips together. "I don't know, Kat. I had a long weekend. I have to do some work, and then I'm going to turn in early."

"Come on. It's only dinner. Tonight at Sushi-Rama?"

A yawn escaped me.

"Oh, jeez. You are tired."

"Very," I said.

She sighed. "All right, then, next time. But let's hope Dr. Heartthrob is still single the next time you're available."

I chuckled and then flipped my thumb up and said, "Let's."

Traffic started rolling again as soon as Kat and I said goodbye. I made one final call to Nick, who was surprised to hear from me.

"You know that lady, Gina? I've seen her before," he admitted.

My neck jutted forward. "You have?"

"It was an arrest for prostitution."

Damn it. I hated that her old life had caught up with her in such a way. "She doesn't do that anymore. And frankly, she had a rough start in life, so…"

"Listen, I'm not judging her. I wasn't one of those cops who wanted a badge so I could crack heads and be the asshole with the power. I cared for people. That's why I remember her, you know?"

"I know." I gave Nick the name, address, and phone number to the rehab facility. I also gave him the date and time that I would be there for Gina's first visitors' day and told him he was welcome to join me if Gina was okay with seeing him.

"If she's up for it, then I'm there," he said.

"Well, you have my number. Thanks for every-thing, Nick."

He hesitated for a beat. "You're welcome, Bryn Blackstone."

Gabriel, the doorman, was shocked to see me back in the building. It had been months since I'd been to my New York apartment. He thanked me for the gift card I'd sent to him as a Christmas gift and asked if he could give me a hug for it.

"Sure," I said.

"That five thousand bucks came in handy." He reached down for my luggage. "And we'll get that for you."

I gently set my hand on top of his. "No need. It's not heavy, and I just have one bag."

"Why can't they all be like you around here? And I'm not just saying that because I'd be a rich man if they were, either," he said, referring to the five thousand dollars.

My laugh was full-bodied and felt good. The ladies at the front desk thanked me for their five-thousand-dollar gift cards, too, and warned me to not be alarmed when I found a bunch of gifts stacked in front of my fireplace. As I gave each of them hugs, Jamison was the furthest thought from my mind. Growing up in the Blackstone mansion, I'd never imagined I would live such a good life with great people in it.

I took my private elevator up to my place. As soon as the doors slid open, I took off my boots and socks and dropped my bag on the floor. I felt the cold marble on the bottoms of my feet as I walked to the large window that looked out over Central Park. There were other apartments with sleeker views of the famous site, some of them more luxurious. But my view was soothing, with the tops of healthy trees pressing forward against the buildings on the east side in the distance. The clouds above were gray and the atmosphere vaporous, but I'd only been in my apartment for several minutes, and I already felt as snug as a bug in a rug.

However, I didn't have long to stand there and decompress. I would wait until later that night to really relax. I breathed in and out deeply as I walked over to the presents stacked in front of the fireplace. I picked up one wrapped in silver paper. Before I could tear it open, the doorbell rang. I ran to my door, suspecting it was a mail delivery from the front desk. Without checking first to see who was there, I swung it open wide.

My excitement collapsed. Luminous whiskey eyes gazed into mine. His sensual lips were parted, and his angular jawline dropped. Such handsomeness had always been disarming. That was why my heart thumped like rapid fire as every emotion under the sun attacked me.

"Jamison?" I whispered. I tried to ask what he was doing there, but my voice couldn't form the words.

My skin warmed as he pressed one hand against each side of the doorjamb and leaned toward me. Our lips were in the perfect range for a kiss.

"Babe," he said in a desperate whisper. "I've been thinking about why you don't want to hear me out. And I've come to the conclusion that it's about you more than me. You know that if I'm standing in front of you, asking for another chance, then I have a rational explanation for what happened. But you don't want to hear it because you don't want me to hurt you again. And I get that. But, Bryn… I won." His face was lit up like a firecracker.

I frowned in confusion.

"When I left the resort with Bree," he continued, "it had to do with my father. I know you understand that I had to fight like a Titan to take down a tyrant. I've been fighting for you, for us, since the moment I walked out of that resort. If you let me in, I'll explain everything, and I'll leave nothing out."

I BLINKED RAPIDLY AS MY HEART, AT LIGHTNING speed, plucked away each hurtful emotion it had nurtured due to losing the love of Jamison. The only thing left to feel was how head over heels in love with him I still was. I glanced anxiously over my shoulder. I hadn't expected to see him that day, but it wasn't as if I had believed I'd never run into him again. Apparently, he was doing business with my brother, so that put him in my universe. Before that moment, I'd clung to the sobering fact that I would have to know him as Bree Lovell's husband. My brain dropped that hurtful belief like a hot potato.

Before he'd arrived, I had actually had a day planned. *But first...*

Jamison was still leaning close to me, his lips still at the optimal position for me to do it. I inhaled his scent and the warmth of his nearness, but his lips devoured mine before mine could his. His tongue was like satin, curling around mine, making my head spin and my sex throb. Jamison had taken me into his embrace, and my arms were around him. My fingers were in his hair again and my hands sliding up and down his strong back. Jamison held me so tight that his hard body and cock felt like steel against my softness.

"Wait," I whispered, forcing my mouth away from his. "Wait."

"Huh?" His eyes were dazed, his mouth open. He looked confused.

My lips pecked his. "I'll be right back." Holding up one finger, I gently closed the door in front of him.

Twenty-Seven

JAMISON COX

I could hear Bryn's footsteps running away from the door. Then the room went silent until something crashed onto a hard surface. I licked my lower lip to taste the sweetness her kiss had left behind. My cock was hard.

Why am I standing in the hallway? I should have been on top of her bed and seconds away from being inside her. I also had to worry about Creed showing up. He'd mentioned that he was going to try to get in touch with her today and asked if I had her number.

"I have it, but I'm not giving it to you," I said instead of lying. *I don't have to lie to him.* Bryn Blackstone was my soul mate, not his. But he gave a "game on" smirk.

I guessed that she was flying back to Colorado. On the way to the airport, I called Alex to tell him that I didn't need him to keep my secret anymore. If Bryn didn't want to hear from me, I was hoping she'd listen to him.

"Bryn's not flying out. We're having bad weather," he said. "You should be able to find her at her apartment in Manhattan. I'll text you the address. This time of day, Gabriel should be working door. He's a beast about not letting people in who aren't supposed to be there. If you're going now, I'll call him and let him know you're on the way."

"That'll be greatly appreciated." I got into the far lane to take the first exit off the expressway. When I looked over my shoulder, I saw Creed drive right past me. He didn't look my way. He must have gotten wind that Bryn was flying back to Colorado from Karen Diploe. He wouldn't learn that Bryn's flight had been canceled until after he arrived at Teterboro.

The thought made me smirk. *Finally, I'm winning.*

But it wasn't hard to believe that Creed would spend the afternoon tracking down a woman who showed no interest in him whatsoever. The research that I'd done on him pointed to the fact that he was single, but he wasn't celibate. He was drawn to extraordinarily beautiful women like Bryn, but he liked to chase them, catch them, and then toss them back in the water. I agreed with Jasper about Creed being able to wear Bryn down. The snake wouldn't stop slithering until he swallowed her whole, but unlike all his other prey, she would be the one he'd try to keep.

I heard another loud crash and shoes running toward the door. She'd been barefoot when she answered the door the first time. I remembered thinking how convenient that was, because I didn't have to worry about taking off her shoes before getting her out of her pants.

What is she doing in there, anyway?

The door opened again. I threw up my arms. *What the hell?* She had on her coat, boots, and a cute beanie with a pom-pom on top, looking as sexy as a siren.

"What's this about?" I asked, knowing that I was about to go far away from where I wanted to be —which was between her thighs. I'd been missing her body since last Wednesday morning.

Her eyes were as bright as the sunrise. "I have work to do while I'm in town today. Do you want to join me?

Once, a friend of mine tried to get me to invest

in his fishing company. He took me out on a boat and sent electrical currents through the water. All these fish started jumping out of the ocean. Not only did I say no to investing, but I'd told him to get me away from the whole process. At that moment, with Bryn, I felt like one of those fish.

I guided her against me so she could feel me. The blood was already down there. "Umm…" I moaned after I slipped my tongue into her sweet mouth.

"Jamison," she whispered as my greedy lips continued to chase hers. "I have work."

I was ready to pull back and let go, but her tongue pushed deeper into my mouth, her soft body closer. Then I heard the door close. She moaned. Her body was no longer against mine. Bryn interlaced our fingers, and her palm pressed against mine.

I was on cloud nine as she led me away from the entrance of her apartment. "Jamison, we have to get out there before the stores close," she said.

I was confused, and so was my cock. "What stores?"

"The furniture stores."

My heart knocked against my chest all the way to the elevator. A woman who wanted to go shopping—there was no way to persuade her to see it my way. "What were you doing in there?" I asked after we got into the elevator.

Her beautiful face smiled up at me, beaming like my own personal Venus. I wanted to take her in my arms, but if we couldn't make love, the next best thing to do was to keep some distance between her and Fido, my cock.

"Other than nearly killing myself, I was getting ready to leave with you." She shook her head rapidly. I noticed she did that when she was ready to change the subject. "Anyway, so what was it that made you leave me alone in Vail?"

The elevator doors slid open, and in walked a family made up of a mom, a dad, and two kids. We scooted to the back, but the mother did a double take when she looked at Bryn and then slapped a hand over her mouth as her eyes expanded. "Oh my God!"

"What is it?" her husband asked, appearing ready to slay a dragon for her.

"You're the Blackstone sister."

Bryn smiled graciously, as I knew she would.

"Bronwyn Henrietta Blackstone. I heard you lived in the building. Oh my God." The woman said she'd left her cell phone in the apartment but asked if Bryn would mind taking a selfie with her, using her husband's cell phone.

"No, sweetheart," her husband said, shaking his head adamantly. "This is her private residence. She's not the only celebrity in the building. We've got to give her some peace."

"You're right. You're right, sorry," the woman said, nodding spastically.

"Mom, Blackstone was last month," one of the kids said.

Bryn laughed. "Just one wouldn't hurt, though."

In the lobby, the mom asked one of the women at the front desk to take the picture with her family and Bryn. "Your boyfriend, or husband, too," she said, waving me over.

I smirked at Bryn, whose smile grew. "Come on over, honey," she said playfully.

I liked being referred to as her husband. When I stood next to her, arm around her, Bryn Blackstone felt like mine forever. The woman taking the photo told us to say cheese, but I couldn't. I was too captivated by the allure of my future wife.

We held hands under the portico as the valet fetched my car. The guy knew Bryn and was thanking her for a gift card, saying it came in handy. He never divulged how much she'd given him, but it must have been a lot, because he said he was able to add the amount to what he saved up for a down payment on a house.

I still believed she was being negligent about security, being a Blackstone and all. The next time I was with Jasper, I would ask him what the hell he was thinking, letting her traipse about without proper security. I grunted thoughtfully. Leaving her vulnerable didn't seem like something Jasper would do, though. There had to be security around there somewhere. My car arrived as I searched up and down the street, looking for any sign that there was someone posted nearby, watching her back. I hadn't seen anyone.

When we got into the car, I reached for her hand, and when she set her palm on mine, the simple sensation of skin on skin made my cock want more. It was like the early days, when we used to work together. I wanted to touch her, kiss her, and always be close to her, but I couldn't.

"By the way, where are we going?" I asked before pulling away from the curb.

"White Plains," she said and asked if she could plug the address into my navigation system.

I felt my eyes burn with lust. "You can do anything you want."

Her eyebrows flitted up. "You really are horny, aren't you?"

"Yeah," I said, nodding.

"Me too. I mean, horny for you, but I really have to get this done. The storm is keeping Alana from shopping, and since there's no storm here, I can get the furniture we need."

As Bryn plugged the address into the system, she talked about Alana being great at her job and taking over her position. She mentioned the woman named Gina, whom she'd flown to the recovery center in LA with. Being with Gina had inspired Bryn to go back and study to become a therapist.

"Good idea," I said.

"You really think so?" She sounded highly curious and almost uncertain.

I kissed the back of her soft hand. "Absolutely." I could feel her beautiful smile burning into the side of my face. I had to keep my eyes on the road.

"Okay, so what happened in Vail?" she abruptly asked. "Or maybe I don't care to know."

I kissed her hand a second time, and since we were stopped at a red light, I turned my face to hers, and my tongue dipped between the seam of her soft lips. Dizzy, I kissed her until the car behind me honked.

Z. L. ARKADIE

"They waste no time doing that in this city," I said.

Bryn laughed, and then I recounted what had happened in my life, from the moment a front desk clerk at the resort called our room to tell me that Bree was in the lobby until Bryn and I came face-to-face at the BFE building in Lower Manhattan. She listened attentively. I loved that about her. I could trust that she heard everything I said.

"So Bree thinks you're getting married this weekend?" she asked.

"I guess so."

"And... you don't have your old cell phone, so neither Boomer nor Bree knows where you are?"

I swallowed hard, wondering if that made me seem like a liar. "No."

"Humph," she grunted as if intrigued. "Nicely played, Jamison Cox."

My head jolted back against the headrest. "Really?"

"Don't you think so?"

"Well... yeah. But I'm not being honest with her."

"No part of her showing up at the resort to collect you and then being part of a plan to blackmail you into marrying her was done out of honesty and dignity and in your best interests. I know you don't like those feelings associated with being slimy, but unfortunately, your father lives in the slime pit." When I glanced at her, she wrinkled her cute nose. "Sorry."

I could have kissed her again. More than that, I wanted to pull over and sit her on top of my erection. Instead, I glanced at her, keeping my craving for her under wraps. "Don't apologize for being right."

"Okay, then, not sorry."

We shared a laugh. I missed doing that with her. I had no intention of letting Bryn Blackstone out of my sight. Where she went, I would go. After a quick glance at the road to measure the space between my bumper and the car ahead of me, I reached out to tuck a wayward ringlet of her wavy hair behind her ear. It was getting in the way of my glances at her pretty face, which, even as the years passed, I would never get tired of looking at.

"So, what were you doing at Jasper's office?" she asked.

I told her about how I'd started my own business and that, thanks to Jasper and Spencer, I would be managing Mike Dunn.

She snorted. "Funny how life comes full circle. He's a winner."

"I know he is."

"And so are you."

I couldn't stop grinning, especially when she leaned over to kiss me on the cheek. When I turned just a little to connect with her lips, she kissed me quickly again. That would have to suffice for then.

I readjusted my position, giving my cock room to expand in my crotch. *Screw nature.* "How are we going to work things out?" I asked.

"Meaning?"

The navigator's voice instructed me to move over to the far-right lane to take the next exit. "You're going back to Colorado. I'll be in DC."

Bryn sighed as she applied a gentle squeeze to my shoulder. "We'll figure something out. Where there's a will, there's a way. Are you going to call Bree and let her know you're not marrying her this weekend?"

"That's none of my concern." I made a right turn down a street with unmarked buildings on each side. It was the sort of area where you had to already know what exactly was there if you wanted to shop there. Grinning, I glanced at her. "Unless you want to marry me this weekend."

She chortled. "Are you asking me to marry you?"

"Yes, I'm asking," I said, feeling no need to hesitate. "And I'll be asking again."

"What does that even mean?" she asked with a laugh.

"It means this is a bad way to propose to the woman of your dreams. The next time I ask you to marry me, it won't be in the car on the way to buy furniture."

"This is fine. But do what you feel."

"What I feel?" I asked.

"Your destination is on the right," the navigator voice said.

I turned my frown on her as I pulled into a parking spot.

"I'm not blowing you off," she said rather astutely. Then she pressed a hand against her chest. "I mean, me, married? I never saw myself married to anyone. But when I look at you, I don't know. I see my Adam."

"Your Adam?"

"I'm made for you, Jamison Cox. And you're made for me."

I released a long exhalation. "I agree," I said breathlessly.

"Okay, then, we don't have to worry about much if we know that already." Her eyes sparkled and danced.

I turned to look out the driver's-side window. *Damn it.* A car had pulled into the spot beside me, and our windows weren't tinted.

When I turned my hungry eyes on Bryn, she was cheesing rather cutely. "That's why you should've rented an SUV."

I laughed. "Then let's hurry up and get the hell out of here so we can follow-through with what we both want right now."

"Deal," she said, aiming her palm toward me so that I could slap her hand.

Instead, I wrapped my fingers around her slender wrist and tugged her to me. When our lips melded, I tongued the hell out of her. Her mouth tasted like honey, igniting me with desire. I suddenly knew what I had to do, and I had to do it fast.

I ASKED BRYN TO GIVE ME A FEW MINUTES TO MAKE a phone call as she shopped. The sales guy was all too enthusiastic to assist her. I didn't want to leave her alone with him, but I had to. This love crap and wanting a woman to be mine was driving me up the wall. I'd never been territorial over any of my girl-friends in the past, but Bryn was my special one, and that was why I was calling my mother to let her know I was ready for the ring.

Twenty-Eight

BRYN BLACKSTONE

Chris, the salesman, had just told me that my soft skin went well with the mustard-colored armchair. I almost blurted a laugh. I'd been in the warehouse store on numerous occasions, and he'd always flirted, but I believed seeing Jamison and me together made him turn up the heat.

"Well, it's not for me—it's for a client," I said, even though he already knew that.

He sneered. "Is that guy your boyfriend?

The answer to that question still seemed unbelievable. "He's more than that."

"Then you're married?"

I started to say no, but my tongue remained stuck on the roof of my mouth when I saw Jamison standing behind Chris, his face seeming drained of blood.

"What is it?" I asked.

His mouth caught open, he blinked until he was able to say, "My mother told me…"

I walked over to stand in front of him, and he continued to look at me as if he was in a daze. "Your mother told you what?"

"My father." He cleared his throat, and I waited patiently for him to finish whatever he was going to say about Boomer.

But Jamison just continued looking me in the eye, shaking his head.

"What about your father?" I asked.

"He, um…" His frown intensified. "He had a heart attack. He died."

I pressed my hand over my mouth and gasped into my palm. "I'm sorry." I was barely audible.

The deep creases between Jamison's eyes turned more pronounced. I could tell he was struggling to believe what he'd just revealed, and frankly, so was I.

I INSISTED ON DRIVING BACK TO MY PLACE. JAMISON was on the phone with his mother. He didn't say much more than "Yes" and "Uh-huh." He asked, "How?" but whatever answer his mother gave made him massage one of his temples.

Before we got into the car, he'd told me that he'd called his mother to ask for his grandmother's wedding ring. She'd always promised to let him have it when he found the woman he wanted to spend the rest of his life with. His mother said she'd been trying to call him. No one could reach him. I could see the guilt eating Jamison alive.

"In the morning." He scratched the side of his face as he sighed. "No. It's not for Bree. Why are we talking about this now?" He stretched his legs. "Okay. I'll try. I gotta go, Mom." He inhaled sharply as he listened to her. I wondered if he knew he'd forgotten to breathe.

I reached over to rub his leg. His muscles were rock hard. "Exhale, baby," I whispered.

He did as I said. "Yes, I'm with someone." He paused. "Mom, I'll see you when I get to California." Then he repeated "Yes" until he ended the call.

The silence felt heavy. I hadn't known what to say to him, and frankly, his uncomfortable conversation with his mother had taken me back to my own dark places with Amelia, the woman who I grew up believing was my mother.

"Sorry about that," he said as if I could hear the things his mother had said about Bree Lovell.

"You don't have to apologize," I whispered. "I'm the one who's sorry for your loss."

"Yeah..." he breathed.

He must have found it hard to believe that such a force of nature was actually dead. It was sort of how I'd felt for about two seconds after Randolph was pronounced dead. Then my sentiments had leaned more toward, *Good riddance, you old lecherous snake.*

Finally, Jamison rubbed my shoulder. "Thanks for driving." He was massaging the nape of my neck, making my folds moist. "Umm... I want to ask... could you come with me? Be with me?"

"Of course," I replied without hesitation. "Of course."

Jamison shifted my hair off my neck. Cooler air brushed my skin until he planted a kiss there, one that included tongue and suction. "Thank you." His voice was thickened by lust.

"You're welcome," I whispered, wanting him so much I could hardly stand it.

WHEN WE MADE IT BACK INSIDE MY APARTMENT, I asked Jamison if he would like anything to drink.

Without answering, he walked up to my large living room windows and gazed out over the killer view of the park. "Bryn."

My steps were light as I went to stand next to him. I felt as if I didn't want to disrupt or disturb his sadness. After all, grieving was part of the healing process. I rubbed his back gently. "Yes, Jamison?"

His hooded, whiskey-eyed gaze bathed me in his lust. My body flickered with lust of its own and in all the right places.

"Take your clothes off," he whispered.

As a matter of fact, he takes them off for me. I assist him out of his clothes too. Then Jamison swipes me up into his arms and cradles me. His mouth is hot and possessive, our kissing greedy and sensual.

Umm… he tastes so delicious. "The bedroom…" I whisper against his mouth, my tongue barely able to let go of his.

"*I know…*" *he says passionately against my lips.*

No directions are needed. Our sensual tongue-brushing, lip-petting kissing continues. Then our eyes flicker open at the same time. I know Jamison feels what I am feeling in my soul—a rush of emotion beyond love. But passion makes me close my eyes again to experience him deep down in my bones. Lightning fast, our kissing turns fiery. I am so set aflame that I'm about to burst. My sex creams and is eager to have his cock stretch me, as I cling to his every stroke.

My breaths quiver when I feel myself being lowered until my backside presses against the fluffy comforter on top of my bed. His body separates my thighs, and I know it's coming. Anticipation makes me toss my head back and sigh and then say, "Ha!"

His fullness is inside me. My hands caress his back, sliding up and down his muscles and soft skin.

Holy… *I bite my swollen lip until he takes it from my teeth and sucks it then slides his tongue around it until he deepens our kiss.*

"*Mm…*" *My eyes widen when I feel it.*

He still remembers all my hot spots, because my nerve endings flicker and are on the verge of catching fire.

"*Ha!*"

I can hardly take it as I toss my head from left to right. Oh my God. *It's just overwhelming.*

Jamison makes low moans and groans and sighs.

Umm... *My nose is against his neck as I hold on tight, allowing my sex to take the ride. He smells so divine that I suck his skin into my mouth. His bittersweet taste, an ambrosia of fading cologne, sweat, and Jamison Cox, saturates my tongue.*

Slap... our sexes collide.

Slap.

Slap.

Slap.

And then, I cry out, face tense, as pleasure bursts and spreads through my womanhood.

"Oh damn, baby," *Jamison mutters.* "I love... oh!"

He shudders and quakes, and I hold him tight so that we can take our pleasure rides together.

COOLING OFF, WE LAY WITH MY LEG ON TOP OF HIS and the sides of our bodies against each other. We held hands too. Jamison and I could never be in bed together without touching. I wondered if one day that would end. *Don't all good things eventually come to an end? Do I even believe that?* I wasn't that fatalistic—not anymore.

"Despite everything, I feel pretty satiated right now," Jamison said.

I flipped onto my side and trailed the tip of my finger up, down, and all around his hilly chest. "So do I."

"That feels good, babe," he whispered.

I cut a tiny smile. "I'm glad you like it." I kissed his skin, and he quivered as I ran my tongue around his nipple. "So when do we leave?"

He sighed. "In the morning."

"How are you feeling about Boomer being gone?" I ventured to ask.

After a long pause, he said, "I don't know."

"It's unreal, isn't it?"

"Yes, it is," he said as I flopped down on my back. Jamison's strong hand brushed the inside of my thigh. "My mother didn't want to give me the details about how he died over the phone."

"I thought he had a heart attack."

"He did, but there's a story behind it that she wants to wait to tell me. I figure there's shame associated with why he had a heart attack. Otherwise, she would have said he died in a meeting or in his sleep or something. He must've been screwing someone who was too young for him." His jaw tightened with force.

I grimaced. That was a large leap for Jamison to make. "You think?"

"I know it."

"Wow."

Somehow, one of his fingers found its way to my clit and rolled circles on top of it. I was wrong. He was still in the mood for sexual activity. Then he captured one of my breasts within the confines of his mouth, rolling his tongue around my swollen nipple and raking his teeth across the tip. Jamison played my body as if it were a brand-new instrument. The pleasure overwhelming me was through the roof.

"Ooh... ahh... mmm..." I thrust my neck forward and my head up off the bed. "Ha!" Then it hit me. "Ahh!"

Then, shifting abruptly, his mouth ended up on my bud, sucking, stroking, and stimulating. I dug my fingers into the sheets, closed my eyes, and gasped. My breaths stayed rapid and shaky until Jamison's efforts procured his desired results. But he didn't stop then. He made me come over and over again until he was aroused enough to thrust his newest erection deep inside me.

I WAS ON TOP, HEAD BOBBING, JAMISON'S MANHOOD in my mouth as I ran my tongue around the tip of his cock and then took him as deep as I could down my throat.

"Damn, baby. You're making me come," he muttered, holding two handfuls of my hair.

His girth stretched my mouth, making my jaw and tongue ache. I could already taste his juices, salty and slippery, and knowing he'd belonged to me since the first night we ever made love allowed me to enjoy the texture and flavor. I moaned with vigor, my hand around his shaft stroking him faster. I also took him in deeper, feeling his fullness at the back of my throat, lathering his manhood with warm saliva until…

THE HOURS HAD PASSED, AND NIGHT WAS IN FULL bloom. Covered with sweat, the sheets damp, Jamison and I separated ourselves far enough for our bodies to cool, although we still held hands.

"You know I'm going to marry you, right?" Jamison said.

I turned to see him staring at the ceiling, one of my favorite sets of dimples on display. "I know."

He faced me, still smiling. "Then that's a yes."

"Are you asking me to marry you right after sex?"

Jamison chuckled. "I have to or else."

"Or else what?"

"The sharks are circling."

I chuckled. "What sharks? I don't see any sharks."

"There's Dale and Creed and the guy in the furniture store."

"Creed?" I exclaimed. "The guy who was with you earlier?"

"He wants you. I know him well enough to know that if you're not married, then he considers you fair game."

I couldn't help but laugh, especially because Jamison sounded serious about that. "Well, it takes two. And I have no interest in him."

"You weren't interested in me either."

I chuckled and shifted to rest my head on his chest. "Oh, I was interested in you."

"But you said you weren't."

"I wasn't interested in a relationship. I was afraid my picker sucked. But I felt it immediately, Jamison. I feel nothing when I look at Creed. What was he doing there, anyway?"

Jamison told me how he'd had the bright idea of taking initiative and bringing a winning candidate to Jasper.

"If I'd known I would run into you at Jasper's office, I would've never taken him there. He's got all the bells and whistles, but he has a weakness for women."

I snorted. "Like all politicians. There's something about power and sex that makes them go hand in hand."

Jamison got a kick out of that, and we laughed together and discussed the way people got so bent out of shape about sex, which felt good as hell and was fun, but they were okay with consuming violence as if it was buttery, salty popcorn in a gigantic tub. Then our conversation landed on his friends from high school and how they were all cheating on their wives.

"You see," I said as my fingers trailed up and down his breastbone. *Gosh, his body is hot.* "Why not you? When I first saw you, I was attracted to you, but I judged you to be that kind of guy too. Why didn't it happen to you?"

Jamison smirked. "Oh, you're going to meet her tomorrow."

I narrowed an eye curiously. "Your mother?"

He captured my hand. "Yes, my mother." Then he lifted his head and looked down at his pelvis. "Look what you've gone and done."

His erection had risen.

And then it was buried inside my wetness.

Twenty-Nine

BRYN BLACKSTONE

Morning had arrived. My body was warm, and so was Jamison's, as he pumped his cock in and out of my heated vestibule until I came first and then he came second. We had to force ourselves out of bed and into the shower. Afterward, we got into our first real lovers' spat over one glaring issue that certainly needed to be resolved if we wanted to make a go at forever. Jamison would rather have taken a commercial flight, but since I had the family airplane fueled up and ready for takeoff, I thought it would be more convenient if we flew out to California privately.

He expelled a heavy breath as he scratched his eyebrow.

"Jamison, we can't let money get between us."

"I want to be the one providing for you, that's all."

We stood in the living room, right where the hallway led to the foyer. I uncrossed my defiant arms and stepped over to stand so close to him that when I looked up, our mouths wanted to merge.

"I have no problem with that. I'm not one of those pampered rich people who can't exist without a mansion, two butlers, and three cooks—my brothers are." I smiled widely, hoping he caught my joke.

He chortled.

"All I'll need is you." I unleashed my mouth to let it have his. My head felt as if it floated beyond the Big Apple while we smooched.

Jamison twisted to look over his shoulder and in the direction of the bedroom. He frowned.

I chuckled. "Let's go before we never make it at all."

Jamison let me go and then picked up my suitcase and briefcase and slung the strap of my purse across his shoulder. "This way," he said, pointing his head toward the foyer.

I bit my lower lip anxiously. "Let's take the

private elevator. We don't want a repeat of what happened yesterday."

"Ah," he said, letting his head fall back. "That's something else I'm going to have to get used to. My wife is a famous Blackstone."

I snorted. "Or infamous, depending on what story you read."

We had a good laugh over my last remark as we made our way to the private elevator. Life was so easy with Jamison. There he was, carrying my belongings again, making me feel so well taken care of.

On the way down to the lobby, I replied to the flight service, confirming our trip from Teterboro to SFO, while Jamison let the parking garage that kept his car know what time to pick us up from the airport.

When the elevator doors slid open, our tasks had been completed, and we were at the start of a kiss.

"Oh, Jamison?" a man said.

Our lips let go of each other, and to my surprise, there stood Creed.

"What the hell are you doing here?" Jamison snapped.

Creed's shocked eyes darted over to me and

then back to Jamison, who took my hand and led me out before the doors could close us in again.

"Um—friends," Creed said, turning to face us.

Jamison grunted. "Right. Have a good day. We have a flight to catch."

"Oh, your father," Creed called after us.

Jamison and I stopped in our tracks. He turned to face Creed, and I followed his lead.

"My condolences," Creed said, sneering. He'd said the right thing to get his way. "Richard was a good businessman." He set his attention on me.

Creed was definitely smirking at me flirtatiously. It was sort of creepy, and what a bold move he'd made, showing up at my building uninvited with some BS story about "friends."

I tugged on Jamison's arm. "Babe, we have to go."

Jamison looked as if he wanted to rip Creed's face off. Without saying another word to him, we turned and walked out of the building and let the cold air cool our heads as we got into a hired car, which was waiting for us in front of the building.

ON THE WAY TO THE AIRPORT, I CALLED ALANA AND let her know about my change of plans and the fact that I was able to get pieces sent to Eden's. She informed me that everything was going swell, but for some reason, Dale was back without Eden and was asking about me.

"You should've seen the look on his face when I told him you were still in New York. He thinks you're coming back today. I can't wait to tell him otherwise. He's such a tool."

There was no way I was going to let Jamison know what Alana had said to me. *Damn, maybe Jamison has a sixth sense.* We'd run into Creed in the lobby, and the slippery, slimy Dale had figured out a way to ditch Eden so that he could spend time at the vacation home, hoping to have a shot at me without his new girlfriend being there. It felt as if everyone was trying to get in the way of me and Jamison being together, even Boomer, who'd unexpectedly died.

Jamison made a few calls of his own. One was to Mike Black's former campaign manager, Jeff. Piecing together their conversation from Jamison's responses, I gathered that Jeff didn't like having to spend so much of his time in Washington, DC. He missed hot weather and blue skies. He wanted to bow out as Mike Black's chief of staff and wasn't going to be around for the next election. Jamison said he had some great candidates in mind to replace him. Jeff couldn't wait to meet them. Boomer was mentioned, and Jeff must have sent his condolences, because Jamison's "Thanks a lot" sounded flat and forced. I had a feeling he hadn't truly processed his father's death. To him, Boomer was still alive. He needed to see the body and, after that, bury him. Only then, perhaps, would his new reality truly set in, and when that happened, I would be there for him.

"Is that all you're doing for Jasper? Taking over as Mike Black's campaign manager?" I asked when Jamison got off the phone and the car stopped near the airplane.

Jamison grimaced as if he wanted to divulge whatever he was supposed to do for Jasper but didn't know if he could.

"No worries. I'll ask Jasper," I said to put his mind at ease.

Jamison shifted. "No. You're going to be my wife, so I'll tell you."

The fact that he loved me more than remaining loyal to Jasper was a turn-on. I needed that quality in a future husband. So I listened attentively as he told me the plan concerning hundreds of political candidates and elections around the country.

"Is that even legal?" I asked.

He rubbed the side of his face. "I'm pretty sure that's my job."

"What do you mean?"

"To make it legal."

Next, he told me about Boomer's Ponzi scheme and how he'd used money from that to fund Cox and Cox. And to add insult to injury, Jamison wasn't the named partner in Cox and Cox.

My head was spinning. Jasper was always going way too far, taking way too many risks with his bottomless pit of money. We could have kept talking about his association with my brother, but I had to expound to Jamison, since he was now associated with my family, that rule number one was to never talk business on an airplane that hadn't been security checked. We both looked at the large aircraft looming beyond the window.

"I guess I'm pretty much part of the family now, aren't I?" he asked.

I chuckled. "Yeah. Get ready, because we're not a light bunch."

He winked at me. "Neither are we."

We shared a chuckle then hurried out of the car

and up the ramp. Carrie and Ronnelle, my favorite flight attendants, welcomed us aboard. They seemed caught off guard by Jamison's natural sexiness. They couldn't stop grinning as Carrie took our breakfast order and Ronnelle brought black coffee for him, a cappuccino for me, and hot lemon-and-honey biscuits for both of us.

Soon we were up in the air, and we finally had a moment alone. Jamison looked at me with a perceptive grin. Of course, he knew the effect he had on the female sex. His eyes turned naughty. "Are you a member of the mile-high club?"

"Unfortunately, yes," I said, rolling my eyes, recalling the tedious sexual experiences I'd had on private flights with Dale.

"Well…" He licked his lips and pressed the call button.

Flustered, Ronnelle came racing out into the cabin as if she'd just beaten Carrie to the punch. "Yes, Mr. Cox?" she said, smiling giddily.

His smoldering eyes lapped me up. "We're going to need a whole lot of privacy."

"Oh. Well…" She cleared her throat. "Okay, privacy. Just let us know when you're ready for breakfast."

"Done," Jamison said, still regarding me with hungry eyes.

Ronnelle was gone. He unzipped and unbuttoned his pants. I dropped my jeans but kept on my black lace panties, since they turned him on. I pushed Jamison's shoulders down, and he sat back down. His manhood was up and ready, though. I adjusted the crotch of my panties. He sucked air and muttered unintelligibly as I straddled him and lowered my wet heat over his engorged cock.

He grabbed my hips and nailed me against his groin.

I gasped.

Thirty

JAMISON COX

THIRTY-THREE MINUTES LATER

I roll my tongue back and forth on the edge of her clit, clinging onto two handfuls of her ass. She tastes so delicious. I've already blown my load, but I try to force my cock to grow another boner.

Um... I love it when her mound vibrates against my mouth and she calls out my name. I slide two fingers inside her.

"Oh Jamison," she cries.

Damn, she's creaming like crazy. I shift my tongue to the opposite side so I can do it again and make her wetter. I want her to suck air, cry out, and let those flight attendants know that I'm only doing this to one woman—Bryn Blackstone.

Grow, boy... *Blood is finding paths to my cock again.* Grow. *Her fingers rub my scalp, squeeze my hair. She repeats my name. Tells me how it feels for her.* Umm... *I suck this clit like it's going out of style.* Grow!

"Ah, Jamison!" *She quivers against my mouth.*

Damn it!

I tug her hole against my mouth and thrust my tongue into her wetness, tasting her. Back and forth, I tongue bang her until I'm ready to make her scream again.

I watch her face. She's so damn pretty. Her swollen lips, angel face, alluring eyes...

Bryn screams and creams for me. Finally, I'm hard.

THIRTY MINUTES LATER

The bathroom door opened, and Bryn walked out, looking as fresh as a daisy. I didn't want to clean her off me, though. On the morning I left her in Vail, I carried her scent on my body for as long as I could. At the moment, I could smell her on the hairs above my top lip. She was also still on my chin and in my mouth. She sat down across from me. That was where I wanted her so that I could have a full view of her beautiful face.

In the future, when someone asked me, "What part of your wife turns you on the most?" hands down, the answer would be her face. Her inherently mischievous facial features included pouty lips and bright eyes well placed on a heart-shaped face. Yes, it was her face. The way she tasted, her sexy long legs, and her cone-shaped tits with nipples sticking straight up, asking to be sucked hard, were bonuses.

Bryn's eyebrows flitted up twice as she sank comfortably into her chair. "That just made us platinum members of the mile-high club, don't you think?"

I looked down at my deflated cock, which told me *Enough already—give it a break*. We still had the night. However, my disposition turned cloudy when I remembered we would be staying in the guesthouse on my parent's property.

"Whoa, that was a sudden change," Bryn said. "What's going on inside that handsome head of yours?"

I lazily lifted one side of my mouth. Bryn Blackstone was my perceptive beauty. To be frank, I didn't know why thoughts of home and seeing my mother again set a gray cloud over my head.

"I'm thinking about what happens when we land," I said.

"Ah, I see," she said, nodding. "When we get to Monterey, we could always stay in a hotel."

I scoffed. "My mother wouldn't hear of it." I was captivated by the look of examination on Bryn's beautiful face.

"People are the sum of two parents," she said.

I ruffled my brows, wondering why in the hell she'd said that.

"There's a reason you're not more like Boomer or the sort of son a guy like him makes. Something tells me your mother has a lot to do with that. But you never talk about her much. Why is that?"

She'd said a lot at once. "I don't?"

"No. I don't even know her name."

"I thought everyone knew Stephanie Ann Cox."

Bryn smiled graciously. "Not me. But why don't you tell me about her?"

Her expression was soft, open, and patient. I loved that. I didn't even know why I said that everyone knew my mother. I was certain that Bryn never gave my mother a first or second thought. Maybe it was because in my mind, Stephanie reigned strong. However, at the moment, I didn't know how to answer Bryn's question, or maybe I was just afraid to.

My anguish must have shown on my face,

because she said, "Okay, well, tell me something you remember about her."

I sighed, trying to think of something. Finally, a memory came to me. "I remember when I told her my father cheats, she said that was between the two of them." I could feel my lips flatten and curl. I hadn't realized that I was still angry as hell about that.

Bryn grunted thoughtfully. "What else?"

I felt stunned by how fast she wanted to leave that subject behind. My head pressed against the seat. "What else?"

"Yeah, that's one memory. Do you have another one?"

I pinched my chin thoughtfully, figuring there was a purpose to her line of questioning. I saw myself at an early age. "We were at my grandfather's funeral, Boomer's father. I was standing next to Stephanie. We were alone at the casket. It was our turn to view the body, and all eyes were on us. She squatted down beside me and said, 'I'm going to make sure your father doesn't do to you what this asshole did to him.'"

"Boomer's father wasn't a good guy?"

I shrugged. "I don't know. I was about six or seven then, and I have no memories of him."

Bryn narrowed an eye. "Did Stephanie hug you, kiss you, say she loves you?"

My mind shuffled through all the memories of my mom asking me, for no apparent reason, to come to her so she could give me a hug. It used to drive me crazy. "Yeah, she did. My mom's affectionate in that way."

"Good." Bryn's tone rang with optimism. "Then why are you still frowning?"

Why am I still frowning? Suddenly, the answer came to mind, but I didn't know if I wanted to say it or not.

"What is it?" she astutely asked.

I squeezed my eyes shut and stretched my neck from side to side.

"Jamison, get it off your chest, babe. You can trust me."

"I don't understand why she never cared that my dad repeatedly had sex with other women. I didn't think women who loved their husbands would allow them to do that. And…" I sighed. "I know for a fact he banged Bree Lovell several times."

Bryn's eyes widened. "Get out of here. No way."

I swallowed and nodded. "I saw them together."

Her jaw dropped. "You caught them having sex?"

I told her how one late night, I returned to the San Francisco office to retrieve a candidate report I'd left on my desk. I heard low moans and grunting echoing in the distance and followed the sounds to the part of the building we kept unoccupied just in case we needed space to run larger campaigns. I swallowed to moisten my dry throat.

"Mm-hmm," she said, encouraging me to continue.

I could picture the hallway and the darkness surrounding me, experiencing it anew. "The closer I got to the noise, the more I knew it was him. I already knew he screwed the stewardesses and some ambitious campaign assistants. Normally, I would've turned around and left. But for some reason, I kept going. The space outside the office was dark, so he didn't notice when I cracked open the door and saw Bree lying across the desk while he banged her. But she saw me."

"She did?"

I smashed my lips together as I nodded. "But we never talk about it."

Bryn and I stared at each other. I wasn't sure

how much better I felt after dumping that load of a secret.

"Keeping their secrets is awful, isn't it?" she asked.

"Very much so," I whispered past my tight throat.

"My father had serious issues with his moral compass too. And, well, you've read the book." She frowned. "Sometimes, it's still hard for me to really believe that you and I will have a happy future and all the bad crap is in the past. But that fear is more like a shadow that haunts me. It's not strong, and I know it's a liar."

The longer I looked at her, the more my stomach fluttered and my heart hammered. I swallowed the lump in my throat. "When it comes to us, I want to stay in the present as much as possible. I'm going to make mistakes. None like the ones Boomer made, though. I might get insecure about your family's money or something like that. Bit I'll never dip my cock into places where it doesn't belong. I want to grow old with you, Bronwyn Henrietta Blackstone. I'll always love and want you, and I hope you'll always love and want me too. I've made my decision. I choose you."

Her cheeks were rosy, and her smile was the

most beautiful thing in the world. "I choose you, too, Jamison Arlington Cox."

I snorted, grinning. "You know my middle name?"

"It was in the report touting how you're marrying Bree Leandra Lovell."

"Damn. I forgot about that."

I fought the urge to officially ask her to marry me. I needed the emerald ring first. When I asked Bryn to be my wife, I wanted to present it to her and then slide it on her finger. But the truth was, I couldn't always ignore Bree. Since Boomer was dead, I couldn't help but wonder what her next play would be. Bree was a survivor, and her family had grandiose aspirations. I could only hope they'd moved on with a new plan to find another sucker to marry their hot but crazy daughter.

Bryn raised both her thumbs. "Together?"

I stopped frowning and smirked. "Yeah… together, babe."

I didn't just say that—I believed it and would make sure nothing and nobody got between us, not even my mother.

Thirty-One

BRYN BLACKSTONE

I couldn't shake the gnawing feeling that Jamison was still holding something back. But I chalked it up to him being only human and, like most of us, having unspoken fears.

Breakfast was finally served. Since we both had a lot of work to do, we did it while eating. Occasionally, he would say something about Mike Dunn, like what came to mind after he showed me several photos of his new client. One-word answers were all he wanted me to give him. Alana and I were instant messaging about my renewed membership in the mile-high club. Then I forwarded her several applications to review for new design associates, project managers, and craftsmen.

So soon, huh? She replied with a sad face.

Better sooner than later, I replied.

I already miss working with you. Maybe you can be my shrink instead, she wrote.

I uttered a laugh and then read the correspondence aloud to Jamison, but not the part about the sex. He chuckled, and we both easily returned our attention to the tasks we were working on.

———

THE AIRPLANE LANDED IN SAN FRANCISCO, AND A transport service drove us to the garage where Jamison's car was kept. Soon, we were in his luxury sedan and embarking on our drive to Monterey. On the way, Jamison and I discussed where we would live and where I would go to school, as if he'd already officially asked me to marry him. He hadn't. Every now and then, we'd stop and drink in one of many spectacular views off the 101 freeway.

We drove off the highway and stood on top of a cliff, gazing out over the rocks along the shore and the ocean in the distance. Cool air pressed against our faces, bringing clarity to my mind.

"I think we'll have to live in New York," I said.

"Me too," Jamison replied.

I turned to him, grinning from ear to ear. "So

when are you going to officially ask me to marry you?"

Jamison's sexy chuckle made my stomach turn flips. "Soon, babe. Very soon."

On that note, we engaged in a toe-curling and head-spinning kiss and then got back on the road.

Soon we entered the gorgeous town of Monterey, which had the essence of a rich-drifter town, with its majestic coastline, grassy mountains, and easy beach community. Jamison was surprised that I'd never been there before, being that I had, as he called it, *a gypsy spirit.*

"Yes, that's even better," I said. "That's what this town reminds me of, at least to the eye—a gypsy spirit."

He rewarded my stab at humor with my favorite chuckle.

"But you didn't grow up here, did you?" I asked as the car slowed and he made a left turn onto a redbrick driveway. Perfectly trimmed bushes sat on each side of the entrance and continued up the hill until the grounds opened up to a freshly mown lawn lined with swaying trees.

It was plain to see that wasn't the front of the house.

"Gorgeous," I said.

"Yeah," Jamison whispered.

I could tell he was just as nervous as I was, so I took his hand in mine. He slowly drove past the grassy part of the estate, and looking through the windshield, I gasped at what must have been the pride and joy of the home. Past the craggy cliffs lay the Pacific Ocean.

"Wow," I said.

"I know. The views are killer."

He stopped the car in the middle of the driveway and explained that the guesthouse was farther down the path, but he wanted to stop in and introduce me to his mother first. We both agreed that it was best to just get it over with. Plus, he said, he needed to have a quick word with her.

When we got out of the car, though, we walked to the edge of the property to get a better look at the ocean. I took his hand and held on tight.

"Jamison, is that you, my darling?"

We turned, and to my surprise, Bree Lovell came slithering in our direction, her face aglow, beaming at him as if I wasn't in the picture.

Jamison turned to me, looking just as dumbfounded as I felt. With everything I knew about her and Boomer, it seemed odd that she would be in the house with Stephanie. Bree stopped less than a foot away from Jamison. I believed her intention was to get so close to him that without thinking, he would let go of my hand so that she could hug him. It didn't work.

"What are you doing here, Bree?" His tone could freeze the sun.

"I knew you would need me here, and I'm your fiancée." She chortled. "The optics are quite important." Bree sort of muttered that last part.

When she fanned her fingers over her chest, I noticed the most gorgeous ring she was wearing. Striking like a snake, Jamison seized her hand.

"Where did you get that?"

"Oh," she said, smiling at the emerald and the encrusted diamonds, "Stephanie said you intended to give it to your fiancée, and that's me."

JAMISON ASKED IF I WOULD WAIT FOR HIM IN THE guesthouse while he conferred with his mother. I didn't want to be separated from him. His eyes held the sort of rage that spewed fire and brimstone. I also pieced together the fact that he wanted to give me the ring that Bree wore, and that was why he'd waited to officially propose to me.

"It's fine. I'll stay with you," I said, hugging his arm.

He placed a hand gently under my chin. "Please, babe." He gave me quick but tender kiss, right in front of Bree. "Let me take you down to the house and get us settled. I have to talk to my mother alone."

First, I breathed him in, and then I nodded. However, I let him know that I was capable of driving down to the house and taking our things in. My eyes expanded in a way to give him a hint that whatever I said next would be wise advice. "You might want to have that conversation with your mother sooner rather than later."

When Bree snorted, I remembered that she hadn't moved an inch. It was as if she was waiting for our intimate moment to pass so that she could resume her version of reality.

Jamison's sexy top lip curled when he glanced at Bree. "Yes. I understand."

Thirty-Two

JAMISON COX

I found Stephanie in Boomer's office, sitting behind the desk. Her neck was bent, and she was massaging her forehead while her eyes were on the glossy wood. It took a few seconds before she noticed my presence. When she looked up, her smile and normally bright chestnut eyes were weighted.

"Yes. I understand," she said to whomever she was talking to. Then she mouthed, "Close the door."

I did as she asked.

"Thanks again. I appreciate your support at this time," she said as I sat down across from her. As if not rattled by her world falling down all around her, my mother composedly set the phone on the base. "Have you ever heard of White Star Investment Group?" Her tone was flat, lifeless.

A knot formed in my throat, and my head soared toward the ceiling. When Jasper had informed me of my father's financial scheme, I never considered how it could hurt my mother. That was a miss of galactic proportions.

I coughed to clear my throat and then tugged at my collar. "Yeah. I heard about it yesterday."

My mother cocked an eye when she studied me. Stephanie was tall but slight, with brown hair the color of milk chocolate and smooth, creamy skin.

Stephanie shook her head and turned to gaze off, unfocused. "Your father had no boundaries."

I was speechless. I'd never heard her criticize Boomer in such a blatant manner.

When she squeezed her eyes shut and inhaled deeply, I realized she and I were trapped in an unknown universe. "How are you doing, honey?" she asked. Her tone had suddenly lightened.

We both stood up, walked to the side of the desk, and hugged. Stephanie's hugs never faltered. She held me just as tight as she had when I was a boy.

"I'm fine, Mom. How are you?"

Her head remained against my chest. "You're going to have to plan the funeral. I hate him too much to do it."

Again, she left me speechless. "I understand." I finally said. "But, um, what's Bree doing here?"

My mother's body had grown tense. "She's here for support."

Dread was like an anchor in my chest. "Mom, we have to talk about Boomer's relationship with Bree."

Stephanie let go of me. When she quietly sat down in Boomer's big chair, which appeared to swallow her whole, I sat in the small seat across from her. As if she could read my mind, she studied one side of the backrest and then the other.

Then she patted the armrest. "Your father liked things that made him feel like a king. Even me." She turned to gaze off. "He considered me a beauty amongst beauties. Is that what you think of Bree Lovell?"

"Not in the least," I said without pause. "And why is she wearing my ring?"

My mother fixed her gaze on me. The wheels were turning in her mind. "How about we talk about that later?"

My muscles tightened as I crossed my arms.

The thought of Bree wearing the ring that had been promised to me and my true bride a minute longer angered me.

"Do you know she had an affair with Boomer?" I said.

Stephanie didn't flinch. Her jaw didn't drop. Actually, she never moved an inch. "Bree would never do that."

"I saw them. And yes, she would. It's in her constitution."

My mother shook her head as if batting the truth away from her brain. She pressed her hand over her heart. "I'm not well either, so don't bring this to me right now." She blew a sharp breath. "The funeral's on Thursday."

Shock made me push back against the seat. "Thursday? That's in two days."

Stephanie opened the desk and took out a pen. Then, as if still angered by what I'd revealed to her, she snatched a Post-it Note out of the holder and scribbled an address on it.

"Make sure the body gets here." She stuck another Post-it on top of the one she'd just written on. "His body is here. Handle the transfer, please."

Not until it started to hurt had I realized I'd

been squeezing my chin too tight. "Bree should leave the house."

"Caroline's here too. She and Bree will be joining us for dinner this evening." She sighed as if the idea of dinner made her tired. "I can't cook like this, so I'm having dinner catered. It's gourmet Italian. Dress casually but not too casual. We are hosting guests."

I couldn't move a muscle. And what could I say? I couldn't stop shaking my head. On too many occasions in the past, I had allowed Stephanie's delusions to reign as truth. Suddenly, I understood how she and Bree were cut from the same stone in that regard. There was no way, this time, I would let Stephanie live in fantasyland. If she was going to forgive Bree and absolve her dead husband for piping the girl she'd given my grandmother's ring to, then she would have to hear about what I'd seen.

"It was three years ago," I said. "I'd left something at the office, so I went back. When I heard Dad, I thought, 'What the hell is he doing here all the way in San Francisco when he should be home with my mother?' But I followed his grunting and moaning all the way to an office, where Bree Lovell was lying across the desk, ass up, being banged by your husband."

The blank look on my mother's face hinted that not one word I'd said had sunk in. *Does she think I made it up? Or has she known all along and simply doesn't give a damn?*

Finally, it occurred to me that Boomer wasn't the only toxic parent, and I knew what I had to do. I put the Post-its in my pants pocket.

"My real fiancée and I will be staying in a hotel."

My mother turned her head slightly. "Your real fiancée?"

"Bronwyn Blackstone."

"Is that so?"

"That's so." I stood. "And we won't be having dinner with you and your guests. I'll see you at the funeral," I said, turning my back on her. "And keep the ring. I don't want it." My hurt had turned to blazing anger.

"Jamison," she called before I could open the door.

I stopped and gathered my bearings before turning to look at her.

"Stay in the guesthouse—please."

I wanted to deny her request.

Stephanie closed her eyes for a moment and then pulled her shoulders back. "Please, son, stay."

My mother standing there, looking vulnerable, got to me. The Lovells knew Bree had been involved with my father. They also thought I was marrying their daughter. They were rats sniffing around the cheese. I loved my mother too much to let them devour her.

Thirty-Three

BRYN BLACKSTONE

J amison and I sat beside each other on the large sectional in the living room. After I entered the guesthouse, I saw that the windows were open, flames were kindling in the fireplace, and meat, cheese, and bread platters were placed carefully on the coffee table. Jamison's mother had clearly been mindful of his arrival. He'd asked if I was responsible for the platters and fire. I said no. His mother's hospitality seemed to weigh on his mind as he recounted his brief but strange encounter.

"That sounds very weird," I finally said.

He scoffed. "Weird is an understatement."

"Why are the Lovells here, though?" I asked, wanting any reason other than the obvious.

"My mother's clearly not in her right mind. I wanted to give you the ring Bree was wearing."

I smiled as I stroked the side of his handsome face. "I figured that was the case."

"I was going to present it to you tonight when I asked you to marry me."

"It's okay. I already said yes twice, so it's a done deal." I broadened my smile, hoping it would influence him to do the same, but no such luck.

"But I was going to get down on one knee. You know, the whole shebang." Even though he couldn't smile, I realized that he was being lighthearted. Then he sighed as if he was being battered by his next thought. "She wants me to handle getting the body to the funeral home to have my father's corpse prepared for the funeral, which is on Thursday."

I gasped. "Thursday?"

His chuckle had an edge to it. "Yeah." He slammed sticky notes with addresses and phone numbers on top of the coffee table, next to his mobile. The way his mother was passing the task off to him seemed so careless.

I took Jamison by the shoulders and looked him in the eye. "I will do it, okay?"

"Do what?"

"Get everything ready for the funeral."

399

"You can't plan my father's funeral, Bryn. Especially after the way he treated you and your family. Your brothers will—"

"You have to stop caring about what my brothers will think. We're not that way. I'm not some special little sister that they all have to tiptoe around and keep in a silk box, protecting her from the world. My brothers have different expectations of me, and taking the load off of you is one of them, because that's what we do for family—we take the load off each other. Got it?"

His lips were coming in for a kiss when his cell phone rang. We both looked down to see the name Jasper Blackstone on the screen.

"Damn. And I have a lot of work to do too," he said.

"Then you'll let me handle the funeral?"

He swiped the phone up off the coffee table. "Yes, you can plan it. I have to take this."

I nodded.

Jamison stood and walked off as he answered my brother's call. Soon, I was sitting alone in silence. Jamison must have gone into the office where I couldn't hear him. Their guesthouse had about the same square footage as my cottage in LA, so there was plenty of space for privacy. I sank against the sofa, unable to shake the image of Bree Lovell slithering out of Jamison's mother's house. The fact that she and her mother were lodging there felt surreal. I fervently wanted to shake things up by insisting we make an appearance at the dinner table. We would touch each other all over, kiss, and announce that we were the actual engaged couple.

A whistle accompanied my sigh as I sat up straight and picked up the Post-its off the table. Forcing Jamison into an uncomfortable situation would have been unloving. Plus, there was no need to show off our relationship in front of Bree and her mother. However, it would have been nice to receive Stephanie Cox's blessing to marry her son.

JAMISON WAS STILL IN THE OFFICE WHEN I CALLED the morgue. The attendant I was speaking to wasn't willing to give me permission to have the body transported until I said I was Jamison Cox's assistant.

"And your name?" she asked.

My eyes darted to the left. I hadn't wanted to

give my real name but figured the odds were that the woman wouldn't know who I was.

"Bronwyn Blackstone," I said.

She went very quiet. I was about to ask if she was still there when she said, "Ma'am, is that your real name?"

I stretched my bottom lip. "Um, yes."

"You're *the* Bronwyn Blackstone?"

"Yes, ma'am," I said.

"And you're Mr. Cox's assistant."

I sighed hard. "Sort of. His father just died, so I'm taking this task off his to-do list."

She excitedly repeated, "Oh my stars," before providing top-quality service. Hannah was her name, and she told me several times that she'd always dreamed of marrying one of my brothers. Jasper was her favorite, but then again, she adored Spencer, too, and Asher, the surgeon.

"They're all so yummy. I just don't know which one to pick."

I got a kick out of that. If only they knew what my brothers had had to endure and overcome to become dreamboats.

We completed our business after scheduling the body to be delivered to the mortuary first thing in the morning. Then I spoke to the mortuary and made an appointment for ten in the morning to select a casket and to drop off whatever suit Jamison wanted Boomer to rest in. Dealing with death was such a dreary task. We'd made Jasper deal with laying Randolph to rest alone. For the first time ever, I felt guilty about not shouldering my portion of that burden.

"Hey, babe," Jamison said as he reentered the room and flopped down on the sofa beside me.

We kissed, and I could feel the exhaustion in his lips. I told him the body would be at the mortuary in the morning. He kissed me again to thank me. Then Jamison kicked his shoes off, and I did the same. I made myself comfortable, resting my head on his shoulder as we gazed out at the sun setting at the end of the ocean.

"That's gorgeous," I remarked.

"Yes, it is." He kissed me on the forehead. "Bryn?"

"Jamison?"

"Thank you, babe."

I looked up at him, and our eyes met. The longer we stared at each other, the more my heart felt like a rose blossoming in the sunlight. I loved Jamison. Of that I was certain. "You're welcome."

We had one last soft, sensual kiss. Then Jamison

turned on the TV, and we watched a documentary about animals in Yellowstone National Park as we finished the meat and bread and each had a glass of the red wine. We marveled at nature, and then at some point, with his arm around me, my head resting on his chest, and his face on my head, we fell asleep.

It's night out. The TV casts the only light throughout the room. Lifting my eyelids feels like a chore, but I catch sight of a figure standing in front of the window, watching us. That's what I see—I'm sure of it. My head is so tired, and so is my body. Jamison's snoring. The woman presses her hands to the glass. She mouths something to me. I'm reading her lips when she says, "Leave."

Ding-ding-ding-ding…

Jamison and I woke up at the same time. Someone was at the door.

I SAT STARING AT THE WINDOW, WHERE THERE wasn't much of a view in the dark. *Was I dreaming, or was Bree actually standing there, watching us sleep?* I tried to remember what I'd seen her wearing only a few minutes before. *Was that only a few minutes ago? Was it light out or dark out?* I couldn't recall. Perhaps my spotty memory and the vision itself were a testament to how tired I was.

Two men wearing white culinary uniforms and chef's hats carted in aluminum food carriers. Jamison explained that his mother had had dinner brought to us. It was after nine o'clock at night, and Jamison and I had eaten meat, cheese, and bread to hold us over until the next morning. We put the containers of food in the refrigerator and went directly to bed.

FINALLY, A SEMBLANCE OF REALITY. JAMISON AND I did not make love after we stripped off our clothes and made ourselves comfortable in bed. He mumbled as if he was intoxicated when he said, "Good night, babe," and then yawned.

My "good night" was mixed with my yawn. But remembering the vision of Bree in the window, I told Jamison I wanted to get some water, and he let go of me. I got up and made sure all the doors were locked and, so I wouldn't have told a lie, took a few swallows of water before dragging myself back to bed. As soon as I was under the covers again, Jamison collected me in his arms.

In the morning, Jamison ground his pubic bone against my ass, sliding his erection up the crack. "Knock-knock," he whispered thickly against my ear.

I smiled as I stretched and sighed. "Come in."

"Really?"

"Mm-hmm."

His hand seized the round of my hip and...

"Ha!" I cried out as his cock surged through me. He reached around my hip, pressed a finger against my clit, and commenced giving me double the pleasure.

Thirty-Four

BRYN BLACKSTONE

J amison and I gave each other space as we cooled down and caught our breath. We started out light and sensual and ended up hot and passionate.

"I think we should go up to the main house for breakfast," Jamison said.

A slow smile formed on my lips. "Really?"

He turned to face me. "Are you ready to meet my mother?"

"Yeah... yes, I am."

We stared at each other, drinking in the other's face.

"BFE's private bank is bailing out White Star Investment to the tune of six hundred and five million," he said.

I wondered how long he'd been thinking about that and if that contributed to how exhausted he'd been after he got off the phone with Jasper.

"What do you think about that?" I asked.

"I don't know." His eyes narrowed a bit more. "Are you sure I can trust your brothers? Did I sell my soul to the devil?"

"No, you didn't," I said in a sincere tone. I wanted him to hear that my answer came from the bottom of my heart. "I once heard Jasper say that he doesn't like making people useful tools because they'll never be loyal to him." I lay on my side, propping my head up on the palm of my hand. Jamison couldn't stop himself from viewing my tits. "Don't get me wrong—he likes loyalty and will always reward it. You went to Spencer for help, right?"

Jamison swallowed as he nodded. "Yeah," he whispered.

"The way my brother thinks, that was the right move. You humbled yourself and made the smart decision, asking them for help."

Like the final hook in a comedy act, Jamison reached out and pulled me under him. "Thanks for the explanation, baby," he said, salivating with his face close to my breasts. Then he sank one of my breasts into the depths of his mouth, spiraling his tongue around my nipple and then tugging it gently enough with his teeth to make my vag tingle. He did it over and over until he was hard enough to enter me again.

———————

By nine o'clock in the morning, Jamison and I had showered, dressed, and driven up to the main house. Round two of making love had made us late for breakfast, but we still walked inside so that I could officially meet his mother. However, Jamison seemed taken off guard to see three women sitting at a window bench, comparing notes.

"Janet, Cora, Diana," he said, his tone ultra formal and his body tense.

"Hi, Jamison," they called and each leaped up to come shake his hand.

"Is my mother home?" he asked.

"No, she's not," one of them said.

"Where did she go?"

"Shopping."

"For the funeral?" he asked.

"And other things."

Jamison's skin was red, and he was pressing his

lips too tightly together. As we made our way upstairs, on our way to pick out a suit for his father, I asked him what was wrong.

"Nothing," he muttered, scowling at the stairs.

"Jamison, it's obviously something," I whispered.

He sighed hard and turned to glance over his shoulder. "My father used to bang those girls. What the hell is going on?"

We made it to the top of the stairs.

"Your mother hired them, apparently."

Jamison's expression remained hard as he continued leading us. "I don't know if she's okay."

That made sense. "She has to be grieving."

"Yeah," he whispered when we reached the top.

"Oh, and congratulations, Jamison," one of the girls called.

Jamison looked at me with raised eyebrows. "I have to put the rumor about me marrying Bree to rest."

"You're telling me," I whispered as we entered a large bedroom that had a lot of dark, classically designed furniture pieces and a great big bed. I didn't know if I was repulsed or intrigued by the large square-cut mirror with a metal-leaf frame that sat on the glossy wood dresser. The piece was just so ugly and yet so grand. The entire space was in need of what I called a fresh-over. The room gave me the willies. It reminded me of the sort of lair Randolph would have felt comfortable in.

I folded my arms and let the chills pass as we crossed the carpeted floor and entered a walk-in closet. I was first struck by the sheer number of suits hanging on the posts. They were arranged by color, and the cuffs of each suit extended to the same height. Basically, a lot of attention and care had gone into displaying them.

"He hardly wore any of them," Jamison remarked as he studied them. "He used to like to come in here and look at them."

Suddenly, I was struck by an illumination in regards to Boomer. "Did your father grow up poor?"

"His family was dirt poor until he was twelve," Jamison said as he shuffled through the suits. "Then the bank gave him a loan to open a feedstore. It did well."

"Need help?" I asked.

"Um, if something jumps out at you, let me know."

I searched through the suits hanging on the

opposite side of the closet. "I take it your father didn't continue in the livestock business?"

"Boomer went off to college and studied economics." Jamison snorted cynically. "I guess that's where he learned all about pyramid schemes."

My chuckle shared his cynicism as I put my hand on what I thought would be the perfect gray suit. "What about this one?" I took it off the rack and showed it to Jamison.

He grunted and looked it over. A small smile flowered across my lips. He cared what his father wore to his burial. "I like it, babe. We'll go with it."

When Jamison took the suit out of my hand, he wrapped me up with one arm and guided me against him. "Have I said thank you already?"

My lips gently kissed his. "Yes, you have."

He kissed me back. "I wouldn't have gotten through this without you."

Our tongues dove deeper into each other's mouths, coiling around each other, sending my soul to the moon. "We have to go," I said against his lips. We had less than an hour to make our appointment at the mortuary.

"Plus, we probably shouldn't do it in my father's closet."

I chuckled. "No. We probably shouldn't."

A naughty glint came to Jamison's eyes. "Although I can make him roll over on the table if his spirit catches wind of me making love to Bryn Blackstone among his favorite collection of suits."

I rolled my eyes and took Jamison by the hand and led him out of the closet. "No. Let's adios, mi amor."

He chuckled on his way out of the room. I was happy our suit search had lightened his mood. However, that changed when the girls working downstairs said goodbye to him on our way out. It seemed as if it pained him to respond.

"I just don't know what the hell is going on," he whispered as we walked out of the house.

I rubbed his back consolingly. "You'll get to the bottom of it."

Jamison sighed as he opened the passenger-side door for me. "Yeah."

A chill ran through me before I climbed in. As Jamison walked in front of the car to get in, I turned to look out the back window. I swore I felt someone watching us, but there was no one else around.

WE ARRIVED AT THE MORTUARY TWO MINUTES
before ten. We kissed as soon as we entered, cele-
brating making it on time. On the way over,
Jamison had let me know that Jasper wasn't
expecting him to officially start working on the
candidate's campaign for two weeks.

"Two weeks," I said. "Why so long?"

"Because, babe, after the funeral, we're getting
the hell out of here, and I'm going to buy you the
ring of your choice, drop down on one knee, and
ask you to marry me for the—what, fourth time?"

I chortled. "Something like that. Maybe third."

"Will you marry me?" he asked.

"Of course."

"There, that's number four."

I rolled my eyes as I shook my head. We
mentioned how we were starving, given that we
hadn't left ourselves enough time to stop by a fast-
food place and order something.

"Let's go feed our faces when this is over," he'd
said.

"I'm all for that."

When we entered the mortuary, an attendant
showed us to his office. He asked if Jamison would
like to see the body. After hesitating, he said,
"Sure," and asked if I would come with him.

We stood over Boomer's lifeless body for a while, just staring at him. That was my first time ever seeing him. I had never even googled him before then. His hair was salt-and-pepper and his skin as white as a ghost. I hadn't met Jamison's mother yet, but he only faintly resembled his father. Perhaps if Boomer's eyes were open and held their life force, I would see more of a resemblance. Jamison was robust. He would live to a ripe old age, and I hoped to be by his side all the way to our last breath on earth.

"I loved him," Jamison said past the frog in his throat. "He didn't treat me like he loved me, but I loved him. Does that make me…?"

I rubbed my hand across his back in circles. "It makes you his son. And you know what? Love isn't black or white."

"I didn't like him," he said, shaking his head. "I never did. When I was a kid, he was a jerk to my buddies. He never had much to say to me unless it was 'Mow the lawn, clean the shed, your mother cooked, you wash dishes.' We were never friends. I didn't want to be his friend because, as I said, I didn't like him."

I remained silent. There was nothing sweeter

for me to do than to let him work out his feelings on his own.

"That doesn't even look like him," he whispered.

Then he closed his eyes, and finally, they came —the tears.

I GAVE THE ATTENDANT THE SUIT. JAMISON WAS UP for picking out his father's casket. He chose a metallic-gray one that matched his suit. It also contained white silk padding. I realized that Jamison was burying his father in a light color. It had to be his way of making Boomer the man he always wanted him to be.

Raymond, the attendant, asked Jamison if there were any special objects he wanted buried with his father. Surprisingly, Jamison said yes. I watched with bated breath as he leaned over to take a fingernail clipper out of his pocket. "He gave this to me when I was young. I don't know how old I was or why he gave it to me, but I felt like he did it because he loved me." Jamison sat it on top of Raymond's desk. "I want this to be with him, from me."

"Sure," Raymond said with a nod.

He asked if we had any more questions about the ceremony on the following day. The service would start at eleven o'clock in the morning at the gravesite. There would be words from family and friends, and then the minister would commit Richard Arlington Cox to the ground.

WE ATE AT ROSINE'S RESTAURANT, SINCE THEY served breakfast until three in the afternoon. The drive to the restaurant was quieter than the one to the funeral home. I believed that Boomer's death had finally sunk in. I found myself sort of envying Jamison. He at least had made peace with his father's demons. I, on the other hand, had just written Randolph off as a monster. I never wanted to know what made him the man he was. I didn't want to have any empathy for someone who could do what he'd done to Gina. *That was it.* When Asher found Gina and brought her to his room and then showed her to me, I knew right away Randolph had hurt her badly. I also knew right then and there that he was beyond exoneration.

Talking about Boomer and Randolph together wasn't comparing apples to apples. Boomer was an apple, but Randolph was a rotted, shriveled-up lemon.

The waitress had come to our table, and Jamison ordered what seemed like half the menu and then asked what I wanted. His smile suggested he was ready to get back to being happily in love.

I chuckled. "I'll have what he's having."

The waitress frowned at us.

"Like, literally," I said. "He can order for the both of us."

He winked at me. "Unless you want something else."

I closed my menu. "I think I can find a few things to eat from what you ordered." I smiled at the waitress. "Oh, and he'll have dark coffee, and I'll have a cappuccino."

Jamison asked what I'd been thinking a few minutes before, and I told him my thoughts about Randolph. When our drinks came, we moved on to me answering the question of what it was like growing up at the Blackstone mansion. I told Jamison things I'd never shared with anyone. Heck, I told him stuff I hadn't remembered until then, like about the time I caught William, the butler, sneaking into Amelia's room.

"How did she treat you—Amelia Blackstone?" he asked.

Before I could speak, we were served all the dishes Jamison had ordered. There were seven plates in all—two types of eggs Benedict, chili egg puff, Italian omelet, tortilla scramble, banana pancakes, and blueberry pancakes.

Before we dug in and I finished telling him about Amelia, I made him pinky swear that we would work together to burn off any love pounds we might gain in the next two to three months.

Jamison laughed and then hooked his pinkie around mine. "Deal."

Then I told him Amelia Blackstone had always been kind to me but never mother-like. She never guided me or taught me a thing about being a woman, at least not directly. She would filter any kind of parenting through Jasper. When I started my period, Jasper had Sally Preacher, who was like a modern-day governess, take me to the drugstore and show me how to buy and use tampons.

"Deep down, I knew," I said to Jamison. "That's why I hired Holly to uncover the secrets. I wanted her to put it out there, and oh boy, did she do that."

"*The Dark Blackstones.*" Jamison put a forkful of

banana pancake in his mouth. We were scarfing down food as if we hadn't eaten in weeks.

I nodded. "I like this town a lot. Especially this restaurant. Do you think we could live here?"

"We can live anywhere you want, babe. We'll make it work."

———

CONVERSATION WAS BOTTOMLESS WITH JAMISON AND me. After eating, we drove back to the house. Again, to our chagrin, we'd missed Stephanie. The strange thing was that not only was she gone, but Bree and her mother were gone too. Jamison and I guessed at what they all could be doing together.

Jamison gave Diana the time and address of the funeral. She thanked him and said the invites had already been sent out.

"And where is my mother?" he asked.

"She's out."

"I know she's out. Out doing what?"

"Shopping for the wedding."

"The wedding?" Jamison and I asked.

For the first time, Diana paid more than fleeting attention to me. Her eyebrows ruffled. "Do I know you?"

I frowned at Jamison and then at her. "No. You don't."

She grunted thoughtfully and went back to doing whatever they were working on while sitting at the window.

Jamison and I walked outside. Then we stopped and looked at each other. "Do you really think they're planning a wedding?" I asked.

He shook his head. "I hope not."

TIME HAD FLOWN BY YET AGAIN. IT WAS GOING ON six o'clock in the evening when we made it back to the guesthouse. While Jamison made more calls, I went to the guest bathroom, which had an egg-shaped tub in front of a large window with a view of lots of pruned rosebushes and flowering green shrubs. I filled the tub with warm water, using the milk bubble bath, and soaked for as long as my thoughts would allow me. I was at a crossroads in my life. Four times, I'd said yes to marrying a man I'd never seen coming. I had a laundry list of things I wanted to do for the rest of my life. It didn't seem as if Jamison sought to cut that list short. He was so supportive of my plans to become a therapist. I'd

Z. L. ARKADIE

said yes to the sort of man whose answer to all the tough issues was, "Let's find a solution" and "Let's make it work."

I felt reinvigorated when I got out of the bathtub and bent over to towel dry my feet and legs. Facing the window, I caught sight of a woman in a red dress. I stood up swiftly. Gazing out the window, I saw nothing but green.

Thirty-Five

BRYN BLACKSTONE

"I had the strangest conversation with my mother," Jamison said.

I lounged on the chaise section of the sofa in the living room, answering emails, wearing nothing but a robe. Mostly, Jamison had been in the office with the door open. I could faintly hear him having phone calls with others. Jasper had graciously given him time off before jumping head-first into their gargantuan project, but that hadn't stopped Jamison from doing what he called the preliminaries. We'd been two people in our separate spaces, getting work done, but now he stood at the edge of the sofa, looking mystified.

I closed my MacBook. "What did she say?"

"She says she doesn't want to talk about me not

marrying Bree until after the funeral. When I asked her why, she said that the Lovells are quite fragile after Richard's death. She wants me to give them time to deliver the bad news."

I shook my head as I rolled my eyes. "The bad news has already been delivered, don't you think?" I threw my hands up and waved them. "Hello, here I am. The bad news."

"Yeah…" He said sounding distracted. "Then Bree stops by, and she gives me this." He walked over to the credenza and picked up a delicate white box, opened it, and showed me the boutonniere inside. "And she looked crazy in the eyes. I'm worried."

I frowned. "Did she have on a red dress?"

He jerked his chin, turning his head slightly. "How did you know that? Did you see her?"

I told him I thought I'd seen a woman in a red dress when I bent over to dry my legs off after taking a bath. Then I told him about seeing the woman in the window the night before while we were asleep on the sofa. "But I thought it was a dream."

Jamison scratched his right eyebrow. "Bree is capable of the kind of craziness you never thought was possible, babe."

"Humph," I said, twisting my mouth as memories flickered in my mind. Bree Lovell was the sort of entitled witch who believed that if she didn't get whatever she wanted, she was permitted to do whatever she needed to appease herself. The old Bryn Blackstone used to annihilate chicks like that. I was not afraid of Bree Lovell. She'd lost, and that was that. However, I hadn't come all the way to Monterrey for Jamison's father's funeral to go to war with an insane person like Bree.

"Don't worry about Bree," I said. "If necessary, let me handle her."

"No," he said, shaking his head adamantly. "I don't want you anywhere near her."

"Let's hope we can keep it that way." I grinned to lighten the mood. "I have three brothers, you know, and Jasper always wanted to make sure I knew how to defend myself the best way I could. So I'm a pretty good fighter... and lover."

Unfortunately, my attempt at humor didn't change Jamison's worrisome disposition. "We should just go to a hotel." He clapped his hands. "Come on, babe, let's go."

He was really flustered. I patted the cushion beside me. "Jamison, sit down for a second, please."

Jamison searched across one shoulder and then

the other. He sighed forcefully and walked over to sit on the edge of the sofa.

"I can't lose you, Bryn. What's happening between us feels too good, and someone like Bree can ruin it."

"Yes, babe, she could, and she wants to."

Jamison closed his eyes and massaged his temples.

"Okay, then," I said.

His arms dropped to his sides. "Hotel?"

"Yes. Hotel." If that made him feel that I was safe, then yes.

WE PACKED QUICKLY AND LOADED THE CAR, leaving our breakfast leftovers and the food Stephanie Cox had brought the other night in the refrigerator. Jamison drove slowly off the property, keeping the headlights off. He didn't relax until we arrived at the cute cliffside spa and resort hotel. Our room faced the ocean. I had to admit, I felt more relaxed away from Bree Lovell and the crazy, toxic environment that existed on Jamison's mother's property. That night, we went to bed with the French doors open, allowing the ocean breeze to engulf us as we made love until we fell asleep.

In the morning, we ate breakfast in bed. We ordered crepes with scrambled eggs, turkey bacon, and a cappuccino for me and black coffee for him. While we were eating, the TV landed on a morning gossip show. I was about to turn the channel when I heard my name.

"You know, the Blackstones. *The Dark Blackstones*. Have you read the book? Everybody's read the book," the woman said, using animated body language that made us feel as if she was gossiping with us, her best friends.

My mouth was caught open as I hung on curiously to her every word. Jamison sat up beside me as our arms touched.

"Anyway, she's been gallivanting around Monterey with an engaged man who's getting married this weekend. His fiancée's name is Bree Lovell, and sources tell me this Lovell girl is pissed. The guy, Jamison Cox, is a very successful political strategist. He makes winners and has a whole list of politicians he's put on the map, but we're not talking about that right now. So Jamison Cox has been with the Blackstone girl, and she's beautiful, like drop-dead gorgeous, so this Bree Lovell is going to have a problem prying him out of her hands. But sources say he had the Blackstone girl plan his father's funeral." She said that as if it was the worst thing in the world.

The woman folded her arms and then shook her head as if it was all a shame. "You don't have just any random chick doing that. But this Bree girl is mad as hell. Now, she has a past. Sources also say she set an ex-boyfriend's house on fire. What's his name...? Darby Huntsville, the famous polo player. Someone said she messed with the brakes on the car belonging to her ex-boyfriend actor, Delta Foster—well, allegedly. Remember, he drove off the side of the road, and it nearly killed him. But I don't know if Bree will be messing with Bryn anytime soon. Those names..." She chuckled. "Bree and Bryn, rich people's names. Well, Bryn's older brother is someone you don't want to mess with. Heck, I don't want to talk about him, so we'll continue following this story."

She rolled her eyes and leaned closer to the camera so that we could see a close-up of her face. "But the Lovell girl is wearing the grandmother's emerald-and-diamond ring, which is said to be worth sixty million dollars."

"Sixty million?" Jamison blurted.

"Sixty million," she repeated for effect.

"She should fire her sources," he said.

Then the hostess sighed, sat back, and crossed her arms. "We'll see where this hot mess ends up."

Jamison and I stared at each other, speechless. *What the hell?* The longer we looked at each other, the more hilarious what we'd just seen became. I laughed first, and then Jamison, seeing that I hadn't been shaken by the gossip report, laughed with me. However, I understood why Jamison insisted we get far away from Bree Lovell. I'd heard about what happened to Delta Foster, and I'd known him well. I'd sent him get-well flowers and a card. He was an eccentric guy with an unconventional kind of sexual appetite. Basically, Delta wasn't someone a girl—or guy—should get serious about. Of course Bree would try to shove someone like Delta into her box.

"But I'm actually shocked that she would even go for someone like Delta Foster," I said, musing aloud.

"Bree has several personalities, babe."

Then Jamison received a text from his mother, which said that the funeral would start at two o'clock in the afternoon instead of ten in the morning.

Again, Jamison and I looked at each other and shook our heads. It was all so very weird.

"I can't wait until this is over," I said.

Jamison reached around me and lowered me down onto the bed as he positioned his pelvis between my thighs. "Same here," he whispered as he thrust himself inside me.

I cried out from pleasure.

OUR SEX SESSION HAD WIPED AWAY THE THREE-HOUR grace period we'd been given when Stephanie, at the last minute, changed the time of the funeral. Jamison and I found ourselves rushing to keep from being late. As soon as we were dressed and ready to go, Jamison seemed nervous again. "We leave tonight," he said as we stopped in front of the door so I could fix his tie.

"Deal." I gave him a quick kiss.

His eyebrows rose intriguingly. "Thank you."

I kissed him again. "You're welcome."

When we made it to the car, we remembered the gossip report. Jamison opened the hood, and I stood next to him as he checked the wires. There wasn't even a speck of dirt on any of the parts.

Basically, we were cleared to get in and get on the road.

I let Jamison remain with his thoughts on the drive over. Mentally, we'd filled our minds with just about everything but the funeral. When we arrived, about fifty or more people were sitting in chairs around the casket.

Jamison sat behind the steering wheel, reading the scene. Then he inhaled deeply through his nostrils.

"Are you ready, babe?" I asked.

"Yes." He sighed. "But wait. I'll open the door for you."

He got out and walked around the front of the car. Quickly, I tried to locate Bree Lovell. *Bingo.* There she was, having a conversation with a man in a blue suit. Strangely, the man made eye contact with me as he turned his back on Bree and walked away. He wasn't a guest.

"What the hell was that about?" I whispered.

I would have to watch her closely throughout the day.

———

AN ELEGANT LADY WEARING A BLACK PILLBOX HAT with a fishnet veil over her face walked over to us. "Jamison?"

Jamison let go of my hand to hug her and introduced her to me as his mother. I instantly noticed the resemblance. He'd gotten his dimples, scrumptious lips, whiskey eyes, and carved face shape from her.

"Mother, this is Bronwyn Henrietta Blackstone," Jamison said.

Stephanie put on one of the fakest smiles I'd ever seen as she grunted and told Jamison that she'd reserved one seat in front for him.

Damn, she just blew me off.

"No," Jamison said without a pause. "I'm sitting with Bryn."

His mother's features grew wide. "You're the son."

"Mother, I'm not doing this here," he muttered.

It took all the willpower and decency inside me to say, "You should sit up front with your mother, Jamison. It's the right thing to do. I'll be fine." The optics were important, and him sitting in the back with me was not a good look.

Stephanie's gaze brushed over me approvingly.

Her smile was small. Then she focused on her son. "Remember what I asked."

Jamison's lips drew together tightly. "I still don't get it."

"You don't have to. Come." She guided him up front.

To my chagrin, Bree sat on Jamison's left and his mother on his right. *He's mine,* I kept repeating to myself. *And after the service, we're leaving together.*

I watched Jamison closely, even though just about everyone was watching me and whispering. I had a feeling I was the villain of the day. But ever since I was a kid, I hadn't cared what people thought about me, especially the pompous sort, and I wasn't going to start caring then. Bree kept saying things to Jamison, who never opened his mouth to respond. I could tell by how rigid his shoulders were that he wanted to get up and move.

His mother said something in his ear right before the service started. A few of Boomer's friends went up front to talk about him. They shared memories of a proud, fearless man. If I had to pick a theme, then it would have been all about his boom. I wondered if a lack of softness, kindness, and love was a great thing for a man or woman to be remembered for.

Then Jamison was called up front. He twisted around to find me. I smiled at him. He pressed his lips into a small but tight smile and tugged at his tie as he stood. Once again, our gazes connected, and I nodded, letting him know he could get through it.

Jamison captured his mother in his gaze. Bated breaths lingered in the air as people waited for him to say something.

"Boomer," he finally said. "The boom. You all like that, don't you? My father…" He closed his eyes, and when he opened them, he narrowed them at his mother. She must have warned him to keep his words nice. Jamison swallowed. "My father is the man who raised me. He liked everything done his way, including me. I'm not going to stand here and say we have, or had, the perfect relationship, because we didn't. You all thought you got hit by the boom? Well, I lived under the gavel. But he was the man who took me fishing and showed me how to put a worm on the hook and cast the line out into the water and wait patiently for a bite. Of course, the exercise came with a lesson about fishing for money. He was also the guy who, when I fell out of a tree at about five years old, told me to get the hell up and run around the yard because boys don't show their hurt, and they sure don't cry." Jamison's gaze had fallen on me.

I gave him a sympathetic smile.

Then he looked at his mother again. "But I want you all to know what real power looks like. It was Stephanie who later came to my room and said human beings should cry, boys and girls, because God gave us tears to heal our souls and our hurt legs. Then she took me to the doctor, and I learned I'd cracked a rib. So Boomer was the boom, but my mother, she was the blast. Rest in peace, Richard, because that is your name." Jamison looked up at the sky. "I don't know what happens when we die, Dad. But next time, leave the reputation in the grave."

It was so silent when Jamison walked back to his seat that all we could hear was the breeze gliding past our ears. I was proud of him for being honest. That was one of many reasons I loved him so damn much. Stephanie whispered something else in his ear, and he kissed her cheek. She must have liked what he said too.

THE SERVICE ENDED, AND RICHARD COX WAS committed to the earth. Jamison seemed strong as he stood beside his mother, shaking their guests' hands. Bree and her family remained close. The optics made it look as if she—not I—was his partner. Every now and then, I'd catch Stephanie tossing a glance my way. I so badly wanted to push Bree out of the way and take my position beside Jamison, but I didn't need to make that kind of scene.

I kept my eyes on Jamison as much as I could. People kept coming up to me, wanting to shake my hand and saying how much they admired my interior design work. Some said it was an honor to meet a Blackstone. I used to hear that a lot before my father died and the truth about him and his decrepit acts was revealed. But I heard it more after Jasper and Spencer, along with Holly, had worked their asses off to rewrite our family's story and strengthen our reputation. Wherever I went, the response of the people I encountered was proof that their efforts had paid off in a big way.

"Let's get the hell out of here," Jamison whispered in my ear.

He whipped me around to face him. He was smiling from ear to ear. I was shocked to see that he was all of a sudden in good spirits. I wondered what had happened. I'd lost sight of him until then.

"Are you ready to head back to the hotel?" I asked.

"No... somewhere else."

I dipped my head to the side, eyeing him curiously. "Somewhere else?"

Bree and her mother stood across the grass, watching us with quizzical expressions. Then Stephanie approached them, and whatever she said made them focus on her and not us.

"Meet me in the car," Jamison whispered in my ear.

I pressed my lips together and looked around. The guests weren't disbanding. The chatter was about Boomer and old friends apologizing for not keeping in touch before then. Then I observed Bree and her mother again. Stephanie held Caroline's attention, but Bree couldn't stop glancing at us. Her arms were folded tightly across her body, and she looked worried. Had she not gotten it yet? Jamison wasn't going to marry her. She was still wearing the ring, too, even though she hadn't shown it off like I thought she would. It was as if she was holding onto hope by a thread.

"Sure," I said hesitantly and walked alone to the

car. Part of me felt sympathy for Bree. I wanted to go over and talk her into accepting reality. But then, maybe Jamison was right about us leaving town that night. Maybe it behooved us to get as far away from her as possible before she could go all *Fatal Attraction* on us.

———————

JAMISON FINISHED SAYING HIS FINAL GOODBYES AND then joined me in the car. He was still smiling.

"You're happy to get all that off your chest?" I asked.

"There's a lot I'm happy about."

I narrowed my eyes. "Like what?"

"You'll see, babe." He navigated the vehicle with his left hand and took my right hand in his.

I decided to relax and go for the ride. When I tried to bring up Bree, he shut me down by saying it wasn't the time to talk about her. "Not yet."

We ended up at the beach, where we took off our shoes. I peeled off my stockings and Jamison his socks, and we walked along the shore. The foamy waves rolled up to our calves.

"So, how many times have I asked you to marry me?" he asked.

I snorted. "Too many."

Jamison guided me up to dry sand and then got on one knee.

"Bronwyn Henrietta Blackstone, will you please be my wife?" He pulled a ring box out of his pocket and opened it.

I gasped, covering my mouth as my eyes expanded at the sight of an emerald stone surrounded by encrusted diamonds.

"Yes," I said with a whimper. "You got the ring back."

"Bree has the fake," he revealed as he slid onto my finger the most gorgeous object I'd ever laid eyes upon. It fit perfectly too.

"Oh my God, it's magnificent," I said, admiring the way the sun caught the emerald.

"We'll have to get another fake made, though," Jamison said as he rose back to his feet.

We hugged each other like our lives depended on it. It was finally official—I would be the first and only Mrs. Jamison Arlington Cox.

Thirty-Six

BRYN BLACKSTONE

EPILOGUE

THREE YEARS LATER

No one would ever forget the travesty of Bree Lovell's life. After the funeral, Jamison and I had remained in our suite and made love for the rest of the day and into the morning. On Friday afternoon, we flew into Manhattan, went straight to the courthouse, and with all of my family present, we got married. Stephanie watched from her desk in her husband's old office in Monterey via FaceTime. Jamison still couldn't tell me what was going on. All he could say was that his mother's only words were that in the end, everyone would get what they deserved.

On Monday morning, Alana called me and then sent me a link to log into her DVR so that I could see the morning gossip show that had talked about Jamison and me the Thursday before. Then Holly called and asked if I'd seen it. My phone beeped, and it was Kat, and then Jada, who wanted to know the same.

"Give us a minute," I said. "We're about to watch it now."

Jamison was hooking my computer up to the television in my bedroom. The report detailed how Stephanie Cox had hosted a wedding on her estate and planted a fake groom, who had her son's height and build, at the end of the aisle. When the wedding march started, all five screens, which were supposed to play lovely videos of doves and sunsets, aired security footage of Boomer gasping while screwing Bree, Janet, Cora, Diana, and another girl —a flight attendant whose business card Jamison dug out of one of his pants pockets. He said he'd forgotten she'd given it to him, but she'd offered him her services. She was a prostitute.

Three years later, people were still talking about that. Bree was still keeping out of sight, licking her wounds. The man I saw her talking to at the funeral was named Nestor. He'd warned her to keep her distance from the Coxes and Blackstones, or she'd end up in jail. Until that very day, we still had no idea what Jasper had in the vault on Bree, but whatever it was, it must have been explosive, because we hadn't seen hide nor hair of her.

Jamison and I were almost at the end of a big year. I'd just finished my third year of studying for my PhD in psychology at Teachers College, Columbia University. I'd never felt so fulfilled in my life as I did while studying clinical psychology. I would make the fifth doctor in our family, and all my brothers liked the sound of that. So did my husband.

It was election night, and Jamison and his team had worked their asses off to get a horde of candidates elected. Despite how much he worked and the amount of school I had, we managed to sleep together most nights of the week. We still could hardly keep our hands off each other.

Jamison was in his pajamas, and I wore my nightie. His team was uptown at a hotel, watching the results of all the elections on monitors. My husband and I wanted to spend the night alone. With each victory, he would receive a phone call from Jason, his right-hand man, and we would listen to an eruption of applause. We'd been holding our breath on the final call of the night, which was the president of the United States. Mike Dunn was in an embittered race with a man who'd rolled in the mud from start to finish. Jasper had called us right before BCN was about to announce who won Florida.

"With Florida, he's got it," Jasper said, his voice projecting through the speakerphone.

"Bryn, you there?" Spencer said. He was on the line too.

"I am," I said excitedly. "Jada, Holly?"

"We're here," they said at the same time.

"We are too," Asher and Pen said together.

"So are we," Gina said, meaning she and Nick. Gina had given him permission to accompany me for the first visit. The two of them hit it off immediately. Then Nick began visiting her without me. It took her a while, but one day, Gina realized she was deserving of love. Nick Bondi and Gina Jones were married at the Vail estate that summer. The entire family was there. I'd never seen Asher cry before that day. He'd shed tears of joy.

"The gang's all here," I declared excitedly.

Then Holly shushed us all as the anchor declared the winner.

It was so quiet we could hear a pin drop. I turned to Jamison, my mouth open.

"You did it, baby." I was so choked up that my words hardly came out.

Jamison took me by the face and kissed me deeply.

"We won!" Jada cried.

The phone rang, and Jamison tore his lips away from mine to answer it. It was Mike Dunn. Jamison jumped around as he congratulated him.

"Jasper? We won," I said.

"Yes, Bryn, we won," he replied in his usual calm and controlled fashion.

"Get your ass down here," Mike said to Jamison over speakerphone.

Jamison's eyes smoldered when we looked at each other. "Oh no, brother. I'm going down somewhere, but I don't have to go far to get there."

I tossed my head back and laughed. Jamison said goodbye to everyone we were in communication with before sweeping me into his arms and carrying me into our bedroom.

You can now start The Lords of Manhattan series written by Z.L. Arkadie and her alter-ego Zoey Locke.

Whereas Z.L. gave you mystery with your romance, Z.L. and Zoey focus on bringing you romance with your romance. But there are still plenty of twists and turns, along with angst and steam to keep you turning the pages!
Also, each book is a standalone, ending with happily ever after!

***

CROSSING THE LINE
THE LORDS OF MANHATTAN

A relationship between them is strictly forbidden, but they are drawn to each other like moths to a flame. Neither was willing to cross the line...until now.

Start *Crossing the Line* today!
READ NOW

About the Author

Z.L. has been writing romance full-time since 2011, which has allowed her to amass quite a catalog of romance novels. She loves what she does, and as she's evolved, so have her stories. Now, she's focused on writing angsty, sensual, and emotionally deep romance.

When Z.L.'s not writing, she loves to cook and read good books, which have the power to take her somewhere she's never been.

For more information:
zlarkadiebooks.com
contact@zlarkadiebooks.com

Printed in Great Britain
by Amazon

23378205R00255